THE KID THAT SPARKLES
BY
ANTHONY ROCHE

ISBN: 9781726793919

Disclaimer

Although based on true events, this is a work of fiction. Names, characters, businesses, places, events, locales, and incidents are either the products of the author's imagination or used in a fictitious manner. Any resemblance to actual persons, living or dead, or actual events is purely coincidental.

Foreword
Acknowledgements and Thanks...

Firstly, my family for putting up with me during the last two years writing this novel. They could read it backwards I've read it out-loud to them that many times.

The famous Gary Bird whom I think is due a stint on Countdown - his spelling is that precise. *Countdown Birdy* sounds good. Gary has been on this journey with me from the start. *Thanks little fat man.*

Terry Melia (author of *Tales from the Greenhills*) for helping me with the editing and for his encouragement throughout, spending a lot of Saturdays in Arthur's cafe.

Ryan Worthington for taking time out from his wonderful family to capture the fabulous photos for the front cover.

Our Billy for all his help to get this book up and running.

Playwright and author Nicky Allt for the guidance and helpful tips he passed over to me.

Steve Fairhurst (of *Regenic Creative Marketing)* thank you for the book cover you did a marvellous job thank you very much.

Sarah Durkin for taking time out to proof-read this novel. You were a great help.

Lee Grant for helping set up *The Kid that sparkles* email address and for his technical advice.

I would like to thank all the football team for making this book possible, and if you're lucky enough to get your hands on a copy don't share it and pass it around. Make your mate buy his or her own copy. That way you can read it over and over again and have endless hours of belly laughs

Please feel free to comment and follow on my Twitter page
https://twitter.com/KidSparkles

I hope you all enjoy the book as much as I have in writing it.

Anthony Roche.

Chapter 1

The last day of school

It's a bright beautiful spring May morning in Liverpool and young scouser Brian Cassidy is in bed, dreaming of scoring the winning goal in the World Cup final for England. As the ball comes over from the right wing he leaps up and rises above everyone to head the ball towards the back of the net.   As the goal is scored, he's woken by a real football hitting him on the head. He looks up, half asleep and sees his best mate Neil Parks laughing, with the football back in his hands.

"What the fuck are you doing and who let you in my room?" growls Cass throwing back the bed sheets exposing his pale muscular body.

"The milkman." replies Neil laughing. "Talking about him, have you been on a sunbed?"

"Don't try and take the piss Neil. Get the fuck downstairs yer dickhead," snarls Cass as he climbs out of bed in his Armani boxers, his impressive six pack on display. As he leaves the bedroom, Neil is hit with a slap on the back of his head. Brian's dad, Derek Cassidy, has overheard Neil's comments.

"I'll milkman yer Neil," says Mr Cassidy, "he only comes twice a week. How are you doing anyway soft-lad?"

"I'm doing great Mr Cassidy. The Blues have offered me a two-year apprenticeship earning £800 a week. I'll start on the 2nd July for pre-season training with the first team squad. I'm still with the schoolboys for now but I'll finish with them next week."

Neil climbs on the bannister rail and slides down the stairs. "Big Duncan keeps asking me to get your Brian down to sign for the Blues Mr Cassidy."

"He's not signing for no-one 'til he leaves school."

Neil reaches the bottom of the stairs puzzled and confused because today is the last day of his and Brian's school days. He enters the kitchen. The radio is blasting out Adele's latest song. Mrs Cassidy has bacon and sausages cooking on the grill, the smell is making Neil hungry. Mrs Cassidy pops into the kitchen boogieing.

"Hello Neil, you looking forward to your last day in school? I remember when you and Brian started nursery... it seems like only yesterday, how life goes so quick."

"I can't wait to leave."

"Oh, don't be stupid Neil! Your school days are the best of your life. How's your mum anyway? Bet she was made up with that big win from the Gala bingo, ten thousand pounds wasn't it? You never get anyone from Liverpool winning the National Bingo. I bet she shit herself when her last number was called out."

"She's okay Mrs Cassidy, but she won't part with any of her winnings. She's a right tight arse. Me old man still has to do overtime and work on Saturdays 'cos she won't part with a penny of it. There's more chance of a sub from the homeless."

Mrs Cassidy laughs. Neil smells the bacon, a big smile on his face. "Is that bacon for me and Brian, Mrs Cassidy?"

"No, it's not for you two, sorry Neil, it's for Mr Cassidy for work. I need to feed him up so he's bringing home big wages for me."

Cass walks into the kitchen still grouchy with the rude awakening, but when he smells the bacon his attitude changes. "Mmmn is that bacon for me mum? It smells lovely."

"No, it's for your dad for work, here's a fiver, get something from Arthur's café. Now fuck off and get to school."

Cass and Neil look at each other and burst out laughing, pushing and shoving each other as they leave the house. On the way to school, they have arranged to meet Lee Cambo at the sweet shop. At the shop, Cambo is moaning that they're late and that Cass has not answered his phone.

"Sorry" says Cass, "It's broke, I'm getting it fixed. It's in the shop now, I get it back on Saturday. Anyway, Neil, tell us all about Everton, what was it like signing for them? Have you met any first team players yet? Have you been in the manager's office?"

"Yeah, of course I have Cass. I had to when I signed the pro-forms. I shit myself when I was in the office waiting for the manager to arrive."

"I'm so jealous... I'm made-up for you Neil, I wish it was me in the team with you but my dad won't let me sign for anyone till I leave school. I've been to train with every top club during school holidays for the last five years and every one of them wanted me to sign schoolboy's forms but my dad always said no. It makes me so sad. He only let me sign for our Reid's team to make me stronger but I think I'm ready now Neil."

As they get near the old Victorian school building Lee Cambo leaves Brian and Neil because he's in a different form class and doesn't want to be late.

He starts to run, shouting back, "You two, don't be late for Art after form class."

Cass and Neil walk snail pace. They don't give a fuck if they're late or not.

Cass turns to Neil, "Art with that horrible self-centred Yorkshire bitch Miss Murray. I hate her! She always has a go at me. I get all angry and frustrated in her class."

"Do you blame her?" laughs Neil, "you locked her in the art storeroom."

"She wasn't in the room for that long."

"Not long? She was in there all day. She only got out when the cleaner opened the door with her master key."

"She must have been tidying up in there and blamed me."

"No, Cass she wasn't, at one point they were thinking of putting her on the front of the milk cartons as a missing person," laughs Neil.

As Cass and Neil reach the school yard, six-foot-two Mr White is standing at the school gates like a bouncer.

"Hurry up you two," shouts Mr. White. "Or you will both be late for class."

"Behave Sir," replies Cass, "we can't be late, it's our last day of school. How can we be late?"

"It's not school you have to be early for lads, it's life in general. It's always better to be early than late."

"Nah, that doesn't apply to us two Sir," replies Neil, "we're both going to be footballers."

Mr. White stares at them shaking his head.

With a smirk Cass adds, "Hey Sir, don't be giving us them Bette Davis eyes and shaking your head as if you're Elvis. We're both centre forwards and if we get in the box too early, we'll be offside."

"You've always got an answer for everything, don't you son?"

"Yeah, I do Sir," laughs Cass. "That's why I'm so clever because I always have the answers."

Mr. White's cheeks turn bright red, shaking his head, he tells them to hurry up and get to their lessons.

As Cass and Neil turn the corner they bump into Fezo.

"Alright Fezo?" bellows Cass.

"Yeah, I'm good Cass, what's happening?"

"Not much you know, we got stopped by Les at the school gates."

"Les? Who's fucking Les when he's about kidda?"

"Mr. White is Les, get with the program lad."

"Oh him. The science teacher with the moustache. The one that looks like a seventies porno star."

"Yeah that's the one lad, but he's sound you know Fezo. I saw him at Wembley with his lad at last season's cup final, he was looking for tickets."

"Fuck off. Did you have any tickets for him kidda?"

"Yeah lad, I gave him tickets for him and his son."

"Did yeah Cass, two cup final tickets for the arl Porno Muzzy?"

"Yeah, of course I did lad. They we're forged tickets like."

"No way kidda, did he get in with them?"

"I don't know lad. I never asked him, but I've never had a detention off him since."

"Do you know what Cass lad, you're sorted with him now. I remember my uncle telling me a story about arl Porno Muzzy, he was their form teacher many years ago. Every time he gave them the cane, that Mr. White would say: 'Giving you lot the stick, will hurt me more than it will hurt you.' But that fucker never walked away with bruised fingers like all the kids did. He's like the rest of them."

"Nah Fezo lad, he's not you know. Mr. White is sound. It pisses me off when people slag the good teachers in the school. Now that twat we have for next lesson, Miss Murray is a right cow."

"Okay, calm down Cass. I'll see you pair of ragarses in Art. I'm off," shouts Fezo as he heads towards class.

"Okay Fezo, see you in Art." Cass pauses…Ragarse? He shouts back at Fezo "Have you seen your own fat arse? You've got an arse like a Bombay money lender."

Ten minutes into registration, they enter their form class. Mr Price, their form teacher, looks up from his desk and says, "I'm glad you two could make it. Was there no red carpets last night? Sit down and be quiet."

As Neil sits down Cass hits him on the head with a ruler. Mr Price looks up, "What are you doing Cass?"

"I'm showing Parks who's the ruler sir."

"Well. That's okay Cass, can you do it quietly please?"

Mr Price takes the register and wishes them all the best for the future. Then he tells them how much they have been a pleasure to teach and how he wants to read about them in the local papers, when they have left school. "Only good things!" he adds.

The bell rings and the class get up to leave for their next lesson. On the way to Art, Cass and Neil see Susie Doyle, the pin up girl from the sixth form. She's heading their way, with her long blonde hair swaying like it should be in a shampoo advert.

As she comes face to face with Cass she smiles and says, "Hello Cass, you okay?"

Cass, cool as an ice cube says. "Yeah Susie, I'm fine. Are you okay? Coming to watch me in the final on Thursday? I'm playing for Golden Dock at Prescot's ground."

"I would love to Cass. I've got a modelling shoot that day though. What time is kick-off?"

"The match starts at half past six."

"Okay, I'll be well home so I'll be able to make it. I'm looking forward to seeing those sexy muscular legs of yours in football shorts."

"Stop that Susie. You're making me blush." As Susie walks away smiling, Cass and Neil stare at her.

"She fancies a piece of me her Neil."

"Fuck off Cass. You're having a laugh mate. She's eighteen. She's teasing yer."

"No, she really does. I get that vibe from her. Hey! By the way are you coming to watch me in the final on Thursday?"

"Yeah, of course I will, I'll be there cheering you on"

"Aww is that because you're my best mate and you want to support me Neil?"

"No, don't be stupid Cass, it's so I can get a grip of Susie when you score a goal."

They enter the art class.

"You're late Cassidy" barks Miss Murray. Cass looks puzzled, wasn't Neil also late?

"Sit down boy," yells Miss Murray.

He sits down and nods over to Lee Cambo who has got to the class early. Ten minutes into the lesson, Neil is bored. He walks over to Cassidy's table and squirts him with red paint. Cass jumps up and takes the paint off him, but as he does it squirts over Neil's' blazer.

"Behave you two," yells Fezo, "I'm trying to finish my drawing here."

"Fuck me Fezo. I'm covered in paint here and you're moaning about a drawing" laughs Cass.

"You're covered in paint? Look at me," Neil squeals.

"Miss...Miss. Look what Cassidy has done to me!"

"It was an accident Miss. I was stopping Neil putting paint on me."

"Get out Cassidy! Get out my class! In fact, get out of this school. You're good for nothing, you will end up a nobody. Now get out of this school."

Cass can't believe this. Neil Parks is laughing his head off, he's waving goodbye to Cass asking him who the ruler is now. Cass laughs, Parks has stitched him up. As he leaves art class, Miss Murray tells him he's a waste of space who will amount to nothing in life. Cass tells her to go brush her teeth because her breath stinks.

Miss Murray bristles with anger, "You're a horrible child, get out of this school!" Shooing him out, she watches as he leaves the school premises muttering. "That lad will amount to nothing, he's a waste of space."

Cass looks back and shouts "Why don't you get in? You ugly smelly rat."

Miss Murray is out of earshot but Cass carries on with his rant as he exits the school's gates.

Cass heads to Arthur's Café. On his way there, he sees two lads off his estate, driving a brand-new Range Rover. As the two lads pass him the car stops. They're older than young Cass, both in their early twenties. Ginger Lee the oldest with Burger a few years younger.

"Where you going?" Burger asks Cass, "do you need a lift?"

"I'm going to Arthur's Cafe" replies Cass, "and I'd love a lift in that mean machine."

"Get in Cass. We're passing that way."

"Nice one Burger." Cass gets in and is so impressed with the car. "Wow! This is fucking boss." his eyes are checking it out like it's a spaceship. "Where are you two off then?"

"We're going grafting, all over Europe!" says Burger, "Paris first, then a good long smoke in Amsterdam -"

"- Hamburg Zurich," says Ginger. "Wherever we feel like going." Do you want to come Cass?"

"What in my school uniform? Bet you two earn a fortune. You must do having a motor like this."

Ginger Lee laughs. "This is a hire car Cass, you should see the motors we drive."

"Yeah this is a run around" sniggers Burger.

"Why do they call you Burger?" Cass asks politely.

Ginger Lee, laughing says, "Why do you think Cass?" as he points to Burger who is munching on a Big Mac. "It's not because he drinks healthy smoothies every day."

Laughing, Burger, with his mouth full says, "It's because I liked the film 'Hamburger Hill' Burger stuck as a nickname."

"I knew that it wasn't because you were fat Burger. I knew it was because of a nickname." Ginger Lee sniggers at Cass's remark. As they pull up outside Arthur's Cafe, Cass gets out of the Range Rover still in a daze.

"Have a good trip, lads." Cass bids them farewell. He skips away from the motor with a big smile on his face.

As he walks into the dark dingy cafe, he gets a whiff of burned fat. The café is empty except for the owner Arthur, who is standing in the cooking zone with a cigarette in his mouth. The radio in the background is making a crackling noise.

Cass goes to the front of the café to place his order.

"Hey Arthur. I thought you weren't allowed to smoke in a public place?"

"Public place son? Can you see anyone in here?"

"Arthur, do you ever wonder why? You're smoking in the cooking zone."

"I can smoke where I like son. I'm the cook. I'm the owner. That's a stupid rule the government brought out. I pay my taxes, I can do what I want."

"That's not a very good advertisement for this five-star café Arthur, is it? It's like a crack den in here with all that smoke."

"That smoke is because of the smoky bacon I've been cooking all morning son."

Cass points to the wall at the hygiene sticker. "Where have the other four stars gone Arthur?"

"What four stars son. It's always been a one-star cafe, that's why I give the council a back hander."

"I thought it was five stars because you had such posh rats Arthur."

"Why aren't you in school Cass?"

"I've left school."

"Left school son?"

"Yeah I've left school."

"Are you taking the piss kid, it's only eleven o'clock. Schools have gone soft. When I was a lad, we had no messing in school."

Arthur starts reminiscing about his schooldays. "What are you going to do now son?"

"Now, I'm going to order a cup of tea and two toasts. Bring it over when it's ready."

Arthurs looks and thinks cheeky bugger. Cass makes his way over to an empty table. A few minutes later Arthur brings over his tea and two slices of toast.

"Two-pound son."

"Two pounds? Two fucking pounds? Fuck me Arthur, even Dick Turpin wore a mask when he robbed people."

"Cheeky bugger," laughs Arthur.

Cass sits at the table staring at two soggy burned toasts and tea like piss water. No longer a school-child. He looks out of the window and ponders what the future has in store...

Chapter 2

William's Big Bet

It's a bright sunny Thursday afternoon. Liverpool in May, the day of the Sean Quinn challenge cup final. 2 pm, Cass is in his bedroom listening to Sam Smith on the radio as he gets his football bag ready for the game. He puts his gleaming New Balance football boots into the bag along with shin pads, sprays and Vaseline. He's ready now for the big cup final. He's waiting for his cousin Reid Johnson to pick him up to take him to the restaurant for their pre-match meal. He's wearing a black Hugo Boss hooded tracksuit with Balenciaga trainers.

Walking down the stairs, he hears a car beep. He looks out of the window and sees Reid Johnson in his BMW convertible, beeping constantly. Cass walks out the door and jokes, "Okay, okay I thought I was on Family Fortunes then with all the beeps. I was half expecting Les Dennis to be picking me up."

Reid Johnson laughs and shouts, "Hurry up Cass, it's *big money*." As Cass gets in the car, he shakes his head at Reid.

"Reid. You have all the Sky channels and you're watching Family Fortunes on Freeview on the Challenge station."

"Maybe I like that station."

"You're old before your time Reid, old before your time."

"Get in the car and get your seat belt on soft-arse." Cass notices Reid is wearing a new Givenchy top. "Lovely top that." Reid is the fashion icon in the team. He's wearing a pair of Giuseppe Zanetti's shoes and Dsquared jeans.

As they are about to drive away, Cass notices two workmen next to a BT van digging up the pavement. He calls them over.

"What are you two doing mate?"

"Why? Who wants to know pal?" replies the elder of the workmen.

"I do mate. I'm Brian Cassidy, chief neighbourhood watch warden."

"You're a bit young for a watch warden son."

"I just look young for my age mate. I'm 32."

"32? My arse son. I've seen you delivering newspapers last week."

"You're the dog's bollocks you mate. There's no kidding you is there?"

"No son, they're isn't. You've got to get up early to pull the wool over my eyes."

"So, what are you doing?"

"We're fixing the cables son. They melted, so we're replacing them. The phone lines are all down kid."

"How long will it take to fix?"

"It could be one week or two weeks. The phones would have been fixed last week, but some thieving bastards robbed the cables we had put down. The robbing bastards."

"That's no good," says Cass. "You should have got the other fella down here as your security guard. You know that big fella, the big muscle man, thingio, what's his name? You know that *gladiator* fella. What's his name? Robby? No that's not him... Bobby, hmm that's not him either. It's Johnny, Johnny Crowe! That's who you should have had as your security mate."

"We didn't think of that son. I'll ring our boss now to see if he's available."

"Yeah Johnny boy is your man mate." Reid and Cass drive away.

The workmen both look puzzled. Workman Joe says: "I think the kid has got a bit mixed up there with the names Billy. I think he meant to say Ronnie Crowe, that fella who played the Roman..." The elder workman, Billy, shakes his head saying, "You're just as bad as that kid. It's Russell Crowe. Not fucking Johnnie or Ronnie Crowe. It's Russell Crowe, he plays the part of Maximus Decimus Meridius. He was a Roman legend made into a gladiator."

"Yeah, that's him. They're twins them two." Billy glances at Joe shaking his head in disbelief...

.

In the car, Cass asks Reid if they are heading straight for the restaurant.

"We're going up to Maghull for our pre-match meal in the Chinese restaurant *Chow Wong.*"

"Nice one, I love our pre-match meals in Wong's,"

"Are you looking forward to the final Cass?"

"Yes, it's the reason I signed for the Golden Dock, so I could play in cup finals."

Reid smiles, "You have a bright future in football Cass. There will be plenty of finals and big games for you if you take the right path in life and steer clear of shit. That's why I'm here to look after you and push you in the right direction."

"I think there'll be lots more finals for you too Reid, because you're so talented."

"Thanks Cass. You sure know how to bolster a person's confidence."

"I just say what I see Reid. Boy you can play."

They both smile and give each other a high five. Pulling into the Chow Wong car park, Reid and Cass are greeted by Bobby Arrow – team captain.

"You both fit and raring to go?" asks Bob.

"Of course, we are Bob," says Reid with his chest pumped out as if he's about to go into battle. As they enter the building the rest of the team are at the tables.

The team reads like this:

KEVIN CHIVERS goalkeeper age 24, His nickname in the team is *The Bull*, because of the way he charges out of his goal. He's 5ft 11 in height and 5ft wide. He likes the arcade games. His other nickname is *Magnet*. He says it's because the ball attracts to his gloves.

BOBBY ARROW right back, age 29, 5ft 9. The captain and leader of the team. He lacks pace but reads the game better than any other player in the league. His nickname is *Serious* as he's always serious.

MARK BARROW left back age 27, 5ft7. Mark is a left foot free kick specialist. His nickname is *Harvey Wallbanger.* Lots of people think it is because of his sweet left foot which scores lots of free kicks, but many of the players snigger at this.

BOB HOPE centre half age 36, 6ft 4. Bob is the oldest in the team. His nickname is *Big Bob* because of his height.

ALAN JONES centre half age 25, 5ft 8. Alan is not the tallest of defender's, but he has a big head that wins most of the headers. His nickname is *AJ* or *Desperate Dan*. Because he always has a beard no matter how often he shaves. He also loves food. He loves pies. He's the pie man.

ANT HODGE centre midfield age 25, 5ft 10. Ant is an all action player, who always has a smile on his face. His nickname is *The Engine*, because he never stops running. He can play a bit also. He kicks just as good with either foot. Ant is a popular member of the team.

JOHN CULLY centre midfield age 24, 5ft 9. The team joker has lots of skill. He's a bit of a show off. He also likes his fashion. His nickname is *Pitbull*, because he's always chewing the ball. He's a popular member of the team.

REID JOHNSON right midfield age 24, 5ft 6. Fiery red head, Reid has so much talent he always gets stuck in and never shirks a tackle. He's the fashion icon of the team. His nickname is the *Raging Bomb* as he always explodes when anyone kicks young Cass. Reid looks after him on the pitch.

KEVIN PARRY left midfield age 28, 5ft 11. Kevin always works hard for the team and does the business on the pitch. He's very annoying and upsets a lot of the team members.

BRIAN CASSIDY centre forward age 16, 5ft 10. Young Cass has a bright future in the game, if he takes the right road. He loves to score a goal and has so much talent he can dance around players like he's invisible. His nickname is the *Boy Wonder*.

KEVIN BIRD centre forward age 28, 6ft 2. His nickname is Steptoe because of his fashion sense. He loves to wear his Wrangler jeans and Next jumpers and his Nike hoody. He's very gangly and is a great header of the ball.

The other members of the squad are:

JOHN PAUL ANDERSON age 23, 6ft. JP had the world at his feet at 18. He was a pro footballer with the Blues until he was tested positive for cocaine and cannabis. He was released and since turned to drink. He plays as a bit part player now. He's a waste of talent. Often, he's sub if he's not drunk or stoned.

TODD ELLIOTT sub, age 26, 5ft 8. His nickname is *Speedy* because he's so fast over 100 metres. He's the team sponsor and only work commitments prevent his full-time involvement with the team. So, he just plays a bit part. He has lighting pace.

FRANK ROX sub, age 24, 5ft 8. He's a team member but not a very good player. He's a favourite and popular figure in the team. He's always making the team laugh and is always committed to the team His nickname is *DJ* because he always plays music in the dressing room.

PAT ARROW sub, age 28, 5ft 8. Pat is the brother of Bob. He's also a committee member who does anything that is asked of him. He's a popular member of the team and likes a drink and a laugh. He's the team joker.

ALEX SHARP assistant manager, age 36, 5ft 9. He has long hair like a girl but all the players love him because he's always there for them. He helps them every way he can. He's the players' favourite and helps out as sub if the team are short. He's still a good player. His nickname is *Brandy* not because he likes his drink but because he looks like Russell Brand.

PETER SPRINGSTEEN manager, age 45. He thinks he's a rock and roll star. He's not very approachable but always seems to pick the winning team.

Heading to his seat, Cass notices Alan Jones munching on a pork pie. John Paul is standing at the doorway smoking a joint. He's leaning against the post. He lets on to Cass and Reid.

"Have you been drinking John Paul?"

"No Reid. What makes you say that?"

"Well, for starters you look pissed and it looks like that post is holding you up."

"Reid, I've had a few pints to warm me up for the match."

"For fuck sake John Paul. It's the cup final."

"I'll be okay, Gazza had one of his best games for Everton when he was pissed. And he scored in that game."

"You're not fucking Gazza, John Paul. Gazza was at the end of his career in that game. He could afford to do it. You've not even started your career yet. That's why Everton fucked you off. Yer gobshite."

John Paul puts his head down as he takes a pull of his joint. Reid pokes Cass in the back.

"That's the direction you're not going down Brian. Keep clear of drugs, okay? Drugs are for mugs. That John Paul had the world at his feet, he's a fucking waste of talent."

They both enter the eating area where the rest of the team are sitting at their tables. It's a buffet meal, most of them have soup and water for their meals. John Paul has vodka in his water and Alan Jones has two meat pies before every match. The lads all sit round the big table talking about the match.

Frank Rox has the iPod blasting out playing the tunes 'All together now' sung by indie band The Farm. He's trying to bond the team as they eat.

Bob Arrow takes a phone call. It's William Henry, the manager of Jersey Croft the opposing team in today's final.

William Henry is one of those managers who had a season ticket for Liverpool in the seventies and eighties, who thinks he knows everything about football but knows fuck all about football. He's rumoured to be paying his players wages which is illegal in amateur football. He always strongly denies this. He's a very rich businessman, who is known to like a bet or two. He's on the phone asking Bob if he wants a thousand pound bet for winning the final.

Bob Arrow puts William Henry on hold and asks his team are they up for it tonight and tells them about the bet.

Kevin Chivers yells "Fuck me Bob. So, William big bollocks wants a thousand pound bet on the outcome of the match?"

Frank Rox jumps up shouting: "Take the fucking bet. Let's take William big balls to the cleaners."

Bob looks at Cass and asks him how he's feeling.

"I'm feeling good skipper. Let's take the bet. Rinse the bastard."

"Rinse the bastard, hey Cass? Well kid... Let the bet commence."

The team all jump up and down, they are going wild.

"Let's have him," all the team shout. Bob gets back on the phone and accepts the thousand pound bet. The players go wild, they are right up for the Cup Final match now.

Bob Hope reminds the players that they will be going to Amsterdam tomorrow Friday - *if* they win the Cup.

"How does that work again Bob?" asks Kevin Chivers.

"Well if you win the cup, two local businessmen have agreed to sponsor the trip to Amsterdam to play the Dutch champions," replies Bob Hope.

"It's pre-booked so we have to win," says Bob Arrow.

"What happens if we lose Bob?" asks Kevin Parry. Frank Rox slaps Parry around his head.

"Hey, Parry there is no lose in our mind-sets," yells Rox.

"If we don't win the trip is cancelled," says Peter Springsteen.

"We'd best win the cup then," says Bob Arrow.

Mark Barrow pays the bill by credit card. As Cass walks past, he notices Mark Barrow signing the receipt in the name of Harvey Smith. This confuses Cass.

As the team leave the restaurant, Alan Jones scoffs down another pork pie.

The team are all up for the game. As they leave, they join in a chorus of *'we're going to win the cup,'* banging on the walls and the ceilings led by Frank Rox and Pat Arrow.

In the car park they separate to make the twenty minutes journey in their own cars to Prescot stadium where the final is being held. It is now 4.35 pm.

Golden Dock's opposition today is Jersey Croft, who have lots of semi-professional players in their team. It should be a tight hard fought game.

A rundown of Jersey Croft:

David Bryons goalkeeper, age 25. He's a top goalkeeper. He plays semi-professional for Southport, he would be in the football league only he's always in and out of jail.

Nico Valente right back, age 29 and 5ft 8. He's the Italian member of the team. He's the cousin of Tommy Rossi. He's an attacking full back. He was released by Napoli age 24 and has been in the Jersey Croft side since.

Gary Eagle Bird left back, age 36 and 5ft 6. He's an actor. The elder statements of the team, he's very dirty in a tackle. He's the arl arse of the team. His nickname is *The Eagle* because he glides down the wing as an attacking full back. His best days are past him.

Phil Lightfoot centre half, age 29 and 6ft 3. He's a big gangly player. He's a great header of the ball and plays non-league for Winsford. He's dangerous at set pieces.

Lee Grant centre half, age19 and 6ft 2. He has two good feet, who plays the ball out with his feet. He's a great passer of the ball and was released by Newcastle, so Jersey Croft snapped him up. He has played for England at under 16 level.

Mark Wynn centre midfield, age 27 and 5ft 8. He's the team captain and the hard case of the league. He takes no messing, he has a left foot that can-do magic with the ball. He played for Tranmere, but he left to box professionally. He still plays Sunday football and he's a good friend of William Henry, who also sponsored him when he boxes.

Vinny Newton centre midfield, age 25 and 6ft. He's a tough tackling no nonsense midfielder. He runs all through the match, box to box, covering every blade of the grass. His nickname is *Vinny The Stare* because if he makes eye contact with you, he's going to blast you in his next tackle. He plays non-league for Prescot, so he has covered every inch of the cup final pitch.

Danny Kelly right midfield, age 18 and 6ft. He's a skilful right footed player. He has just been released by Wigan. He's another youngster snapped up by Jersey Croft. He's also a DJ in nightclubs.

Curly Rossi left midfield, age 27 and 5ft 10. He's the son of assistant manager Tommy Rossi. He tries to tell the referee how to ref during games. He has a good left foot and he's fast down the wing.

Joey Egg Head centre forward, age 29 and 6ft 2. He's another arl arse member of the team. He's a good header of the ball but he's a bit lazy. He likes the glory and plays non-league for Runcorn.

Joey Worthington centre forward, age 24 and 5ft 11. He's a very skilful player with bags of talent. He plays non-league for Runcorn and likes to dribble with the ball.

Bobby Henry sub, age 18 and 5ft 11. He's the son of William Henry. He has a lot of talent and he's skilful.

Giorgio Pearce sub, age 26 and 5ft 10. He has a lot of energy and will run all day.

Neil Saint John sub, age 28 and 5ft 8. He's an attacking full back. He was released by Motherwell because of a serious knee injury. He's the nephew of Liverpool legend Ian Saint John. His nickname is the *Flying Scotsman*.

William Henry manager, age 48 and 5ft 9. He puts on a subs shirt but he hardly ever plays. He just likes being part of team. He has played twice in 5 seasons.

Tommy Rossi assistant manager, age 65 and 5ft 6. He used to be a referee in non-league football. He shouts for every decision that is not given to his team. He's known to video the football games and send them to the league committee when he's not happy with a decision.

As the Golden Dock enter Prescot's ground, there's already a big crowd gathering.

It's 5pm, the weather is good, it's a warm bright May Day. Kick-off is scheduled for 6.30 pm and the referee for tonight's match is Brian Barton, who's a fair referee who can handle the big occasions. Both teams were pleased with the choice of the referee. The linesmen for tonight's final are:

Joe Tootle who is also a top referee in the league and Nicky Holt who has also been a linesman in the football league and he's known for being able to read the game well and for his precision in spotting an offside correctly.

The Golden Dock players take a look at the condition of the pitch and make their way to the home dressing room. As they enter the dressing room, the smell of ligament oils hits them flaring their nostrils. They sit on the benches. The door is wide open. John Cully is kicking the football in the dressing room.

As the team chat and joke, Jersey Croft enter their own dressing room making lots of noises and start banging on the walls trying to intimidate the Golden Dock's players. Mark Wynn yells out a war cry as he passes Golden Dock's open dressing room door.

Peter Springsteen looks up and asks Kevin Bird to shut the dressing room door. Frank Rox puts the team's iPod on and starts playing 'The eye of the tiger'. The tune gets them all fired up. Ant Hodge puffs out his chest and does an impression of King Kong. Mark Barrow jumps up and does some shadow boxing as if he's Rocky Balboa. Frank Rox comes from behind him and slaps him on the back of his head.

He starts dancing around him like Ali shouting: "I am the greatest."

The whole dressing room burst out laughing. Again, Frank Rox has got the team in good spirits. Bob Hope, Peter Springsteen and Bobby Arrow are all in the corner in a deep discussion. After five minutes, Peter Springsteen walks over to address the team, he asks Frank Rox to turn off the iPod. He gets the reply: "Yes sir, sir yes."

The team piss themselves laughing.

Peter Springsteen reads out the team and reminds the players that if they win the cup, they will be rewarded with a five day trip to Amsterdam courtesy of two local businessmen. They will be leaving the next day, on the Friday morning, as a big thank you for doing the double. They have already won the league a week earlier. This news gets them all fired up as they know if they lose the final, the trip is cancelled.

Pat Arrow starts singing: *"Today is going to be the day we're going to win the Sean Quinn cup final."*

The whole team join in. John Paul Anderson, who is mixed race, starts dancing like a disco diva. The team all join in dancing, it's like being on the dance floor on *Top of The Pops*.

Peter Springsteen gathers them into a circle and tells them that it's time to win the cup.

The team gather together. They are all up for this cup final. The sound of football-boot-studs rattles the tile floor of the dressing room.

Frank Rox pipes up "HEY LADS. This must have been how General Custer felt when he was going into the battle of Little Bighorn."

"I can associate with that," replies Peter Springsteen "I had my own battle with Little Bighorn. I won that battle with Viagra."

The team look toward Peter Springsteen in total shock.

Frank Rox yells, "Did you hear that? Our own manager won his battle with Little Bighorn. So now you see. Custer went into battle as brave as fuck and our manager went into battle as hard as fuck. So, let's mix them together and let's go out and win this cup."

The team roar like lions as they get into line and the captain Bobby Arrow leads them out of the dressing room into the corridor to await the arrival of Jersey Croft.

John Paul Anderson taps Ant Hodge on the back.

"What's up John Paul?"

"Hey Ant, I thought it was only Pelé who suffered with that problem?"

"No John Paul, all soft dickpots suffer with that problem."

"It's lucky that I'm a hard case then. Isn't it Ant?"

Ant Hodge, shocked, looks at John Paul and whispers to himself. "The lights are on upstairs but there is definitely no one in." Cass overhears Ant whispering and starts laughing.

As Jersey Croft emerge out of their dressing room, the referee Brian Barton and his two linesmen lead them out of the corridor out onto the pitch.

"Come on Golden Dock! Are we ready to rumble?" yells Bobby Arrow.

As the team jogs out all fired up, Frank Rox yells, "This is it. It's the start of the Sean Quinn challenge cup final."

Chapter 3

The Sean Quinn Challenge Cup Final

Golden Dock	Versus	Jersey Croft
1. Kevin Chivers		1. David Bryons
2. Bobby Arrow (Captain)		2. Nico Valente
3. Mark Barrow		3. Gary Bird
4. Ant Hodge		4. Phil Lightfoot
5. Bob Hope		5. Lee Grant
6. Alan Jones		6. Mark Wynn (Captain)
7. Reid Johnson		7. Danny Kelly
8. John Cully		8. Vinny Newton
9. Kevin Bird		9. Joey Egghead
10. Brian Cassidy		10. Joey Worthington
11. Kevin Parry		11. Curly Rossi
Subs		Subs
John Paul Anderson		William Henry
Todd Elliott		Bobby Henry
Frank Rox		Giorgio Pearce
Pat Arrow		Neil Saint John
Manager: Peter Springsteen		Manager: William Henry
Asst. Manager: Alex Sharp		Asst. Manager: Tommy Rossi

As the team runs out, Joey Egghead pushes Cass in the face, trying to put him off his game.

Cass barks, "Fuck off you, yer baldy twat."

Reid Johnson sees this and squares up to Egghead. Whistle blowing, they get pulled apart by the referee Brian Barton.

"Calm down," he yells, "let's have a clean game."

As the teams take their positions, Alex Sharp reminds the players that win this and they win the double. The Golden Dock players look up for it. At sixteen, boy wonder Brian Cassidy is the youngest player in the final yet he seems so relaxed and focussed.

Mark Wynn wins the toss and decides his team will kick off.

There is a crowd of over five hundred watching the final today with chief scouts from Liverpool, Everton, Man United, Man City, Bolton, Wigan and many other clubs all watching boy wonder Brian Cassidy. In the VIP section Liverpool chief scout Ian Barragan is talking about the boy wonder Brian Cassidy with Everton chief scout Bob Pendleton and Man City's chief scout Terry Anderson.

Cass looks up to see his best mate Neil Parks with Susie Doyle in the crowd. Both have made it to watch him. He smiles at them both as they wave. Cass is focussed and raring to go.

As William Henry passes Bobby Arrow, he shakes his hand, and wishes him all the best.

"May the best team win Bobby."

"Yeah, that will be us William."

"I hope you do otherwise you have to pay me a lot of money Bobby boy." Both smile and take up their positions.

The game gets underway. Tommy Rossi is already moaning about a double sided coin, his team have won the toss. Jersey Croft kick off and start brightly. The big battle will be in the centre of midfield. This is where the game will be won – where men show they are men and not little boys.

The local radio station is doing a live commentary on the game with local DJ John Kelly. Bob Dring is on the touchline with his radio as he lets the crowd listen to the live commentary.

(Commentary by John Kelly)
In the opening minutes, John Cully is chewing the ball.
Mark Wynn hits him like a runaway train, sending him flying.
Mark Wynn stands over him and tells him to get up.
John Cully doesn't know what day it is.
Pat Arrow runs on the pitch with the magic sponge and squirts water over his head.

John Cully squeals, "Fuck me it's World War Three." He gets up and limps away.

Ant Hodge tells him to release the ball quicker to stop the opposition whacking him.

(Commentary by John Kelly)

As the game goes on it evens itself out. Ant Hodge takes control, picking up all the loose balls.

In the fifth minute, Brian Cassidy dances past three players. Out of nowhere, Mark Wynn whacks him in the ankle sending him tumbling down to the ground. Cassidy goes down, wincing in pain, holding his ankle.

Mark Wynn stands over him and picks him up by his armpit hair yelling, "Fucking get up Billy Elliot. This is a man's game, not a fucking dance show…"

Cassidy gets up and smiles at Wynn not knowing what to hold first – his ankle or his armpits to ease the pain.

Reid Johnson rushes over and shouts, "Fuck off you, yer big prick."

Wynn jogs backwards laughing, "You're next Johnson."

"You don't scare me," Reid replies.

Cassidy winces in pain, his armpits are burning and his ankle is throbbing.

(Commentary by John Kelly)
From the resulting free kick Reid Johnson sends over a pinpoint accurate cross to Kevin Bird who heads it over the bar. That's the closest to a goal yet.

David Bryons hits a goal kick, long up field. Joey Worthington knocks it on to Danny Kelly who is clear on goal only for the linesman to flag for offside. Tommy Rossi is furious. He's effing and blinding at the referee.

Tommy watches it back on the video player he has set up to record the game. He notices Kelly was two yards offside but still calls the linesman a fucking wanker.

(Commentary by John Kelly)
In the eighth minute, Reid Johnson beats the Italian fullback Nico Valente, cuts inside and shoots. The ball flies towards the near post. David Bryons makes a world class save.

In the tenth minute Mark Wynn receives the ball from Lee Grant in the centre circle and nutmegs Kevin Parry before sending an inch-perfect pass to the ageing Gary Bird. He flies down the wing like an eagle, turning back the clock, he eases pat Bobby Arrow to send an inch-perfect cross to Joey Egghead who rises above Alan Jones with the use of his elbow in Alan Jones's nose. He heads the ball towards the far corner of the goal but it's just an inch too high. That was a huge let off for Golden Dock.

`Tommy Rossi is complaining that Egghead was getting held back while William Henry is smiling thinking his money is safe and it's only a matter of time before he's a grand richer.

"Shut up Rossi let the game flow," come the cries from the crowd.

"Yer dirty bastard Egghead," yells Alex Sharp.

The game is end to end for the next ten minutes.

(Commentary by John Kelly)

It's that man Brian Cassidy - the boy wonder who opens the scoring. Reid Johnson starts the move, beating two players then sends in a cross to the head of Kevin Bird at the far post who heads the ball back in to the eighteen-yard box for Brian Cassidy who, with his back turned, performs an overhead bicycle kick - volleying the ball in to the far right corner of the goal, where it smashes the back of the net giving David Bryons no chance in goal.

The crowd can't believe what they have just witnessed. They will be talking about that goal for years and years. Unbelievable goal. The kid is a boy wonder. The scouts have sat up and taken notice. Golden Dock 1 – 0 Jersey Croft

Reid Johnson is the first to congratulate young Cassidy, rubbing his head. He's mobbed by the rest of the players. William Henry is not smiling now. Rossi is shouting for offside.

That was typical Golden Dock teamwork with a finish from the boy wonder. That is why they're league champions.

"Boy Wonder, that was more like a young Pele," shouts Lee Cambo.

"Cass, yer beauty," yells Parks.

(Commentary by John Kelly)
Jersey Croft kick off and attack all guns blazing. Phil Lightfoot carries the ball forward unmarked. Phil Lightfoot strikes the ball, it flies like a scud-missile hitting the bar before going out for a goal kick.
Ant Hodge and John Cully control the midfield passing the ball about. It's looking like Golden Dock are going in at half time one-nil up. The match is as exciting as anything the crowd has seen in years. It's end to end. "Pass It to Cass, let him do his magic," yells Frank Rox.

"Give the ball to the boy wonder," come the cries from the crowd.

(Commentary by John Kelly)
The referee looks at his watch to blow for half time. John Cully is chewing the ball in midfield. Mark Wynn robs the ball from him and sends Vinny 'The Stare' Newton clear on goal. Kevin Chivers rushes out of his goal to cut the angle down, Vinny The Stare sees this and chips the ball over him to make it one all. Class goal!
The referee blows up, it's the last kick of the half.
William Henry has got his smile back on his face. He skips back to his team's dressing room like he's just won the lottery. Tommy Rossi stays in the dugout checking the video playback of the first half.
Golden Dock walk off the pitch gutted.
Golden Dock 1-1 Jersey Croft

As they enter the dressing room Frank Rox has the iPod speaker playing 'Don't Stop Believing.' The team are all a bit flat after conceding that late goal. Peter Springsteen tells them to do more of the same in the second half as they were the better team.

They sit down having their energy drinks. Alan Jones goes into his kit bag and pulls out a meat pie, scoffing it down. They have a team talk and as the bell goes make their way back out on to the pitch.

(Commentary by John Kelly)
The game kicks off. Cassidy tries a shot from the half way line, it whizzes just over the bar.

Jersey Croft start taking control of the game with Mark Wynn and Vinny The Stare Newton bossing the midfield.

"Subs warm up," shouts Alex Sharp from the dugout.

"Get tight to their midfield Cully," yells Peter Springsteen.

(Commentary by John Kelly)

John Cully picks up a loose pass, it's a close fought contest, he holds on to the ball too long.

Mark Wynne treads on his ankle leaving John Cully squealing like a pig on the pitch turf.

Pat Arrow runs on with the magic sponge but it's all to no avail - he can no longer carry on. Pat Arrow helps him off. Peter Springsteen is telling John Paul Anderson to get stripped and ready.

John Paul Anderson moves in to the centre and starts to control the game. He passes the ball about making Mark Wynn chase shadows.

"John Paul work your magic lad," yells Pat.

The pace of the game has slowed down in the last ten minutes.

(Commentary by John Kelly)

In the seventieth minute Jersey Croft attack down the left. The ageing Gary Bird bombs down the flank sending a cross over. Alan Jones intercepts and sends Kevin Parry free down the wing, he swings in a cross but Lee Grant heads it over the bar for a Golden Dock corner. As the players take up their positions, Brian Cassidy is at the near post marked by Gary Bird and Vinny The Stare Newton.

Vinny shouts over to Gary Bird. "Hey Birdy, see that little shit Cassidy?"

"I fucking see him Vinny, why what's up?"

"When this ball comes over you fucking tee him up and I'll volley the little twat."

"Yeah, alright Vinny will do, you take the little shit out, fucking chop him in two."

Cass is stunned, he can't believe what he has just heard, he's bewildered and relieved when the ball goes over him to the far post. The crowd are lapping the game up.

(Commentary by John Kelly)
Nico Valente picks up the loose ball and sends Joey Worthington free, he's about to shoot. Bobby Arrow slides in and wins the ball. To the dismay of the Golden Dock players, the ref blows the whistle and awards a penalty.
Tommy Rossi is jumping up and down shouting, "yes ref, defo a pen, defo was a pen." the crowd can't believe it. Bobby won the ball cleanly.
Mark Wynn steps up and strikes it smoothly in to the far-right hand corner with his sweet left peg.
Golden Dock 1 – 2 Jersey Croft.
The game resumes. The ball goes out for a throw in. Golden Dock make a change bringing on the speedy Todd Elliott for Kevin Parry.

Bobby Arrow is on the touchline taking the throw when William Henry stands next to him rubbing his hands, pretending to count money, smiling.

Bob looks and shouts, "William, it's not over 'til the fat lady sings and your birds still in McDonalds." The crowd piss themselves laughing.

(Commentary by John Kelly)
Mark Wynn and Vinny The Stare start to feel the pace of the game, it has tired them both out. John Paul Anderson skips past two players then lays it off to Todd Elliott who sends in a cross. Phil Lightfoot half clears but only heads it straight to the feet of Reid Johnson, who bursts in to the box only to be fouled by goalkeeper David Bryons. The referee has no choice but to give a penalty and also gives David Bryons a yellow card.

Tommy Rossi is furious. He storms on to the pitch yelling, "You fucking wanker ref, it was never a penalty." He races twenty yards demonstrating that it wasn't a penalty.

(Commentary by John Kelly)
The referee shows Tommy Rossi a red card! Tommy is furious, stomping up and down.
William Henry has to come on the pitch to remove him. Curly Rossi is pleading with his dad to leave the pitch, reminding him it's only a penalty and they're still winning.

Tommy Rossi leaves the stadium and heads for his car outside the Prescot's ground.

The crowd cheer as he leaves.

William Henry tells Bobby Henry to take over videoing the game. Up steps the sixteen-year-old wonder boy Brian Cassidy to take the penalty.

As he places the ball on the penalty spot he checks David Bryon's position in the goal. Cassidy takes two steps back, watching Bryons every movement. As he moves forward to strike the ball he looks David Bryons in the eyes, as he dives to the right Cassidy passes the ball down the centre of the goal, cool as you like, dinking the ball into the empty net.

The crowd can't believe what they have witnessed. How could he be that cool in the eighty-sixth minute?

It's now 2 – 2. Reid Johnson jumps on Cassidy, head hugging him, "Well done kid, fucking brilliant."

Frank Rox runs on from the touchline, hugs Cass then spins and performs the *'Ali shuffle'* shouting "You're the greatest Cassidy, you're the greatest."

(Commentary by John Kelly)

As Jersey Croft are about to kick off they make a substitution bringing on Giorgio Pearce for the tiring Mark Wynn.

The game is heading for extra time with Golden Dock looking the stronger of the teams. The referee blows the whistle.

Extra time starts.

(Commentary by John Kelly)

Tempers begin to flare. Gary Bird, and Kevin Bird – cousins on opposite sides – square up to each other after Gary fouls Kevin, both teams pull them apart. John Paul Anderson skips past three players before unleashing a shot that hits the post.

On this form clubs will want him back, he has been outstanding since he was introduced as sub for John Cully.

Todd Elliott has a run with the ball down the line leaving Gary Bird in his wake. Todd sends over a cross but there is no-one on the end of it.

Both teams are feeling the pace.

Joey Egghead is replaced by young Bobby Henry.
The ref blows his whistle signalling the end of the first period of extra time.
The teams have a quick drink on the pitch then turn around for the second period of extra time.

Second period of extra begins.

(Commentary by John Kelly)
It's still warm on this spring May evening. Both teams have half chances with Kevin Bird going close and Bobby Henry hitting over the bar.
Kevin Chivers sends the ball up field, Ant Hodge brings the ball under control and passes it to Brian Cassidy who does a 'Cruyff turn' leaving two players in his wake. He skips past another two before he nutmegs Lee Grant. He's clean through on goal. David Bryons comes charging out. Brian Cassidy sees this and chips him. As Bryons goes to ground the ball bounces in to the empty net. The young wonder boy has scored a hat trick. The crowd will be talking about this game for years to come.
As Jersey Croft restart the game the ref blows the whistle.
That's it! Golden Dock have won the Cup. The Jersey Croft players fall to their knees, exhausted.

The crowd go wild and start to chant;
"HIS NAME IS CASS AND HE'S WORLD CLASS."
"HIS PACE IS FRIGHTENING HE'S FAST AS LIGHTING."
"HE ROARS LIKE THUNDER HE'S THE BOY WONDER."
"HIS NAME IS CASS AND HE IS PURE CLASS."

William Henry is going around all the players, patting them on the back. As he crosses Bobby Arrow's path he shakes his hand, congratulates him and tells him he will settle their bet later.

The scouts on the touchline have just witnessed a world class player in the making.

Mark Wynn walks over to young Cass, puts his arm around his shoulder and tells him he has a bright future in professional football if he takes the right direction and that he needs to get his head down and work hard with no distractions.

Wynn smirks saying, "If Billy Elliott could dance like young Cassidy plays football he would have been a top ballet dancer in Swan Lake." Cass thanks Wynn as he hobbles away.

Reid Johnson jumps on John Paul. "Was that lager you drank before the match John Paul?"

"Yeah Reid, I'm sorry it was just to calm my nerves down before the match."

"Don't be sorry, John Paul you were brilliant today. That rocket fuel you drank made you play better than Gazza."

"Thanks Reid. I'll drink to that."

As Cass walks off the pitch he's greeted by his best mate, Neil Parks, with a big smile and a high five.

"Well done Cass. You were brilliant. The scouts will be queuing at your front door to sign you now."

"I hope so Neil, I really do hope so." Susie Doyle runs over to Cass and gives him a big kiss.

"Well done babe, you were great."

"Thanks Susie, watch that lipstick on my face, the women will be wanting pictures with me now."

"They sure will after that performance babe."

"Thanks, Susie but you're the only want I want my picture with."

"Oh, you're such a little charmer Cass."

"Charmer more like a piranha," whispers Neil.

"Now now Neil. Don't be jealous because Susie kissed me and not you."

"Shut up Cass, you gobshite, you only scored three. I think you were falling backwards when you scored that overhead bicycle kick."

"Yeah Neil, just like Susie is falling for me."

Cass has stolen the show. The scouts leave buzzing. They will be remembering the name 'Brian Cassidy' for years to come.

Lee Cambo greets Cass, gives him a big hug and shouts, "Brain Cassidy you fucking beauty, you will play for England one day if you take the right road through life. You are a star in the making."

"Fuck me Cambo, That's the first time I haven't heard you moan about something."

Peter Springsteen gathers the team together as the Jersey Croft team receive their medals from the Lord Mayor.

William Henry looks disappointed as he picks up his runners up medal.

Golden Dock applaud the Jersey Croft team.

Now it's time for Bob Arrow to lead the team to pick up the cup.

As Cass picks up his medal, young loveable Downs Syndrome local lad – Stevo - climbs onto the team's dugout and starts chanting,

'CASSIDY FOR ENGLAND, CASSIDY FOR ENGLAND.'

He repeats this louder and louder, jumping up and down on the tarmac dugout roof. The crowd all join in, the noise is deafening.

All the Golden Dock players join in the singing.

Cass goes bright red. His dad watches, feeling ten feet tall and so proud of his lad. He winks at Cass telling him to enjoy the occasion.

Stevo, still standing on the dugout roof, starts singing, 'We are the Champions.' This little stadium has never seen anything like it. As he jumps up more and more the roof of the dugout collapses. It doesn't deter Stevo, he chants even louder.

'WE ARE THE CHAMPIONS.'

The crowd help Stevo up and carry him out of the ground. All the crowd are buzzing, singing and dancing as the Golden Dock players head towards the dressing rooms on a high.

As the team enter the dressing room Frank Rox showers the team in Dom Perignon. There is a happy feeling in the room.

Bob Hope is outside the dressing room with the two business men who have sponsored the Amsterdam trip. They are two local gangsters, Max and Ronnie. Both in their mid-forties. It looks like a serious conversation.

Bob Arrow announces to the team that there are free drinks and a buffet back at the Golden Dock pub and reminds the team that they should be at the pub car park at 10am on Friday morning to depart for their trip to Amsterdam.

Bob Hope returns to the dressing room and announces he won't be going on the trip and that this was his last game as he's retiring from football. The team are in shock. Frank Rox squirts Bob Hope with Champagne.

"Don't worry Bob, you're shit now anyway. With you playing we had no hope, and with you gone we have no hope." The whole team burst out laughing. They all jump up and down in the dressing room like wild cave men, dancing like Michael Jackson minus the rhythm.

Rox has 'We are the champions' blasting out of the iPod.

The team are buzzing, they're all getting their pictures taken with the cup, pouring Champagne into it, swigging it like it's water. The players get showered and changed then head for the Golden Dock pub.

As the team enter the pub it's jam packed. All the crowd have gone there. The Landlord, Charlie Reece, greets them. "Well done lads, another trophy for behind the bar. Well done Cass, man of the match I heard but you're still too young to drink so, orange juice only for you kid."

Cass looks Charlie Reece in the eye. "Charlie why would I want to drink your piss like water lager? I would get more pissed on milk."

"Don't blame me it's the brewery's fault, they're cheeky fuckers just like you Cass." replies Charlie smirking. "That's why I stock my own cans of Carling Black Label to keep my regulars happy."

"Oh, I thought it was to line your pockets," mutters John Paul Anderson as he makes his way to the pub garden so he can smoke his joint in peace.

"What entertainment is on tonight Charlie?" enquires Alex Sharp.

"We've got a comedian on tonight Alex, Colly Stone, and a DJ."

"Fuckin' Colly Stone! She used to work here as a barmaid serving pints. She wasn't funny then," rages Kevin Bird.

"Don't blame me. Blame Todd Elliott, your team mate, he booked her," replies Charlie. "She's on his books 'Ultimate Star Entertainment.' It's his company."

Mark Barrow shouts over to Todd Elliott, "Some business mind you got Todd. We only won the cup an hour ago and you booked the entertainment already."

"Great business minds make top dollar Mark."

"Did you sort it out whilst you we're warming up as sub?"

"No, she's local and was the only one available at such short notice, and she's funny," reassures Todd as he slides away and heads towards the bar.

Pat Arrow sits down next to John Paul Anderson in the pub garden, cracks open a can of lager and hands it to John Paul, telling him he was fucking brilliant when he came on and that he was a fool wasting his talent.

John Paul takes a swig of lager, pulls on his joint and shouts, "Let's get high."

Pat Arrow laughs, "You get high, if Charlie Reece catches you smoking that shit out here he'll throttle you by the throat up against the wall."

"Fuck him," Replies John Paul.

In the far corner, Peter Springsteen, Alex Sharp and Bob Arrow are in deep discussion with local gangsters Max and Ronnie who have sponsored the trip.

Kevin Chivers is on the fruit machine, the drinks are flowing and Colly Stone went down a treat. She's a better comedian than barmaid. She ripped into Kevin Bird, he was terrorised by her because she heard he said she was a shit barmaid. The disco is booming. Cass is drinking orange juice. Frank Rox takes over as DJ, blasting out tunes from his iPod.

Cass looks out of the window and notices William Henry pulling up in his brand new Bentley. He gets out of his car and enters the pub, he's heading over to Bob Arrow to pay the bet. He's smiling and laughing, shaking Bob's hand. He walks over to the landlord, Charlie Reece, and gives him £200 to put behind the bar for drinks for everyone. As he makes his way out he passes Cass and shakes his hand, telling him he was the difference between him winning and losing, that he was world class. Brian smiles and thanks William Henry. Just as he's leaving, he asks if Cass fancies playing for Jersey Croft for £200 per week.

Cass smiles, "Thanks Mr Henry but no thanks. I'm hoping to join a league club."

William Henry smiles, "If you follow the right path son, you can go all the way to the top Cass. It's up to you which path you take, just don't be another John Paul Anderson who is a waste of talent."

"I'll do my best Mr Henry."

"You have the talent Cass just don't waste it."

"Mr Henry, I thought John Paul was brilliant today."

"Aye he was Brian. Pity he can only do it in short spells now. That kid had potential. Now you're *the kid that sparkles* Brian.

As William Henry leaves, he hands Cass a DVD of the cup final. "Watch that and enjoy it," he scoffs. "It cost me a grand." He laughs and makes his way out of the pub.

Cass knew William Henry paid his players and he just heard it from the horse's mouth. William Henry offering to pay him money to play for his team. He smiles as William Henry drives off. He has just seen the good side of Henry. He has total respect for him now. In Cass's book he's a true gentleman, a good person.

The drinks are flowing, Kevin Chivers still hasn't won the jackpot on the fruit machine, despite the seventy pound he has put in it. John Paul Anderson is wasted in the corner, fast asleep whilst Frank Rox is banging out the tunes on the DJ decks, rocking the house down. Alan Jones is eating all the pies at the buffet. Bob Arrow announces on the mic that all the players should report inside the car park of the pub in the morning at 10: AM, bringing their passports.

As the night is drawing to an end Cass notices Reid Johnson – his cousin – arguing with three men outside in the car park. Cass grabs Kevin Chivers off the fruit machine to help him help Reid Johnson. As Cass gets to Reid with Chivers. Reid head-butts the fat tall stocky man who he was arguing with. The fat man goes down holding his nose. Fat man's friend goes to kick Reid. Cass sees this and blocks the kick, throwing a right hook in to the stocky lad's chin, sending him tumbling over. Kevin Chivers fronts the six-foot three third friend of the gang who holds his hands up.

"Wow, it's nothing to do with me," says the third friend. He walks away, picking up his mate who Cass knocked over. They back off. The lad who Reid butted is holding his nose.

"You've just broke my nose mate."

"Have I, so fucking what!" replies Reid. "That'll teach you not to bully people now fuck off and don't let me see you in this pub again."

Apparently the three men tried to give a very drunk John Paul Anderson shit for being drunk and asleep. One kicked him, calling him racist names because he's mixed race. Reid had seen this and told them to get outside on his own as in this team, no matter what colour skin or religion you are, they are all one team and all stick together. It's a family.

As the three go back inside the pub, Todd Elliott is on the fruit machine Kevin Chivers had been playing. As Chivers walks by, Todd Elliott drops the £100 jackpot. Kevin Chivers is pig sick, he has spent £80 on that machine. Todd Elliott laughs.

"Don't worry Kevin it's all your jackpot, I was just playing the game for you while you we're away."

They all laugh. That action sums this team up, they are there for each other no matter what. It's a great team to be part of.

The night draws to an end with Charlie Reece calling taxis for all the players. Reid and Cass are the last to leave.

"Night lads," says Charlie.

"Night Charlie," replies Cass. "You can count all your money now."

"Piss off you cheeky get," laughs Charlie as he bolts and locks the pubs metal doors.

Chapter 4

The leaving of Liverpool

It's Friday, 10am in Liverpool on a sunny May morning. Bob Arrow is first to arrive at the Golden Dock pub car park to greet the coach driver Mick Lawrence for their journey to Hull on one of their 'First-Class' luxury coaches. As team captain, Bob likes to be early, to lead by example.

It's Golden Dock's first trip to Amsterdam. Their first as the league and cup double champions.

Mick Lawrence who is the owner of 'First-Class' travel is there waiting for the Golden Dock team to arrive. Mick is doing last minute checks on his coach.

"What is that thing Mick? The lads will go mad when they see this heap of junk."

"Bob, what do you mean?"

Bob points at the coach. "That thing that you've brought, we're going to Hull not the scrap yard."

"Are you being funny Bob?"

"Does it sound like I'm being funny Mick? Have a word with yourself. This is a piece of rusty shit."

"It's the only one available, it's the best I could do at such short notice."

"What do you mean short notice Mick? We pre-booked with you last week, you tosser."

"Yeah, but you had to win the cup first."

"We did win the cup yer gobshite."

"I know that Bob, but I thought Jersey Croft would have pissed all over your lot and won the cup so I booked all the other coaches out."

"Well you thought wrong Mick you prick, we won the cup and don't for one-minute think you're getting the full amount of money, bringing this heap of shit. I want fifty per cent discount and I think your new name will be Mick the Prick for thinking we wouldn't win the cup."

"I'll give you twenty-five per cent discount Bob, if you stop calling me Mick the Prick."

"Okay, Prick that's a deal."

Todd Elliott pulls up in a black Mercedes. Todd looks pleased with himself, as he gets his bags out of the Mercedes boot.

"Bob, I've bought the team a new kit for the game in Amsterdam. It's got our names printed on the back of the jerseys with the squad numbers and I've also got 25 Golden Dock tracksuits for the squad to wear during the trip for the players and committee members."

"Shut up Todd! That must have cost you a fortune."

"Bob, it won't cost me a penny, I've put the company name on the front of the jerseys tops, so I'll claim for it on my tax as advertising. The players will get to keep their kit and tracksuits."

"Put the new kit in the coach baggage area next to our other kit Todd. It means we have two kits for the trip."

Todd waves to his junior manager William Worthington as he drives off in his Mercedes. "I didn't think you would make the trip Todd. I thought you would have been too busy in work making your millions, so the new kit is a bonus."

"I've got my phone Bob that's all I need; the office staff can get in touch with me if they need me. I wouldn't miss this trip for all the tea in China."

John Cully and Ant Hodge are next to arrive. Ant Hodge is smiling as he nods to Todd and Bob who are at the baggage area of the coach.

"Hello smiler." says Todd. Ant Hodge just grins.

"Are you okay Ant?" Enquires Bob.

"Yeah, I'm on the top of the world skipper, top of the world..."

Ant Hodge's nickname is *The Engine*, he's rumoured to have ran two marathons in the same day, back to back, hence the nickname. Ant is the fittest in the Golden Dock team.

John Cully takes a football out of the kitbag and starts trying to hit the pub sign. On his first attempt he's way off the mark and he hit's the pub window. Up pops Pat Arrow from inside the pub shouting out the window for the dickhead to pack it in.

The management team of Peter Springsteen and Alex Sharp arrive with committee member John Arrow in his BMW x5. They'll go in John Arrow's car with Bob Arrow also being in the group that travels in the BMW.

Cass turns up at the car park with Alan Jones. They put their bags in the coach baggage compartment and get on the coach. Walking down the coach aisle, Cass turns to Alan Jones.

"It fucking stinks in here of bad eggs Alan."

"That's not the coach soft-lad, it's my egg and pork pies Cass."

"Fuck me they stink. What's in them, shit and pickle?

"Don't be soft, pies are good for you."

"Good for you maybe Jonesy, but they're not for me, the smell of them is just burning my nostrils."

As they take their seats, Alan Jones notices two local gangsters sitting at the back of the coach. They're both mean looking, stocky built men in their mid-forties with beards and short brown hair.

"Who are they Jonesy?

"They're friends of Bob Hope, they're the two men who sponsored the trip," mutters Alan.

"So, are they the business men?"

"Business men? Don't make me laugh, they're gangsters."

Cass looks towards the gangsters and nods his head towards them and smiles. They ignore this and look right through him.

"They're not football fans then Jonesy?"

"No, they're a pair of horrible twats." mutters Alan.

Cass laughs at Alan, muttering under his breath about the gangsters. Alan Jones gets a pie out of his bag, taking a big bite.

"Hmmm I love my pies Cass, just love them."

The rest of the team arrive in dribs and drabs. Kevin Bird turns up in sandy beige shorts, a Hawaiian shirt short sleeve, white socks and sandals. He's wearing a Mexican hat. The lads take one look and piss themselves laughing.

"When did we sign Barry from *'Auf wiedersehen pet'*?" jokes Mark Barrow.

"It's not Barry, it's grandad from *'Only fools and horses'*, when they were in Spain," Ant Hodge shouts from the back of the coach.

"We're going to Holland not Spain Birdy," says John Paul Anderson.

"Listen lads, there is an old saying. *When in Rome do as the Romans do,*" replies Kevin Bird.

"Do as the Romans do Steptoe?" says Kevin Chivers. "We're going to Amsterdam and you're dressed like that, we would be best to drop you off in Wigan, so you can blend in with the Wigan pie arses and look like a soft twat there."

The whole bus piss themselves laughing. Even the two gangsters raise a smile. The last two players to arrive are Reid Johnson and Frank Rox, who can be seen in the distance making public nuisances of themselves. In tow with them are Fred Kettle and Chopper Moon who is the local district hard case. As they reach the coach they bang on the side of the mint green paint-work.

"What the fuck is this banger we are going in Bob? *'First Class Travel?'* It's a fucking shit heap," complains Frank Rox.

"Take it up with Mick the driver, not with me Frank."

"Are you having a laugh, bringing this heap of shit mate?"

"I'm the driver and the owner Frank, this was all that was available."

Frank Rox looks at Mick in disgust. "This coach is a heap of rusty junk. I could cut this heap of shit in two with a tin opener." Frank Rox storms off and puts his bags in the baggage area.

"Frank just get on the coach and stop being a diva." shouts Kevin Parry.

Peter Springsteen boards the coach and introduces Bob Hope's new replacement Ian Craig.

"Now lads can I have your attention. This is our new centre half that's replacing Bob Hope."

"Are you kidding Peter? He's a fucking donkey." snaps John Cully.

"That cunt got me sent off last season." yells Kevin Parry.

"Pack it in you lot. Ian is a top defender," mutters Peter.

"He's also your brother in law isn't he Peter?" shouts Kevin Bird.

"What difference does that make Birdy?"

"Peter when you said you needed a defender that is solid and can park the bus so we don't concede, I think you got a bit confused."

"How have I Birdy?"

"Well Peter you have only gone out and got a real bus driver that parks the bus in the bus depot and he cannot defend to save his life. He's just a big kick alehouse player. Peter, our style doesn't suit his big ale house style of play."

"Well he's here to play in the tournament so get used to it." yells Peter.

"I've got feelings you know lads, I'm only here to try and help you win the tournament." mutters Ian Craig.

"Take no notice of them Craigie. Sit here next to me, let's let bygones be bygones and start afresh. You'll be playing alongside me. Welcome aboard Craigie make yourself at home." shouts Mark Barrow

"Thanks Mark it's nice to be liked," says Ian Craig with a smirk on his face.

Frank Rox heads towards Bob. "Bob is it okay for my two mates Fred and Chopper to come on the trip with us?

"Yeah two committee members have pulled out Frank, so they can take their places."

"Nice one Bob, they will both pay for the trip, they don't expect a free ride like us."

"It's okay Frank. I'll think of something they can do to pay their way," grins Bob.

"What are the plans then Bob? What airport are we flying from?" enquires Reid Johnson.

"All get on the coach and I'll explain."

Bob grins as he gets on the coach. All the players are seated. Bob tells the players they are driving by coach to Hull, then they are getting the ferry to Rotterdam. The players face's drop.

"Are you taking the piss Bob? Who organised this trip? Was it Del Boy? Is Uncle Albert going to be sailing the ship? What jokers organised this joke travel?" Yells Kevin Bird. The players all laugh and snigger at Kevin Birds' comments.

"No, I'm not taking the piss, it's all been paid for by two local business men Max and Ronnie, who are sitting at the back of the coach. They have kindly sponsored the trip," replies Bob.

Max looks at Kevin Bird and growls. "Don't you like ferries Bird? If you want I can throw you overboard in the middle of the North Sea if you get seasick."

"No, it's okay. I mean yes, I love ferries," stutters Kevin Bird.

Bob gets off the coach to join the management team in the BMW. As the coach revs up to leave for Hull harbour, Pat Arrow jogs out of the pub with three packs of 24 cans of Carling Black Label and jumps on the coach.

"Away the lads," yells Pat Arrow.

"What have you been doing Pat? I'm cold turkeying for a drink here." moans John Paul Anderson.

"Driver, hurry up and pull away before Charlie Reece notices he's three packs of Carling Black Label down."

"Where did you get them from Pat?" asks Ian Craig.

"They're the leftovers from our team's party last night Craigie, but if Charlie sees them he will be saying they belong to him. So, I just grabbed them from behind the bar and legged it onto the coach with them."

"Give us one here then Pat. It can be my introductory drink into the team."

"Fuck me Ian, if I knew you had signed, I would have got the trolley loaded up, the way that you can drink."

Pat Arrow hands Ian Craig a can of Carling Black Label, as the coach pulls away from the Golden Dock pub, upwards and onwards to Hull harbour. This is the start of the leaving of Liverpool. John Paul Anderson lights up a joint. Max and Ronnie get a whiff of a funny smell. Ronnie looks over to John Paul.

"Hey dickhead put that smelly thing out,"

"What! Are you kidding mate? It's only a joint."

"I don't give a shit," snarls Ronnie. "Put it out before I put it out in your fucking eye."

"Okay, chill brother," says John Paul.

"Don't give me that *chill me brother shit*," shouts Ronnie with spit clinging in his teeth as his eyeballs go larger. "I don't want the smell of that shit on my clothes."

Pat Arrow heads towards John Paul and cracks open a can of Carling and hands it's to John Paul.

"Drink that, it's better than smoking that shit, that's why the Blues released you. You we're a world beater before you started drinking and taking drugs."

"Hmmm, thanks for reminding me Pat."

Cass looks at Alan Jones and states that it's going to be one long trip. Alan nods and agrees, before going into his bag as he scoffs on another pork and egg pie.

Todd Elliott walks down the coach handing out the new tracksuits. Todd asks Chopper and Fred Kettle do they want a tracksuit. 'Yeah', they both say simultaneously.

Todd gets to Max and Ronnie. He politely asks them if they want a tracksuit each.

"Do we look like football fans?" snarls Ronnie.

"They're free mate."

"Piss off son, and take your tracksuits with you."

Todd looks shocked and turns away as he goes back down the aisle. Max whispers something into Ronnie ear. As Todd is handing out the rest of the Golden Dock tracksuits, Ronnie calls Todd back, smiles and politely asks him for two tracksuits for him and Max in extra-large. Todd goes into his bag and hands them two extra-large tracksuits with his company name on the back with Golden Dock's name on the front.

"Here you are lads, wear them with pride. You get to keep them." beams Todd.

"Thanks son," mutters Ronnie.

At the front of the coach Frank Rox and Reid Johnson are toy fighting and stumble with both of them falling onto Mick the coach driver. Mick loses control of the wheel and the mint green coach swerves close to the barriers, missing them by inches. Kevin Chivers leans over from his seat and pulls Frank and Reid off the driver, who has gone the colour of boiled shite. Mick regains control of the coach.

"What's that smell? Is it this smelly coach or have you shit your pants Mick?" Yells Frank Rox.

"Hey lads, anymore of that and I'll turn the coach around and head back to Liverpool. Frank, you need to grow up lad." replies Mick.

"Oh, behave Mick we're only having a bit of fun, but I do think you seriously need to change your undies."

Pat Arrow gets up from his seat and shakes a can of Carling Black Label and sprays Frank and Reid. It goes all over their tops and he tells them both to behave and to let the driver do his job without any distractions.

"Ah, fuck off Pat that's gone all over me new Givenchy top," moans Reid.

"Well stop messing. The pair of you nearly made the driver crash the coach."

"Yeah, behave Reid. Stop being a naughty boy," laughs Frank Rox.

Reid Johnson picks himself up and goes to the back of the coach, to sit with Cass and Alan Jones, to get away from his friend Frank Rox, so he can get a bit of peace and quiet. Kevin Bird gives up his seat for Reid and makes his way down the aisle to talk to Kevin Chivers. As he's walking, Kevin Bird stands on chewy on the coach aisle floor. It sticks to both his sandals making it hard for him to walk as the chewy sticks like glue.

"Hey, Mick is this a moon bus you're driving?" yells Kevin Bird.

"No, it's not, why what's up now lad?" replies Mick.

"There's fucking chewy stuck to my sandals Mick it's making me walk like an astronaut. I feel like that Buzz Aredin when he became the first man to walk on the moon and its wrecked my sandals, they were brand new five years ago."

"Birdy, it wasn't Buzz Aldrin who first walked on the moon. That was Neil Armstrong, who was born on the fifth of August, in 1930 on a Tuesday. He was from Ohio, in the United States. He was 82 when he died on a Saturday."

"Okay, Chivers calm down, what have you eaten for your breakfast a Wikipedia with your Weetabix?"

"No Birdy. I've just been swotting up, so when I go on *The Chase* I can win the Beast and when I'm walking away with my winnings, it will be one small step for mankind and you with that chewy on your sandals, it will be one giant step for mankind."

"It's not funny Chivers. My sandals are full of chewy."

"Have you got insurance for things like this Mick?" asks Frank Rox with a smirk on his face.

"No, why would I Frank?"

"Why? Well for a starter, them sandals are priceless. You cannot buy them anymore. They stopped selling them in the nineteen seventies and even then, they only sold four pairs."

"Don't talk shit Frank. He just said he bought them brand new five years ago, so that would be in 2013 that he bought them."

"No Mick, he said they were brand new five years ago, that's because he bought them from a jumble sale in the church fete."

"No, I didn't Frank. My missus bought me them from the St Helens car booty."

"Well take them off Birdy. They're wrecking my coach floor." snaps Mick.

"Wrecking your coach. You're a cheeky git Mick. Your coach is a fucking piece of stinky shit." yells Birdy. Pat Arrow passes Kevin Bird a can of Carling Black Label.

"Calm down Birdy. Have a can of Carling Black Label mate."

"Thanks Pat. You're a true scholar. Cheers mate."

"You're welcome Birdy. Just mellow out and enjoy the trip."

Reid Johnson is sitting alongside Alan Jones and Cass near the back of the coach.

"What happened to you this morning Brian? I phoned you five times on your mobile phone and rang your house phone twice." queried Reid.

"My mobile phone is still in the shop Reid. It's getting fixed. James Fitz's is fixing it for me, he's not charging me, it's a freebie and the house phone is still off. Those BT workmen woke me up this morning when they were fixing the landlines. That's why you couldn't get in touch on the house phone. I met Alan on my way so I walked over to the car park with him."

"That's okay, a freebie Cass. How did you work that?" asks John Paul.

"My mate James Fitz's is doing it for me John Paul."

"I don't know him Cass."

"You will do John Paul, his dad is Jimmy Fitz's. He's a professional footballer for Bolton."

"No, the name is not ticking the boxes Cass."

"His dad is the six-feet-five giant."

"No, I can't picture him Cass."

"He has got that scar over his eye like the letter T."

"No Cass, it's not ringing any bells."

"His dad has got a spiky Mohican."

"No, you have lost me Cass."

"His dad has got bright ginger hair John Paul."

"Oh, do you mean Ginger, Jamie's dad? Why didn't you just say Ginger."

"I didn't think I had to John Paul as I was talking to Reid not you."

"Oh, sorry, but it's always nice to know of these places if I ever need my phone fixed for free."

"John Paul, you've not even got a phone."

"I know that, but I'm thinking of getting one, especially with Gingers lad fixing them for free." Cass turns to Alan Jones and Reid Johnson with his mouth wide open in disbelief.

"He's a fucking bell end him. I can't be doing listening to him. He's a fruit and nut cake, that kid has lost his marbles."

At the front of coach. Frank Rox moans to Mick, the middle-aged driver about the radio and sets up his iPod and goes about setting up the tunes.

"How long are we on this coach Mick?" asks Frank Rox.

"About three hour's son."

"Three fucking hours in this shit heap. Are you having a laugh Mick? No wonder nobody books you."

"Hey Frank, he gets more booking's than Ken Dodd ever did," laughs Kevin Chivers.

"Well, I hope he pays his taxes then," laughs Frank Rox.

Mick looks at Frank straight faced and is not amused by his comments. "I pay my taxes mate."

Frank blasts out the tune he has loaded. *'The tax man'* by the Beatles. The whole bus is in fine sprits. The coach is rocking side to side.

"Hey Mick, can you pull over at the next service station." shouts Kevin Parry.

"We need the toilet," says Mark Barrow.

"I'll just piss on Mick the driver because this is a shit hole," laughs Frank Rox.

The coach settles down as it heads for the next service station. Frank is getting bored and leaves his seat at the front and walks to the far end of the coach. As he walks down the aisle he rips up a piece of paper from his daily newspaper that was in his pocket and crunching it into a ball he throws it at Reid Johnson but it misses him and hits the gangster Ronnie on the head.

"What the fuck are you doing dickhead! I'll break your legs," growls Ronnie.

"Sorry mate," says a stunned Frank Rox.

"I don't give a shit if you're sorry and I'm not your mate you fucking little shit."

"Okay Ronnie big time calm down, it's only a piece of paper, fucking bullhead" says Kevin Chivers.

"It's not as if it has hurt you," pipes up Chopper Moon.

Cass looks over at Ronnie, who glares back at Cass. Unmoved by Ronnie's stare Cass stands up to him.

"Hey mate, I'm sixteen years of age. This my first trip away playing football with Golden Dock and you're spoiling it with your aggressive attitude."

"It wasn't even meant for you doughnut. It was meant for me. We're mates trying to enjoy our trip," rants Reid.

The team have stuck together again. The coach pulls into the service station.

"No longer than twenty minutes lads, we need to get a move on to get to Hull," shouts Mick.

As the players get off the coach, they head towards the service shops. Max whispers something into Ronnie's ear. Ronnie looks for Cass and pulls him aside and apologises for being aggressive and for him spoiling the trip. Cass nods and accepts Ronnie's apology. Max and Ronnie head towards the BMW, Max tells Bob if he will let them swap with him and Alex Sharp in the car, they will pay for cabin beds for all of the players on the ferry trip to Rotterdam and will also pay for cabin beds on the return journey.

"So, you have met the players then?" grins Bob.

As the players make their way to the shops in the service station. John Paul stops at the entrance. He lights up his joint, unaware there are two policemen in a car at the side entrance of the building. They smell the magic cigarette and step out of the car and approach John Paul.

"Excuse me sir?" The black-haired policeman calls out. John Paul looks around wondering where the voice came from as he smokes on his joint.

"It is against the law to smoke cannabis, can you put it out please sir?" John Paul looks up to see the two policemen standing in front of him.

"It's only a joint officer, can't I just have a smoke in peace?"

"Fuck me. It's John Paul Anderson. The best footballer I've ever seen. It's me Mickey Stockwell, we played together for the Blues. We won the F.A. youth cup together," bursts out PC Stockwell.

"No way, no fucking way. Mickey bloody Stockwell last time I seen you was when you were in the treatment room at Finch Farm. Next I knew they released you. I had a few hazy days during my time with Everton, at times it was a big blur. You had that ankle injury I remember that. No one seen you after that. No one could get in touch with you. What you doing now Mickey?"

PC Stockwell bursts out laughing. "You smoke too much of that shit John Paul. I'm a copper now. Isn't my uniform a clue?"

"No. I didn't notice it Mickey. There's no way I would ever make a detective." PC Stockwell laughs as he turns to his colleague PC Dixon.

"He was best player I've ever seen Dixon. He could do things with the ball I could only dream of doing. Look what drugs does to you Dixon. What a waste of talent." Pat Arrow sees John Paul with the two policemen and walks towards them and asks if everything's okay.

"Yes sir, everything is great. John Paul, you smoke that shit away from the public and take care of yourself. I play for the metropolitan police now. I moved back to Halifax when I got released but I'm happy now in my new job. I'm the captain of the team. We get a good bonus."

PC Stockwell gets a call over his walkie talkie.

"I've got to go John Paul, looks like your lot are robbing the shop in the service station blind, you scousers make me laugh, you're all loaded but won't pay for anything," laughs PC Stockwell.

"It's in our genes Mickey."

"Yes, your jeans, coat pockets, down your socks, anywhere you can carry it really John Paul."

"Take care Mickey mate. Don't forget to take Dixon of Dock Green with you. They're a bunch of tough bastards them scousers Mickey."

Pat Arrow cracks open two cans of Carling. He hands one to John Paul.

"You really are a fucking waste of talent John Paul, but it could be worse, you could have ended up a bizzie like your mate."

John Paul and Pat both start laughing as they drink the lager.

In the shop, Bob Arrow calls Fred Kettle and tells him that they want four bottles of big coke and two bottles of orange Fanta for our Jack Daniels and brandy. Fred is told that when he gets them, to put them in the boot of the BMW and to also get some nuts, crisps and teabags.

Fred gets a bag from the shelf and fills it up with the stuff Bob asked for, and walks past the staff smiling. He loads it into the car boot of John Arrow's BMW. As the players walk in the shop they are filling their pockets. Cass is filling his with drinks and Mars bars. Reid Johnson sees what Cass is doing and goes over and asks him what he's up to.

"Put it back or pay for it Cass! What the fuck are you doing? Are your stupid?" Growls Reid.

"Everyone else is doing it Reid. It's easy in here."

"I don't care what they do. I only care about you and I'm not letting you go down that road, now here's 20 pounds, pay for them."

"I've got money but it's easy to just walk out," argues young Cass.

"I don't care. Go fucking pay with this money I'm giving you and do as I say. You're going in the right direction, not down the road of no return."

Cass pays at the till.

As Alan Jones is walking out the shop he puts four pasties inside his coat pocket. The players make their way back to the coach. They are all smiling in a jovial mood. Cass is the last one out of the shop. As he's leaving PC Stockwell arrives with PC Dixon in tow. PC Stockwell looks at Cass and at the bags he's carrying. PC Stockwell calls Cass back.

"What's up, PC Plod. Have you got a problem?" asks Cass.

"Well we might have son. Have you paid for those things in your bag?" asks PC Stockwell.

"Of course, I've paid Sherlock! Why are you asking me that? Is it because I'm scouse? I see you are from Yorkshire, but I'm not accusing you off shagging sheep in the Dales, so why are you asking me?"

"It's just routine son."

"Listen I'm not your son, keep it real Kojak." Cass is not happy. He stares at the two policemen shaking his head.

"Here is my receipt gobshite." Cass throws the receipt at PC Stockwell. "Now check my stuff PC Clueless." says Cass angrily.

Reid Johnson comes back looking for Cass and sees the police and asks what's the problem. PC Stockwell checks the receipt and glances at Reid.

"There's no problem sir, the young lad is free to go."

"Free to go, I was never in your custody, you sheep wanker."

As they both walk away. Reid Johnson slaps Cass on the back of the neck.

"See, soft-lad you could have been nicked then. That's why you should always listen to uncle Reid."

"I was only doing it because everyone else was, but thanks for guiding me in the right direction. That's the reason I look up to you because you always look out for me."

Cass and Reid are last to get on the coach. A big cheer fills the coach because Max and Ronnie are in the BMW.

Frank Rox blasts out a top tune *'nothing's going to stop us now'* the whole bus start singing *nothing going to stop us now Golden Dock Golden Dock*. The whole team are rocking the coach, as the players bounce up and down on their seats. They pass the police car. John Paul waves to PC Stockwell. The rest of the people on the coach stand up. They look towards the police car at the side of them and make wanker gestures at the two police officers and put two fingers up showing them the covers of the porn mags they have stolen.

PC Stockwell laughs as the whole team sing, "Nothing going to stop us now, Golden Dock, Golden Dock."

As the singing gets louder Cass turns to Reid.

"This is the reason I signed for Golden Dock, to have days like this with my big cousin. I'll remember these times for the rest of my life." In the far corner Bob Arrow turns to Alex Sharp. "Alex, you can't buy team sprit like this. If I could bottle that team spirit, I'd be a billionaire, in fact that team sprit would win world wars, if I could bottle it, I could rule the world."

"As I'm assistant manager, will I be your deputy Bob?"

"Of course, you will Alex."

Alex and Bob both laugh then join in the singing. Frank Rox has got the coach rocking. Bob gets up to see Mick the driver, he walks towards Fred Kettle and Chopper Moon. They're both looking at the porn magazines.

As Bob passes Fred and Chopper, "Hmm I see you both went down the porn aisle," mutters Bob. Next, he passes John Paul and Pat Arrow drinking lager.

"Oh, you both visited the alcohol aisle" Next seat Bob passes is Alan Jones who is eating pasties. "I see the pie man ravaged the cooked meats aisle."

As Bob moves further down the seating aisle, he sees Ant Hodge eating oranges.

"Hmm the man from Del Monte Dock ran down the fruit and veg aisle." As Bob gets to young Cass, "Hey Cass I see you went to the paid aisle."

"How did you know that Bob?" asks Cass.

"It was easy Cass as you're the only fucker on this coach with a fucking receipt."

The whole bus is united and begin to sing *"We shall not, we shall not be moved, we shall not, we shall not be moved, just like a coach that has robbed all the shop, we shall not be moved."*

Kevin Chivers asks the driver if the telly works at the front of the coach.

"Yes, it works Kev. It's a DVD player as well."

"Have you got any DVDs for us to watch Mick?" Asks Ian Craig.

"No, I didn't bring any with me. Sorry."

"What you saying it works for then," pipes up Frank Rox.

"It does work, the only reason I didn't put the telly on is because you took over with your iPod.

"Well it's no good without DVDs Mick." replies Mark Barrow.

"I've got a DVD of last night's Sean Quinn challenge cup final in my bag. William Henry gave me it in the pub last night," yells Cass.

"Where's your bag Cass?" Shouts Pat Arrow.

"It's in the luggage part."

"Driver, stop the coach," yells Chopper Moon.

"I can't stop the coach in the middle of the motorway, don't be stupid I'm a coach driver not a stunt man."

"Mick flash them in the BMW to pull over in the hard shoulder, or you're not getting paid," yells Bob.

Mick flashes his lights at the BMW. Bob rings John Arrow to tell him to pull over. The BMW follows suit, both vehicles are now parked on the hard shoulder of the M62.

Cass gets off the coach and goes to the luggage side with Mick the driver. Mick opens the side panel and Cass gets the DVD. They return to their seats. Peter Springsteen gets out of the BMW and stands at the footwell of the coach, asking why they have they stopped.

"Cass has got the DVD of last night's final, are you getting on the coach to watch it Peter?" shouts Bob from back of the coach.

"Fucking too right mate. That Max and Ronnie are miserable bastards, I've only been in the car with them for twenty minutes. It's like being in school with two headmasters. I thought that Ronnie was smiling, but twenty seconds later the car stunk of shit. He wasn't smiling it was wind. He stunk of raw eggs, so yeah I am getting on here. Phone John Arrow, tell him to leave without me Bob."

As the coach drives past the BMW, everyone starts chanting. "Shitty arse, shitty arse, shitty arse, shitty arse, shitty arse."

Ronnie and Max are oblivious to what's happening on the coach. Alex Sharp puts the DVD on. The whole coach sits back to watch the cup final.

The team start chanting. "Golden Dock" and "There's only one Brian Cassidy."

The sixteen-year-old blushes and laughs and takes a bow. Frank Rox throws the pillow he took from the service station at Cass in in a joking way.   "You're shit really Cass, I should be playing up front."

"You can play alongside me Frank."

The whole team laugh and start singing. "There's only one Frank Rox, one Frank Rox." For the rest of the journey the team enjoy watching the DVD.

It's 1.30pm now, as the coach pulls into King Dock road.

"Aww it stinks of fish. Are you meeting your missus here Birdy?" Shouts Frank Rox.

"No, I'm not soft-arse. It stinks of fish because it's a fishing port."

The coach pulls into Hull harbour and heads towards ferry terminal one. The Golden Dock have arrived from their 130-mile journey from Liverpool. The coach pulls up next to a minibus full of female students. John Cully starts talking French to them from his window. The girls look at him and start to laugh, the coach moves off and heads towards the north car park. As they reach the car park the coach pulls over and the driver Mick asks the players to bring back boxes of Golden Virginia tobacco. He offers them one hundred pounds for a box of ten 50 gram pouches.

Kevin Parry tells Mick he will get some as he collects his luggage. As the team get their belongings from the coach the sun is reflecting off the sea water onto the side of the minty green coach.

"Hey Mick the driver, make sure you bring your best coach on Tuesday to pick us up," yells Frank Rox.

"I'll do my best," says Mick.

He checks over the coach, sees there are empty cans, porn magazines, half eaten pies, orange peel and paper all over the floor.

"You could have put all the rubbish in bin bags," he yells at the departing team.

"We did, the whole coach is a bin," shouts Frank Rox.

"You should have bought us a better coach Mick," grins Bob Arrow.

The team retrieve all their baggage. Todd Elliott gets a trolley and loads both sets of kits on to it. The smell of the sea air is all around. In the distance the team see their ferry in the harbour.

"The size of that ferry it's massive," says Kevin Bird.

"What did you think we were going on soft-lad, the Mersey Ferry?" laughs Peter Springsteen.

"Yeah all aboard the Royal Iris," Pat Arrow says sarcastically.

The players all head towards the sign saying *P&O ferries to Rotterdam*.

Chapter 5

To Rotterdam with love

As the players make their way down the gang plank they head towards terminal one and the Port Ferries check in desk. The warm salt sea air blasts them in their faces as the seagulls circle above them dropping shit bombs left right and centre.

Frank Rox dives for cover. "It's like being in a one-way paint-ball battle."

"Frank run, head for cover," yells Fred Kettle. The players run towards the doors to get out of the way of the shitting seagulls. Chopper Moon gets a shit bomb on his head.   "Bastard seagulls." Frank Rox can't help but laugh as he sees the seagulls shit on Chopper Moons hair.

"When did you get white streaks put in your hair Chopper?"

"Don't try and take the piss Frank." Chopper is not amused and kicks Frank up the arse and tells him to get him a wet-wipe. Pat Arrow goes into the kit bag and gets the water spray and a towel and helps Chopper clean up the bird shit on his head. Max and Ronnie give Bob Arrow a bundle of money to book the cabins.

Bob goes to the P&O Ferry desk and books the cabins. It's four to a cabin, except for Max and Ronnie who have got a cabin for two. The ferry sets sail for Rotterdam at 3pm. It's a twelve-hour ferry ride, so they will dock in Rotterdam at 4am Saturday morning. Holland is one hour ahead of GMT time. The team makes their way to passport control. Max and Ronnie mingle in with the team. They breeze pass customs and passport control without a hitch and make their way onto the ferry. They are all excited.

"Aye aye captain," yells Kevin Chivers as he boards the ferry.

"Can I order fish fingers for tea captain Bob?" asks Kevin Bird.

"Piss off, I'm the team captain of Golden Dock not the captain of the ferry."

"Aye aye captain Bob," yells Frank Rox.

Bob tells them all to go to their cabins and that they're to meet on the entrance deck on level four at five pm so that they can all have their dinner together as a team.

As the players gather, John Paul lights up a joint. Bob Arrow looks at him in disgust.

"Are your stupid soft-lad? We are going to Amsterdam and there is going to be tons of that stuff that you're smoking. You must be the only gobshite that has ever smuggled it out of England," snaps Bob.

"It's okay, Bob. It's only a little block of Rocky," mutters a stoned John Paul.

"You need a good kick up the arse Rocky. You're fucking thick lad. John Paul we're a football team not a gang of the most wanted on the run. We're the league champions of the top Sunday league in Liverpool. Smoke that shit away from the team," yells the mild-mannered Alex Sharp.

The players make their way to their cabins to put their bags and luggage away and to freshen up. Cass is put in the same cabin as Bob Arrow, Alex Sharp and Kevin Chivers, the committee members of the team. Cass is still a minor at sixteen so he has to stay with them. He's fuming because he wanted to share a cabin with his cousin Reid Johnson, who is sharing with Frank Rox, Fred Kettle and Chopper Moon.

In the cabins there are four beds and a little wash basin. There are separate rooms with toilets and showers at the end of the corridor. The shower rooms are mixed. Cass has a look at the ship brochure; there is a casino, cinema, sauna, steam room, gym, arcade games room, discos, bars and duty-free shops with two restaurants on board. It's got everything.

Cass meets up with Ant Hodge and Kevin Bird to have a work out in the gym and to try the steam room before dinner. It's 3pm. As the ferry sets sail it leaves Hull harbour full steam ahead with a big blast from the horn. John Paul and Pat Arrow are on the top deck with the sea breeze in their hair, drinking cans of Carling. They're raising their cans saying 'Au Revoir,' to the Hull docks and the shitting seagulls.

"Pat, if only all ferry journeys we're made by Carling Black Label."

"Carling, John Paul. Wrong brand soft-lad that's Carlsberg and we have only got Carling so this ferry ride might not be all plain sailing." They both piss themselves, laughing and singing, *'Rule Britannia'* as the ferry sets sail for Holland.

Meanwhile in Reid Johnson's cabin, Reid and Chopper Moon are trying to fix the bed that Frank Rox and Fred Kettle have broken. They were toy fighting. They entered the cabin and Frank Rox jumped on Fred Kettles back and both of them fell onto the bed, breaking the leg off the bed as they landed on it. Chopper Moon slots the leg of the bed into place and tells Frank and Fred that's their side of the bunks in the cabin.

In the gym Ant Hodge is on the treadmill running like a Kenyan long-distance runner. Kevin Bird is doing stretches. At six feet two he's very flexible and always wins the headers in the air. Cass is talking to one of the female students that the coach passed on entrance into Hull Harbour.

Her name is Chelsea. She has long straight brown hair and stands at five feet four in a size ten matching Nike gym jog suit, with bright white teeth and a dark tan. Chelsea has Cass in a trance. She's eighteen, from London, studying Law at Liverpool University. Cass is flirting and joking with Chelsea, She seems smitten by him.

Ant Hodge and Kevin Bird start singing in harmony.

"I'm not in love… So, don't forget it…. It's just when I get to Rotterdam that I'll be in love with you."

Cass laughs, "That song should be number one like Chelsea." Chelsea blushes as Cass looks her in the eye smiling as she blinks.

"You're such a smooth talker Cass." Chelsea is with two of her friends who seem invisible to her as she looks into Cass's eyes.

Ant Hodge finishes on the treadmill and asks are they both ready to go for a steam. Kevin Bird nods and Cass turns to Chelsea and asks her would she like to have drink with him later. She says yes and that she will meet him in the bar on deck four at seven o clock.

Ant, Kevin and Cass make their way to the steam room as Chelsea and her two friends exit the gym. Cass and Chelsea smile at each other as the both go in the opposite direction.

Ant Hodge slaps Cass on the head smiling. "Stop it lover boy, snap out of it, you're our boy wonder not hers."

"Sorry Ant, but how beautiful is she?" Cass smiles and floats into the steam room.

On deck five, in the free Wi-Fi room Todd Elliott is on his laptop and on his phone to his office, He's checking the booking his company have made. Todd is a workaholic.

New signing Ian Craig is on the phone to his mate Danny Red who is a horse racing tipster. Craig is picking Danny Red's brain getting the best horses in form of him so he can back them. He's checking out the prices on the horse racing web page. He's known to like a bet or two, he likes to gamble. Mark Barrow and Kevin Parry check out the prices in the duty-free shop.

"Mark, you do know it's our duty to take stuff out of the duty free for free," laughs Kevin Parry.

"Of course, I do Kev, duty free means it's free." They both piss themselves laughing as they slot two Gucci aftershaves into their pockets. As they walk out of the shop, they're smiling at the duty-free staff before making their way back to their cabins to freshen up for the team meal in the restaurant.

Alex Sharp and Peter Springsteen are in the cabin checking both sets of kits to make sure it's all there and that they have the right number of socks, shorts and football jerseys. John Arrow is doing the team accounts. He's counting the money from tickets the club sells that helps fund the team.

In the arcade, Kevin Chivers is using a magnet to clean out the ten pence pieces out of the drop machine. He swipes it across the bottom of the machine where the coins fall out, he makes them drop over the edge by the magnets force. John Cully is standing next to him blocking everyone's view of what Kevin is doing with the magnet.

On the top of the ferry in the open roof deck, John Paul Anderson and Pat Arrow are enjoying the warm breeze from the North Sea, singing football songs while they crack open their cans of Carling. Max and Ronnie have distanced themselves from the team but they are expected to join them for the group meal in the restaurant at 5pm.

As the ferry heads further out into the North Sea the waves get choppier as the clock hits 5pm. The team have assembled in the corridor of the restaurant. The last to arrive for the team dinner is manager Peter Springsteen with Max and Ronnie, they are chatting away to Peter in the corridor. As they approach the players, Peter announces that Max and Ronnie's friend Ted Hike who is from Liverpool but resides in Amsterdam is sponsoring the match against the Amsterdam Jets and there will be a trophy to play for with medals for the winners.

"We have done the double. Now let's conquer Europe lads, let's win the treble. We have to beat these Dutch wankers to be European champions. Let's show these Dutch dickheads how the scouse teams win. We will conquer all," shouts Frank Rox.

"Fuck me, when did we sign William Wallace from Braveheart?" sniggers John Cully.

"Are they a Belgium team? They must be named Braveheart," jokes Ant Hodge.

The whole team laugh at Ant's joke. Alex Sharp leads them into the restaurant. It's a buffet meal so all the players can get their own food. They make their way to the two big tables next to each other, they get their food and sit down to eat. Alan Jones has got chips, peas and two fish dishes, which are in square tubs. Peter Springsteen sits next to Alan and looks at his plate in shock.

"Hey Alan, I thought you only ate pies?"

"No! What made you think that Peter? I eat chips and peas also with meals."

"I didn't mean them soft-lad," replies Peter.

"What did you mean then boss?"

"I meant them fish things in the tubs."

All the players stop eating and look towards Alan Jones plate. As he tucks into his evening meal you could hear a pin drop in the restaurant.

"What the fuck are you going on about boss?" Alan is confused and bewildered by Peter Springsteen comments.

"I mean you're eating fish Alan."

"I know I'm eating fish. It's fish, big deal. Ten out of ten for being so observant Peter."

"So, are the fish better than your pies?" The players all stare open mouthed waiting for the pie man's answer. Not one player has moved since Peter first mentioned the fish, they're all in a daze wondering why the pie man has given up his pies.

"They're fish pies soft arse, don't you know fuck all about pies Peter? They're lovely, go get yourself one, there's loads over they're on the buffet bar. Keep your eyes off my fish pies you're not getting one of mine, you can piss off." The whole team piss themselves laughing.

"I give up," Peter Springsteen declares.

Cass has a small plate of chips and gravy. "You not eating Cass?" Ant Hodge enquires.

"No. I'm not really hungry Ant."

"Oh, have you got butterflies in your stomach lover boy?" Hisses Kevin Bird.

"What's *lover boy* about?" asks Reid. Looking shocked, Reid is not amused with what he's hearing,

"Cass has got a date," replies Ant Hodge.

"A date, what are you all going on about a date?" asks Reid Johnson.

"Cass has met a girl in the gym. He's meeting her later in the bar," replies Kevin Bird.

"Well you kept that quiet Cass and there'll be no girlfriends when you're on tour with me," laughs Reid.

"Well it's lucky I'm not with you then isn't it Reid," snaps young Cass.

"Where did that come from Cass? I'm here with you now."

"No, you're not Reid. You're too busy with the three goonies Curly, Larry and Mo, you've got no time for me."

"Why are you saying that Brian? You know I'm always there for you."

"No, you're not Reid, I've got to fight for your attention at times."

"Are you serious Cass? I've more time for you than I've for anyone here, you're more than my cousin you're more like a little brother to me. It's not my fault you're not in my cabin. I begged Bob to let you stay in the cabin with me and swap with Frank Rox but he wouldn't have it," insists Reid.

"I'm not surprised, of course he wouldn't swap with Frank Rox. He's the ultimate pain in the arse."

"Oh, thanks," says Frank Rox.

"Cass you're in with me for one reason only. Your dad said he would only let you go on this trip if you stayed with me at all times. He said that I had to keep a watch over you, that was the deal," points out Bob.

Reid goes up to Cass and jokingly sprays Hugo Boss aftershave on his neck and says,   "Enjoy your date and smell like the champ you are."

Cass and Reid laugh, they're both back in a good place, mates again.

Chopper Moon still looks puzzled about being called one of the goonies but gives Cass a walk over because he's the boy wonder of the team. The rest of the team are eating their meal quietly. Alan Jones finishes his meal and gets apple pie and custard. He shows it to Peter Springsteen.

"Apple pie and custard, do you want a discussion on it or can I eat it in peace Peter?"

` "No, you eat the pie and enjoy," taunts Peter.

Frank Rox gets strawberries and brings them over to the table. As he squirts the cream on his bowl, John Cully knocks his arm and it misses his bowl and flies into the face of Max.

Max wipes it off his face. Frank Rox is in shock. Max stands up and picks Frank Rox up with his two hands across Frank Rox's throat, throttling him. Max has steam coming out of his ears.

Frank is spluttering his words as Max's hands tighten around his neck. "It was an accident, it wasn't my fault, get the fuck off me dickhead." Frank Rox is turning blue. As he chokes, he looks to Chopper for help.

Chopper Moon stands up and grabs Max by his hands and releases his grip from around Frank's neck. Max has red mist he's in the destroy zone.

"That's enough, you fucking bully," bawls Chopper Moon.

"You fucking arsehole," croaks Frank. As he fights to catch his breath, he breaths heavily through his nose and mouth.

"I'm sick of that little cunt," barks Max.

"Well that's tough shit, we're a team and if you doing it to him you're doing it to all of us," yells Chivers.

"Well if that's so, I'll smash all the team then," roars Max.

"Is that so, bad boy Max? Smash me first then," growls Chopper Moon.

Bob Arrow jumps in-between Max and Chopper and calms things down.

"Okay, let's all remember we're here celebrating the Golden Dock league and cup double win," shouts Pat Arrow.

"Let's not spoil the trip lads," mutters Bob.

Ronnie steps in and whispers in Max's ear. Max nods to Bob. "Okay, Bob you're right but keep that little shit away from me." Max and Ronnie leave the restaurant to freshen up in their cabin.

Frank Rox turns to Chopper Moon. "What did you jump in for soft-lad? I had him there, I was on top. I could see his hands turning blue."

The whole team piss themselves and tuck into their meals. Bob Arrow turns to Alex Sharp and states you can't beat that camaraderie, that what makes us all winners. As the players filter out the restaurant Peter Springsteen calls over Fred Kettle. As Fred reaches their table, Peter, Bob and Alex Sharp are in deep discussion. Peter looks up and smiles at Fred.

"Right Fred, time for you and Chopper to pay your way, we need two bottles of Jack Daniels, two bottles of Remy Martin brandy, a bottle of vodka and a carton of Embassy cigarettes, that will pay for yours and Choppers trip.

"Okay, no problem," whispers Fred Kettle.

"I will go the duty free now Peter." As Fred Kettle is about to leave he's called back by Pat Arrow.

"Hey Fred, pick up a bottle of Jack Daniels for me."

"Piss off Pat. I'm paying off my debt to the club by getting this for the committee."

"Fred, Fred, Fred, I've a big influence on this team, I'll get you at least a sub shirt against Amsterdam Jets, if you get me a bottle of Jack Daniels."

"Okay Pat, one bottle of JD on its way, for a sub shirt."

"You know it makes sense Fred."

Fred Kettle leaves to get the drinks. Bob Arrow turns to his brother Pat smiling. "What influence have you got over the team Pat?"

"None at all Bob but Fred doesn't know that, plus we have got a few injuries so we need every one who is fit." Bob smiles at Pat and starts banging on the table.

Bob turns to Alex and mutters, "I'm always saying we have good team spirit now we have spirits, lager and cigarettes and team sponsors that's why this is a grand old team to play for." Bob has a glint in his eye as he thinks of the up and coming trip to Amsterdam.

Kevin Chivers and John Cully head back to the arcade to use their magnet to clean out the ten pence machines, which also have watches and five-pound notes inside them. Alex Sharp texts all the players to meet at a quarter to four in the morning so that the team all leave the ferry together and to put their watches and phones an hour ahead, as Dutch time is one hour ahead. He tells them all to meet on deck at the front exit point.

Fred Kettle and Chopper enter the duty-free shop which has a strong whiff of perfume. Chopper goes to the counter asking the staff can they help him pick a perfume for his girl. As he flirts and jokes with them, getting their utmost attention, Fred Kettle fills his bags with the stuff Peter Springsteen and Pat Arrow have asked for. Fred whistles as he leaves the duty-free shop letting Chopper Moon know he has finished.

Chopper smiles at the girls in the duty-free shop. "Choices, choices, choices girls. I'll have to come back, thanks for your assistance ladies." Fred and Chopper Moon make their way to the bar section of the ferry where Pat, Bob, Alex and Peter Springsteen are all sitting on the deck, drinking glasses of lager. Fred gives them the bags of spirits and cigarettes.

"Nice one Freddy boy, you and Chopper have paid your way now, thank you very much Fred," says Bob. Fred Kettle hands Pat Arrow his bottle of Jack Daniels.

"Thanks Fred, nice one. There is a sub shirt for you against Amsterdam Jets Freddy son." Pat turns to Bob Arrow and gives him a cheeky wink. Bob spurts out his drink at the cheek of Pat.

Cass, Ant Hodge and Kevin Bird are on the middle deck of the ferry. Cass is sitting on the handrail. As the ferry sails up and down in the winds of the North Sea. Alan Jones walks over and throws Cass a bag of cheese and onion crisps. Cass grabs them nearly going overboard, Peter Springsteen sees this and begs Cass to get down before the boy wonder of football falls backwards into the North Sea.

"It's okay I'm a good swimmer Peter," smiles Cass.

"Cass I'm not joking, get down my nerves have gone," begs a worried Peter Springsteen.

"Look Peter no hands," laughs Cass. Seeing Cass in this motion Peter drinks a full glass of Remi-Martin brandy in one gulp.

"Look Peter, I'm that fella from Titanic."

Cass stands up on the rail with his feet still locked into the bottom rail, Cass lets go of the rail spreading his arms out wide dropping the crisps into the sea as he spreads his hands out, he keeps safe by locking his feet into the rail.

Peter Springsteen goes white and starts shaking. "Cass, please, please, stop."

"Why Peter?"

"I can't believe you! *'Fucking no hands'*, you have just wasted a full packet of crisps doing that stunt, they'll be in the North Sea now," moans Alan Jones.

Cass starts singing *'Ferry across the Mersey.'*

"Cass get your feet on the deck or you're not playing in the match," yells Bob.

"Okay, for fucks sake," shouts Cass as he gets down.

Peter Springsteen walks over and gives Cass twenty pounds. "That's for you Cass if you promise not to do that again."

"Okay I won't do it again," laughs Cass. Peter breaths a sign of relief, as Cass puts the twenty pounds into his pocket.

"Peter do I get twenty pounds if I don't sit on the handrail?" Kevin Bird asks.

"Fuck off Birdy, you can fall overboard for all I care, Cass will be worth about twenty million in a few years' time when your worth fuck all. In fact I'll be surprised if you get a shirt next season, so you can sit on the handrail all you want."

Peter sits down with a little smirk on his face and swigs his drink, while all the committee lads burst out laughing.

Cass turns to Kevin Bird. "Never mind Birdy, I'll give you a fiver out of the twenty because as my strike partner you make me look good, you being so bad."

"Nice one Cass, a fiver is a fiver."

The players all laugh and leave the committee lads and make their way into the arcade where Kevin Chivers is using the magic magnet to clean out the ten pence machines with his sidekick John Cully.

Cass gives Birdy a fiver. "Do you want a game of pool Cass, ten pounds a game?" asks Birdy. Cass agrees. Kevin Bird smiles to himself thinking this will be easier than taking candy of a baby, as he's the captain of the pub pool team,

"You break if you like Cass." Cass smiles.

"Okay Birdy may the best man win."

Five games later Kevin Bird hands Cass fifty pounds. "Nice one Birdy five games to me zero to you," laughs Cass.

"You got lucky Cass."

"No not lucky Birdy, my private snooker coaching lessons have paid off."

Cass walks away singing. "Snooker-looper nuts are we, Kevin Bird just lost to me, pot the balls and then the black and then put the money in my sack."

Kevin Bird is gutted, his face resembles a man who found a pound but lost a million.

"Cass, you best go meet that bird. It's five to seven," shouts Ant Hodge.

Cass smiles and looks at Ant Hodge in the eyes.

"A bird is gangly and ugly," whispers Cass as he points at Kevin Bird.

"Chelsea is a beautiful looking princess," says Cass.

"Well whatever she is, you best fucking hurry up before she fucks off," shouts Ant Hodge.

Cass leaves the arcade and makes his way to the bar to meet Chelsea. As he leaves the arcade, all the lads start to make kissing noises. Laughing, Cass walks out with his head held high, as if he's just about to go into combat. Cass makes his way to the bar he looks up and sees a vision, it's Chelsea... she looks amazing in her white dress to her knees with her tanned legs and long straight brown hair and her tanned face. Chelsea is with a friend that Cass hasn't met.

"Hiya," says Cass. Chelsea smiles. Her friend looks at him and turns her head.

"So, Chelsea is that him? He's a drip, why bother, he's so rough looking."

Cass gets onto this comment from her snotty mate. "Sorry, I didn't catch your name, I'm Brian Cassidy, what's your name? And when is your birthday?"

"Pardon?" Says the girl angrily.

"I asked what your name is and when your birthday is."

"It's Sarah and it's April the second, why?" Sarah is standing with her nose in the air like a stuck-up toff.

"Well if you would have been born a day earlier you would have been the April fool, now you're just a fool and I would have thought by now that birthday present would have expired."

"What present?" asks Sarah confused.

"The one where you got that attitude from, surely it has expired now, your birthday was April it's the end of May now."

Chelsea, unable to keep her laughter in bursts into a giggle. "Sarah, I think on this date two's company three's a crowd. I'll meet you later. I'll be okay with Brian." Sarah looks at Cass, pulls a face and storms off.

"Ciao, ciao Sarah baby," laugh's Cass. Chelsea tries to hold her in her laugh as Sarah walks away. Cass goes to get two non-alcoholic drinks, as Chelsea finds a table.

"Chelsea would you like to watch a film in the cinema? Creed is on."

"Creed hey, that's so romantic Cass."

"Chelsea, no it's a boxing film, a Rocky one with a real scouse boxer playing the main role."

"I know Cass, it's about Rocky from Stocky the scouse boxer," Chelsea says in her posh cockney voice.

"Are you winding me up Chelsea? Rocky Fielding from Stocky is real, he's W.B.A. Champion of the world, he's an inspiration to all the kids in Canny Farm, he's a true champion in every way, kids from there look up to him, he gives them belief. He's the first world boxing champion from that manor."

"Yes, I know, I'm taking the piss, Cass it's about boxing with that other Rocky fella Rambo." Cass sniggers to himself and thinks I think I may have just met my soulmate.

"Do you know how you can tell the man in the film is a true scouser Chelsea?"

"Is it because he's ugly like all scouse men?"

"No, you're a cheeky cow, we're not all ugly, we're the salt of the earth, all scousers are. We have the best-looking girls in the world in Liverpool."

"So why are you dating me, a cockney girl?"

"I won't be if you carry on insulting scousers Chelsea."

"Shut up scouse and drink up, get your jacket, you have pulled," laughs Chelsea. They leave the pub and make their way to the cinema.

In the arcade Kevin Chivers and John Cully finish playing the ten pence drop machines and go back to the cabin to count the money. They have three hundred pounds in ten pence's. Kevin gives John fifty pound's worth. John goes to the exchange cashier to change the money, but they don't exchange coins so Kevin offers him forty Euros for the fifty pounds in ten pence's.

John thinks he's losing out and points this out to Kevin.

"Take it or leave it Cully son." John Cully takes it.

"You're a robbing twat Kev, I'm supposed to be your right-hand man."

"You are Cully lad but all's fair in love and war," declares Kevin Chivers. As he finishes counting his money, he attaches his magnet onto his suitcase like it's a permanent fixture. John takes his Euros and meets the other lads in the casino.

On the top deck. John Paul Anderson, Pat Arrow, Mark Barrow and Todd Elliott are singing football songs badly in the pitch dark of the night, with the sea salts of the North Sea bearing up their noses.

"Smoking, drinking and singing, this is the life lads," bellows Pat Arrow.

John Paul Anderson stands up drops his trousers and sticks his arse into the air slapping his arse cheeks as he starts singing.

"Kenny is our King, King Kenny should be knighted, O King Kenny should be knighted."

Pat, Mark and Todd all stand on the ferry bench and drop their trousers sticking their arses into the direction of the moon singing.

"If you think King Kenny should be knighted show your arse."
If you think King Kenny should be knighted show your arse.
If you think King Kenny should be knighted, King Kenny should be knighted, King Kenny should be knighted, show your arse."

They slap their arses in sync with John Paul Anderson.

As they're jumping up and down on the bench. Pat Arrow slips and tumbles off the bench landing arse first onto a cold wet wooden floor. John Paul helps Pat up making sure he's okay.

"Thanks, you're a cracker."

"My pleasure, you're a legend in my book."

The lads stop singing. The beer that has flowed on the ferry has taken its toll on the lads, pissed, they discuss how they will change the world and how they will make King Kenny a Sir, as he deserves it more than anyone in the United Kingdom.

In the casino Reid Johnson is looking for Cass. "Ant, have you seen Cass?"

"He went out for a drink with that bird. I think he was going to the cinema after that."

"Okay, thanks."

Reid nods at Frank Rox. "Let's go to the cinema Frank to make sure Cass is okay, I'm worried about him. I haven't seen him much today I want to make sure he's not missing home."

"Missing home, he has only been gone a day. I've been longer on a message," snorts Frank.

"Shut up Frank! Just because he looks like a man he still only sixteen and I'm going to find him to make sure he's okay."

"Have you got his nappies Reid?"

"Stop being a tit, are you coming or not."

"Okay, calm down, calm down." Frank mimics the scousers from the Harry Enfield show.

"What about Fred and Chopper they will be here in a bit Reid?"

"Fuck them, I'm going now Frank. They can find us, come on let's go."

Reid and Frank head towards the cinema. At the entrance Frank Rox buys a big box of popcorn.

"Do you want a box of popcorn Reid?"

"No, I don't, I'm just here making sure Cass is okay, what the fuck are you buying popcorn for? We're only here checking on Cass we're not film critics soft arse."

As they enter the cinema it's pitch black and the film has started. Frank Rox is walking down the aisles shouting "Are you in here Cass?" A gang of lads ask Frank to be quiet. Not amused he throws popcorn at them warning them he's the real Rocky so it'd be best if they shut up. Reid finds Cass with Chelsea.

"What do you want Reid?"

"I'm just making sure you're okay Cass." Frank catches up to Reid in the cinema.

"I'm fine, leave me alone Reid. Piss off."

"Piss off, piss off? Hey Cass he has been worried sick about you" says Frank Rox

"I'm sorry Reid, I didn't mean that, sorry I know you worry about me but I'm okay I'm with Chelsea, she's the girl I told you about at dinner." Cass turns to Chelsea. "This is Reid my cousin. He's more like my older brother."

"Oh, so you're the one he looks up to, Brian has talked about you none stop Reid, he really does look up to you. I've been looking out for a super hero," says Chelsea.

"Well I'm sorry to disappoint you Chelsea. They do say never meet your super heroes in real life."

"You haven't disappointed me Reid, the fact you have come looking for him to see that he's okay shows me that you're a good person and that you're very close."

Frank Rox introduces himself to Chelsea. "Hi I'm Frank, the star player in the team, I should be the captain, but we gave it to that old man Bob Arrow to keep him quiet. Cass cleans my boots, he might have mentioned me to you Chelsea?"

"No, sorry Frank never heard of you, Cass has never mentioned you."

"Who's on this date me or you Frank?" fumes Cass.

"Me I think," laughs Frank.

Fred Kettle and Chopper Moon enter the cinema shouting for Reid and Frank.   "Reid, you here? Frank, where are you?"

"No fucking way, it's not funny now Reid, get rid of the three goonies."

"Okay I will do Cass as long as you're okay, if you need me just ring me."

"I'm fine Reid. I can't ring you my phone is in the shop getting fixed, just get rid of them please," pleads Cass.

"Let's go Frank, he's okay. Tell Fred we're coming now."

"We're here Fred, I can see you," yells Frank.

As the four of them leave, all the people in the cinema start clapping. Frank Rox turns around and throws his box of popcorn into the direction of the back-row seats.

Cass sinks down into his seat. Chelsea laughs then turns to Cass. "You're all like a close family, they're a lively bunch them lot." Cass is not amused.

"Chelsea can we just watch the film now?"

"Yes, if you hold my hand."

"Hold your hand Chelsea? Are you fucking kidding? You're on a date with a northern lad now not a pappy cockney yuppie. Just watch Creed."

"Yes, Brian we can if you hold my hand." Brian holds Chelsea's hand.

"You're lucky it's pitch black in here Chelsea."

In the casino Kevin Bird, Ant Hodge, Ian Craig and John Cully are playing poker, Todd Elliott is watching the lads play. Fred Kettle, Frank Rox, Chopper Moon and Reid make their way back to their cabin to try get a few hours' sleep. On the top open deck Pat Arrow and John Paul Anderson are still trying to change the world.

Cass and Chelsea are on the open deck gazing at the stars in the moon lit sky. "So, Cass how do you know a proper scouser?"

"Didn't the scouse actor in the Creed film teach you anything Chelsea?

"Yes, Cass I learnt that a scouser who was a big Everton fan won a world boxing title in the film at Everton's football ground which is called Goodison Park."

"No, Chelsea you learnt that proper scousers are Everton fans. That Everton are the peoples club. To support Everton, you have to be a pure scouser born and bred in the city of Liverpool."

"Is that a fact?"

"Yes, that's a fact Chelsea, most scousers are Everton fans, Liverpool is a bigger club and yes, they are more successful and all that shit but all their fans are Norwegians with Liverpool shirts on. I heard that even their advertising boards are in Norwegian, but I can't say if that's true because I won't go to that shitty place."

"Does that not just mean they have more fans Cass?"

"No don't be stupid are you thick Chelsea? Liverpool do have a worldwide fan base but these days at Anfield it's like the United Nations, you have to be able to speak five different languages just to work in their ticket office."

"Is that not a good thing?"

"No, it's not Chelsea, at Everton it's just scousers that support Everton."

"So why in the trailer of the Creed film did it show you that Rocky fella Sylvester Stallone parading around Everton's ground in an Everton jersey? He's not a scouser, he's a yank."

"Oh, shut up Chelsea, you're a cockney what do you know about football, just watch the stars in the sky."

In the casino John Cully has had enough of the poker. "Todd are you going back the cabin?

"Yeah Cully, let's go, it's shit in here."

As Todd walks out of the casino he puts a pound in the fruit machine and hits the hundred pounds jackpot. The rest of the lads can't believe it.

"Fuck me that's the first pound he has spent and he has won the fucking jackpot," groans Birdy.

"Money goes to money they say. I give up," moans Ian Craig.

"I give up too," says Ant Hodge.

All the lads finish their game of poker and head back to their cabins to try and catch up on some sleep. Most of the squad are in their cabins sleeping,

Cass has stayed up, he's out on the open deck talking to Chelsea listening to her dreams of becoming a barrister. They are both in Amsterdam at the same time and they are both on the same ferry that takes them back to Hull. Cass is well impressed with Chelsea, they are sitting out on the open deck watching the stars in the sky, smelling the tulips as they glide up to the Rotterdam harbour. They don't notice what the time is, as they are enjoying each other's company so much. It's like they are in a movie and they are the main stars, they're in their own little bubble.

It's 3.55am and the ferry is pulling into the Rotterdam harbour. All the team are on the deck waiting to get off the ferry except for young Cass.

"Where is Cass?" yells Bob.

"He's supposed to be with you Bob," shouts Reid.

"Reid, he didn't come back the cabin."

"Are you fucking kidding Bob?"

"No, Reid I've had to bag all his stuff and bring it here with me." Reid looks worried. He vomits over the side of the ferry.

"He's with that Chelsea one," says a half-asleep Birdy.

"Ring him Reid, he might answer to you. I've sent him texts and I've rang him about fifty times all I get is the answering machine," says Bob.

"His phone is getting fixed Bob, we need to look for him."

Bob starts scratching his head as he can't understand why Cass is not here at the meeting point. He has a worried look on his face.

"Bob, I'll go and look for him." Reid leaves his bags to go and find Cass.

"Cass. Where are you Cass?" yells Reid as he goes from deck to deck.

Cass is on the top deck unaware that they had to meet at 4am. A shooting star flies through the dark skies of the night. Chelsea sits up from the bench.

"Brian, I had best get back to my Cabin."

"Okay Chelsea, I'll walk you to your cabin door." Cass bumps into Reid as he's walking Chelsea back to her cabin.

"Where have you been Cass? You have had us all worried sick, we were supposed to meet at 4am on the exit deck. Bob has had to pack your bags and he's not happy with you. Why didn't you tell him you weren't going back to the cabin? Bob has rung you and text you about fifty times."

"I'm a big lad now Reid"

"Big lad, a fucking big daft farmer's lad that's what you are Cass, someone who thinks they know everything but who knows nothing. I'm pissed off with you Cass, stop thinking about yourself all the time. I was worried about you."

"Reid I'm sorry I didn't get any texts my phone is in the shop getting fixed, I told you that on the coach but as usual you weren't listening to me."

"I was listening to you Cass."

"Me and Chelsea didn't know what time it was, we were just watching the windmills and the fields as the ferry sailed into the harbour."

"Didn't that give it away Cass? The harbour - time to get off the ferry?"

"I wasn't thinking. I'm sorry Reid."

"Okay, let's forget about it now. I've found you and you're safe and well, go and take Chelsea back to her cabin as quick as you can. I'll go back and tell Bob I've found you."

Cass walks Chelsea to her cabin where her mates are fuming with her. Cass gives her a kiss and says his goodbyes. As he reaches the exit deck Bob is waiting, glancing at Cass like a crazy fat kid that has had his last doughnut robbed.

Bob is fuming he's not one bit happy as he tears a strip off Cass. "Where have you been Cass? Boy wonder or no boy wonder you don't just do as you want. We're a team, this is not the Cass show, and you have had us worried sick. Peter Springsteen is pissed because of you, he drank a full bottle of Remi Martin when he found out you had not returned to your cabin, you could have fell overboard or anything, now get your fucking stuff and check that all your stuff is there, your passport and all your money. Make sure I've left nothing behind, now get out of my sight."

"Sorry Bob."

"Save it Cass, just check your bags."

The whole team feel for Cass but the only way he will learn is if he knows what he did was not that of a team player. Cass checks his bags all his stuff is there, as the team wait to get off the ferry Cass goes to the front and whistles to get everyone's attention.

"Lads, I would just like to say a few words, I'm sorry to all of you for being late, you lot have made me the player and person I am today and the reason I was late was because I didn't get the message or text because my phone is getting fixed, but that is no excuse and I'm sorry that I've let the team down."

"We accept your apology Cass. We were just worried about you that's all," says Reid.

"Yeah Cass it's okay I would have slotted into your place in the side no problem," yells Rox.

"We were more worried about Rox playing than you going missing Cass," mutters Birdy. Bob goes up to Cass and puts his arm around him.

"We all think the world off you Cass. We're all just looking out for you because we care about you."

"Thanks Bob. I'll try not to let you down again skipper."

Bob smiles and looks Cass in the eye with a beaming smile. "Do you know what Cass? You have never let me down, never ever and I believe that girl you were with was like a model but she also had a brain." Bob winks at Cass.

"I think if I was your age in your shoes Cass, I would have done the same thing as you, I just blew my top because I was worried about you. Reid vomited when he found out you never came back to the cabin and you were missing. He went looking for you straight away, he cares for you more than you will ever know..."

The gates on the exit deck open. The players gather their belonging together and make their way off the ferry towards the passport and customs borders onto foreign soil.

The Golden Dock Have Landed.

Chapter 6

The big house in The Hague

As the team make their way towards passport control it's four in the morning and the cold sea air hits them in their faces. John Paul Anderson and Pat Arrow have their arms around each other's shoulders singing as loudly as they can.

"Show me the way to go home, I'm tired and I want go to bed." Kevin Chivers looks puzzled with the song they are singing.

"Go home, go home, we have only just got here you pair of muppets."

Pat Arrow, pissed, shouts, "We know that Kev. We know that but we're here to conquer Europe and make this our new home."

John Paul who can barely stand, is straightening himself up by leaning on the wall.

"We will conquer all," shouts John Paul. Bob Arrow looks over to see the commotion and hears John Paul shouting.

"That's good John Paul, conquer your drink and drugs problem first and sober up before we get to the passport control office."

Peter Springsteen staggers as he's walking to the passport entrance. Cass is walking down apologising to Reid for not being more responsible and tells him he won't let him down again. Max and Ronnie have re-joined the team and blend in talking to Bob and Alex about the match against Amsterdam Jets.

Bob tells the team to sober up and to get their passports ready. They fly past passport control without a hitch. As they reach customs it's empty, they walk past without a problem. They exit the Rotterdam grounds.

Kevin Chivers turns to Bob and asks what's happening now. Bob asks Max and Ronnie the same question. Max explains they have arranged for the team to be picked up and they will be chauffeured around during their stay by two friends of Ted Hike who is sponsoring the game. They will stay in a house tonight in The Hague which is a half hour's drive away and in the morning, they will all book into a hotel. Max gives Bob a bundle of Euros to pay for their stay in the hotel. Max and Ronnie tell Bob they will be back in touch with him the night before the football match. They both leave and jump into a taxi and drive off into the distance.

Frank Rox turns to Bob. "Is this a fucking wind-up Bob, we're stranded with nowhere to go."

"Shut up Frank, just be patient." bellows Bob.

In the distance there is a roar of two big vehicles racing towards where they're waiting. In the space of two minutes two black Mercedes minibuses pull up and two men get out and introduce themselves as Fat Joe and Scouse Ricko.

"Sorry we're late," says Fat Joe.

"All jump in the minibuses lads, we're going to our gaff in The Hague," says Scouse Ricko.

Cass gets in and is amazed by the inside of the minibus. It's got blacked out windows with leather seats, cup holders and a television built into every head-rest so they can watch the telly while they're in the minibuses.

Fat Joe and Scouse Ricko are from Liverpool. They're both in their early thirties, they have moved to Holland to seek a better life. The drive to the big house takes half an hour, most of the players are pissed and tired and head for one of the beds upstairs in the big house. There are four bedrooms with ten beds so some players sit up watching porn on the sixty-inch television. It's spoken in Dutch but this doesn't stop them watching. The house is detached with a six-foot wall built all around the grounds. It's in a secluded spot with beautiful views. It's built on the hilltop looking down into The Hague.

Chopper Moon is in the kitchen with Scouse Ricko talking about the bars in Amsterdam, when Chopper notices the gun in his inside coat pocket, Chopper asks Scouse Ricko could he get him a gun for protection for the team.

Scouse Ricko goes upstairs followed by Chopper Moon. Scouse Ricko goes into the safe and picks out three guns all with boxes of ammunition. He takes the guns downstairs followed by Chopper Moon. They enter the kitchen Scouse Ricko stands at the table putting the guns onto it very carefully. Cass who is watching the television in the other room looks through the doors and sees the guns, he's in total shock. He looks away, pretending he hasn't seen them this is not something he wants to be part of.

Scouse Ricko tells Chopper to be careful and to always have the safety lock on the gun and that at the end of the trip he must return it, where it will go back into the safe.

Chopper nods at Scouse Ricko and agrees to what has been asked of him. He picks up the gun and puts it into his bag.

Kevin Parry is upstairs causing mischief, he walks into the bedroom where Peter Springsteen is asleep. Kevin sees he's flat out snoring. He goes into the bathroom and gets a razor and shaving foam and heads back into his room, where he leans over and sprays the foam onto Peter's right eyebrow and shaves it off.

A drunken Peter didn't even flinch while Parry shaved off his eyebrow. With Peter still asleep and motionless, Parry decides to put foam on Springsteen's moustache and shaves half it half off. He then leaves to go into another bedroom where he finds his next victim Pat Arrow. He shaves Pat's left eyebrow off while he sleeps and moves into the other bedroom and shaves off half of Kevin Bird's right eyebrow. He makes his way downstairs where Cass is nodding off to sleep. He stands over Cass and squirts the shaving foam onto his eyebrow which wakes up young Cass.

"Hey! What the fuck are you doing gobshite?" Cass yells.

Cass jumps up and smacks Kevin Parry on the jaw with a right hook followed by a left uppercut into Parry's eye sending him flying backwards over the sofa and onto the cactus plants. Kevin Parry starts screaming in pain.

"What's that for Cass?"

"You know what it's for Parry."

Curled up, Parry winces in pain from the spikes from the cactus plants, which are sticking in him. He rushes to the bathroom to get tweezers from the cupboard. He stands in front of the mirror picking them out.

"You're bang out of order Cass," Parry shouts from upstairs in the bathroom.

Cass, standing at the bottom of the stairs shouts up to him.

"That's what you get for being a prick and trying to shave off my eyebrow."

Chopper Moon comes into the television room and asks Cass what the fuck has just happened. The noise has woken up Alan Jones, who was asleep on the chair next to young Cass. As Alan Jones stretches his arms out wide, he yawns then reaches into his bag and gets out a pork pie, taking a bite, he turns to Cass.

"Are you okay Cass? What just happened?" mutters Alan.

Both Cass and Chopper burst out laughing as they watch Alan Jones munching on his pork pie at six o clock in the morning.

Cass explains to both of them that Kevin Parry tried to shave off his eyebrow, so he smacked him in the face and Parry fell into the cactus plant.

Chopper and Alan both look at each and in tandem say "The fucking wanker."

Todd Elliott, who is sitting in the big leather chair, pops up explaining how he'd seen all of what had just happened and Cass was right to crack him. He tells them Parry has been upstairs doing the same thing to some of the other players that have crashed out on their beds. They can hear Kevin Parry squealing in the bathroom, as he takes out the spikes from his body. Chopper, Cass, Todd, and Alan all burst out laughing.

Scouse Ricko walks in and looks at his cactus plants on the floor.

"Hey! Parry, get down the fucking stairs and fix these plants."

Scouse Ricko is not happy with Parry.

Kevin Parry walks down the stairs. His eye is closed over and his face, is blotchy from the cactus plants. He picks up the plants and puts the soil back into the pots.

"I'm sorry for knocking the plants over Scouse Ricko," says Parry.

"You're a wanker Parry, you had best piss off out of my sight," shouts Chopper.

Parry tries to plead his innocence. "It's not my fault, blame Cass, look what he did to me." Cass gets up out of his chair and heads towards Parry.

"I'm to blame, you're a cheeky twat Parry. I'll close your other eye you fucking prick."

Alan Jones jumps up and aided by Todd Elliott, both manage to pull Cass back.

Chopper jumps up pointing his finger at Parry. "Get the fuck out my sight Parry, before I kick you all around this house." Parry exits very quickly to a room at the far end of the house, locks the door and lays on the sofa feeling sorry for himself.

It's 6.20am and it's lights out with everyone trying to get some sleep as the birds start to sing and the sunlight hits the windows of the big house on the hill.

At 7.30am Fat Joe is woken by the tune of *'Ground control to Major Tom'* sung by Ziggy Stardust aka David Bowie.

Frank Rox who was asleep in another bed in the room turns around muttering, "Fuck me Joe, are you an alien?"

Fat Joe shakes his head laughing. "No, I'm not an alien, it's the tune on my alarm clock, I had it installed into my clock." Frank Rox turns over and goes back to sleep.

Fat Joe makes his way downstairs to the kitchen to prepare a full English breakfast for over twenty men as he forgot to do a head count at the ferry terminal when he was picking up the team. He puts on his pinny and gets to work. He sets up the table, putting twenty bowls down with boxes of cereals and jugs of milk. He fills up the coffee machines and boils the kettle ready to fill up the teapots. He puts the bread in the toaster and fills pans with beans, chopped tomatoes and gets the bacon and sausages on the go.

He fills up two jugs with pure orange and two jugs with apple juice and puts them on the table. The mushrooms are frying while the black pudding is under the grill. He whisks ten eggs in a tub for the scrambled eggs and stacks the plates and places them at the end of the table. Fat Joe has *Food glorious food* playing on the DVD player. He's dancing around the kitchen as he prepares the breakfast; he thinks he's on the Dutch version of *Master Chef*.

It's now 8am, breakfast is prepared waiting on the hot trays, ready to dish out buffet style. Fat Joe goes to his room and gets a megaphone from his wardrobe shouting,   "Wakey, wakey, eggs and bakey it's time to move your lazy scouse arses from them comfy beds, breakfast is now being served in the kitchen, help yourself."

He moves from room to room repeating the message on the megaphone. The players slowly get the message looking up at Fat Joe with an eye half open, while the other eye is still in the land of nod they start to make their way downstairs.

Peter Springsteen gets out of bed and goes into the en-suite bathroom and washes his face. As he looks up into the mirror he lets out a scream.

"What the fuck! Where has my moustache gone?" The whole house shakes as he lets out a roar.

"I've had that moustache since I was twenty, my wife has never seen me without it, who the fuck did this to me?" He's fuming, the players downstairs are pissing themselves laughing.

Alan Jones shouts, "It was Kevin Parry, he's locked himself in one of the rooms down here at the back of the house."

"The bastard has shaved my fucking eyebrow as well, the fucking little shit, wait till I get hold of the twat."

Pat Arrow walks into the bathroom, to see what Parry has done to Peter Springsteen, he sees him and bursts out laughing.

Peter turns to Pat shouting, "I don't know what you're laughing at, look at your own eyebrow."

Pat Arrow looks in the mirror and notices half his eyebrow missing. "The little shit."

Pat rushes downstairs and kicks the door, where Parry has locked himself in.

"Get out you little shit. I'm going to rip your head off."

John Paul Anderson tries to calm Pat down. "Pat it's not that bad, leave it for now, a bit of black cherry blossom boot polish on it and no one will notice, let's get some breakfast the sausages smell lovely."

"Sausages, sausages, I'll shove the sausages up his arse and feed him to the dogs the little shit."

Cass has his right hand in a Champagne bucket full of ice because his hand has swelled up after he hit Parry on the jaw. Most of the lads are eating breakfast. Chopper tells Reid about Cass and Parry.

Reid is not happy but keeps quiet. As Reid makes his way to the kitchen he bumps into Parry as he walks out the locked room. Reid grabs him by the throat, throttling him and butts him on the bridge of his nose. Parry's nose bursts open.

Bob rushes over grabbing Reid. "Leave it Reid, I'll deal with Parry, we're a team, we stick together."

Reid who is still not happy, kicks out at Parry as Bob drags him away.

"He's a fucking shit Bob, picking on kids. Cass is sixteen," rages Reid. Once again Parry pleads his innocence. "I didn't touch him, look what Cass has done to my eye. It's closed over." Bob sends Parry to another room to eat his breakfast away from all the players.

Peter Springsteen walks into the kitchen minus his moustache, all the players look in amazement. "Peter, you look twenty years younger." smirks Ant Hodge.

"Twenty years younger, my wife will think I'm being Jack the lad over here."

Kevin Chivers who is holding in his laugh trying to keep a straight face, turns to Springsteen. "He said you look twenty years younger, not that you look like Brad Pitt, you're still an old man with one eyebrow."

"One eyebrow, half a moustache. That must be how the twenty first century rock and roll sex symbol looks like," laughs Chopper.

"You're years ahead of the fashion Peter," smirks Rox.

"Yeah, fucking light years ahead," says Kevin Chivers.

Kevin Bird is eating his breakfast, not realising his eyebrow has been shaved off. Mark Barrow points it out to him, being laid back, Bird just shrugs his shoulders.

"I've always wanted to be a punk rocker." Bird jumps up and starts to play air guitar shouting, "Anarchy."

Pete Springsteen joins in with him shouting, "Let's rock and roll."

The whole team are on the floor laughing their tits off. The room has gone wild, the team spirit has shone through once again.

Fat Joe walks into the room, all the lads start singing,

"For he's a jolly good fellow, for he's a jolly good fellow, for he's a jolly good fellow, because he's cooked breakfast, for all of us." Fat Joe takes a bow and gives a little speech.

"It's my pleasure as you're here to conquer Europe, so win them cups and take them back home with you."

This speech is met with a roar from all the players.

"Champions, champions, champions..."

Bob Arrow and Alex Sharp go and have a word with Kevin Parry in his isolated room. The three of them leave the room and enter the dining room where the team are gathered eating their breakfast.

Kevin Parry apologies to all the team. "Sorry lads. I was drunk... At the time, it seemed funny, now I realise it was a stupid thing to do, especially to my great team mates who have a special place in my heart."

Peter Springsteen goes over and hugs him, as he's hugging him, Parry screams.

"Aww, Peter you're patting my shoulder. It's got a cactus spike in it.

Scouse Ricko, walks over, yanks Parry's t-shirt down from his shoulder and takes three cactus spikes out which are embedded into his shoulder with tweezers. Parry winches in pain but thanks Scouse Ricko explaining that he could not reach them.

Parry walks over to Cass with his eye swollen and closed over offering him his hand.

"I'm sorry mate. I was out of order."

Cass takes his hand out of the ice bucket and shakes his hand. "It's sweet Parry lad, no hard feeling."

Kevin Bird turns to Alan Jones and whispers. "That's how Springsteen must have felt when he was going through his own little battle of the big horn."

Frank Rox jumps up and starts dancing around the room, going up to each player roaring like the lion in the Wizard of Oz, shouting "Put em up, put em up."

All the lads are curled up on the floor laughing, throwing the cushions at Frank Rox.

Fat Joe walks in the room looks, "Nice mess lads, you had best all go and get a wash and brush your teeth, go and freshen up. We will be leaving in twenty minutes, to make our way to Amsterdam, to book into the hotel."

All the players start to get organised.

Kevin Parry is in the ironing room about to iron his black jeans and black designer Prada shirt. Pat Arrow notices this and gets John Paul Anderson to call Parry out of the room and to distract him for a few minutes. John Paul calls out Parry, as Parry is talking to John Paul. Pat Arrow goes into the kitchen and gets the bleach, then sneaks into the ironing room to empty the water out of the iron, he then fills it up with bleach, sneaks back into the kitchen giving John Paul the thumbs up. With that, John Paul tells Parry he needs to go brush his teeth.

Parry makes his way back to the ironing room, where he irons his jeans spraying the iron onto his jeans, he finishes his True Religion jeans to iron his black Prada shirt. As he sprays it, he starts to notice white dots on his shirt. He checks his jeans, they're full of white dots also, he looks puzzled, then notices Pat Arrow and John Paul Anderson laughing at the door. Pat Arrow looks Parry in the eye, as he's scratching his missing eyebrow, laughing.

"Karma is a bitch, Parry isn't it, fancy spraying bleach onto your black jeans and shirt."

"Bleach, thanks a lot Pat." Pat Arrow walks away, turning around.

"What goes around comes back around. Hey Kev?"

Parry is not amused but accepts it.

Fat Joe gets out his megaphone, telling everyone that they depart in five minutes time, and that they all should meet at the front of the house and to get into the minibuses.

The team all board the minibuses and are ready to leave. Frank Rox sits in the passenger seat. He picks up Scouse Ricko's walkie talkie and starts fiddling with the buttons.

Fat Joe opens the big metal gates with his remote control that he keeps in his car. Scouse Ricko is in the minibus behind him. It's now nine in the morning and the sun is shining. Fat Joe drives off leaving the big house on the hill behind as they head towards Amsterdam, an hour's drive away.

"Ground control to Major Tom, let's get ready to move these scousers on," says Fat Joe through the walkie talkie, catching Frank Rox by surprise. Frank can't believe what he has just heard. "I knew Fat Joe was an alien, I knew I wasn't dreaming."

All the lads look at him puzzled, Chopper Moon turns to Rox. "Are you still drunk soft-lad? What have you been taking? Angel dust?"

"I told you not to let him watch E.T," smirks John Cully.

The players all start to chant, "E.T. for England..."

Chapter 7

Tulips of Amsterdam

Fat Joe opens his window and aims his fob at the big black metal gates to close them. Scouse Ricko watches from behind in his minibus.

Fat Joe picks up his walkie-talkie from the dashboard and tries again to contact Scouse Ricko. "Ground control to Major Tom, is your walkie-talkie on?"

"Yes, Roger and out fat boy it's on," replies Scouse Ricko.

"Let's get these boys to their hotel then scouse boy."

Scouse Ricko mutters into his walkie-talkie, "Joe, have the big gates been sealed and protected?"

"Yeah, all done Ricko lad, lets travel through space on this fine Saturday morning."

Frank Rox is sitting at the front of the minibus next to Scouse Ricko. "I knew he was an alien, I know you all think I'm mad, I knew I wasn't dreaming."

Scouse Ricko looks at Frank Rox puzzled. "Who's an alien Frank?"

"How much of that angel dust have you taken Frankie boy?" laughs Chopper.

Frank Rox grabs the walkie-talkie from the dashboard. "FJ, not FR phone home, FJ phone home, I knew you was an alien Joe."

Scouse Ricko is now even more confused. In the other minibus. Fat Joe looks at Bob.   "He's fucking mad him Bob."

Bob smiles at Fat Joe shaking his head. "Tell me about it Joe."

The team are heading to Amsterdam, to book into their hotel which is a two-minute walk from the famous red-light district. Kevin Bird has his head out of the minibus window sniffing the Dutch air, filling his lungs with car fumes.

"We must be near, I can smell the tulips of Amsterdam."

Alan Jones opens his window in the Mercedes minibus as he is munching on a pork pie.

"We're definitely near, I can smell the cannabis on the streets of Amsterdam."

"That's not on the streets of Amsterdam soft arse, that's John Paul at the back of the minibus smoking a spliff out of the window," smirks Chivers.

John Paul looks up, he raises his arm. "Power to the people."

Peter Springsteen is on his Apple mobile, explaining to his wife that someone has shaved off his moustache. He's getting a right ear bashing, his wife is not happy with him, he starts stuttering while he's talking.

"Fuck me when did Rigsby become our manager?" Frank Rox says tongue in cheek.

"It's not Rigsby who picks the team, it's his wife," laughs Chivers.

"Mrs. Springsteen wears the trousers in that household," yells Birdy.

All the team piss themselves laughing. Peter Springsteen closes the call and turns to Kevin Bird. "She's not happy with me."

"It's not that bad Peter, take no notice of yer bird you look better now without that tash."

"Don't bullshit me Birdy."

"I'm not, it makes you look younger."

"Yer you're right Birdy, fuck her," yells Peter.

In the same breath Peter Springsteen jumps up pretending to play air-guitar imagining he's a rock and roll star. "Come on lads, let's fucking party."

John Arrow who is a committee member, quietly points out to Peter Springsteen that he's the manager of the team and needs to show a good example to the players.

"Yeah just tone it down Peter," says Bob. Peter Springsteen looks shocked, he points out that he's just getting them in the mood for the trip.

"It's rock and roll, Elvis has not left the building."

"That's because we're on a minibus soft arse," mutters Birdy.

John Arrow shakes his head and turns to Kevin Bird. "I give up, he's a rock and roll star."

The team pull up outside the hotel *Grand Amrath Amsterdam*. They get out of the minibuses and gather together in the hotel car park.

Bob Arrow tells them there will be three to a room, he tells them who is sharing;

Room one… Bob Arrow…Alan Jones… Brian Cassidy…
Room two… Alex Sharp …John Arrow…Peter Springsteen…
Room three…Kevin Chivers… John Cully …Ant Hodge…
Room four…Kevin Parry… Ian Craig… Mark Barrow…
Room five…Reid Johnson…Todd Elliott…
Room six…Frank Rox…Chopper Moon…Fred Kettle…
Room seven …Kevin Bird…Pat Arrow… John Paul Anderson…
Room eight…Fat Joe…Scouse Ricko…

Bob takes the lads into the foyer and tells them that after he's booked them in, they should all go to bed to catch up on their lost sleep and to meet up at 1pm in the foyer. Its ten-thirty in the morning, the sun is shining on the streets of Amsterdam, the tulips are blossoming. Bob books into the five-star hotel, the lads are all made up, it has everything they need. He has booked breakfast, the main meal of the day for these lads, it makes them bond stronger and they already have a bond like superglue, there is such a closeness in this team.

All the lads make their way up to their rooms, except Cass and Alan Jones who go into the lounge area to sit down and have a pure orange juice. Alan hears two young lads speaking English at the next table.

"Hey mate, are you both English?" The two lads both burst out laughing.

"English, no fucking way boyo we're Welsh and proud," says the tallest of the two.

"As Welsh as the valleys can be," grins the ginger Welsh lad

"So, you're from the valleys then?" enquires Cass.

"No, we're from Cardiff," says the ginger Welsh lad. Cass and Alan both look at each other puzzled.

"What are you doing here then?" asks Alan.

"I'm a sports journalist," smiles the ginger Welsh lad.

"I'm a Welsh referee," says the tallest lad.

"I'm here reporting on the Welsh under 18's football team, they have got three matches next week over here. I report on all the best young players coming through the ranks." The Welsh lad introduces himself and his friend to Alan and Cass.

"I'm Jordan Jacobs and this is my friend Sam Llewellyn."

"We're both 24," pipes up Sam the Welsh referee.

"That's young for a referee," says Alan.

Cass turns to the Welsh lads. "I'm Brian Cassidy and this is my teammate Alan Jones, we both play for the Golden Dock."

"Never heard of them," says Sam.

"Well you won't have Taffy, we don't play in Wales do we, but you will hear his name soon." Alan starts pointing at Cass.

"Why's that then, is he on the run for robbing car dust-caps?" smirks Sam.

"No soft-lad, it's because he's the next big thing in football."

"What's his name?" Sam asks politely.

"BRIAN CASSIDY," says Alan Jones proudly.

"Never heard of him," Sam says, shaking his head.

"Fuck me, do you live in the field with the sheep Sam? You haven't heard of anyone, bet you go in the empty fields by yours giving the sheep yellow cards with your ref kit on and your little black book, like a daft referee." barks Alan.

"I've heard of a Brian Cassidy from Liverpool, it can't be you, this Cassidy would be about sixteen, who played for Merseyside boys, you're far too old to be him," says Jordan.

Laughing his head off Cass smiles. "That's me, I'm sixteen." Jordan looks shocked.

"So, are you the Cassidy who scored five goals, in a seven-two win in Cardiff against Glamorgan boys in January, in the British Isles counties cup?"

"Yeah, that was me," smiles Cass.

"My word, you're the best player I've ever seen at that age group, I can't believe you're sitting here at my table. I went to the final against Surrey boys at Wembley to watch you but you weren't playing, a lad named Neil Parks scored a hat-trick, in a three-two win.

"Yeah, Neil Parks is my best mate."

"I was gutted when I saw the team sheet, and you weren't playing. I thought you must have been injured. I asked a Merseyside coach where Brian Cassidy was and he told me that your school had banned you from representing the county from all sports activity, because you locked a teacher in a store room. He told me you were a bad egg, who was taking the wrong road in life. I was shocked."

"Why was you shocked Jordy? He's a scouser they're all mad from there."

"Sam if you see him play you will understand, he was such a talent in Cardiff."

Cass is not happy at what he has just heard, it has annoyed him. "What the fuck do they know, the fucking dickheads! I got that team to the final, me and Neil Parks and that's the thanks I get, a wanker of a head coach calling me a bad egg. I've changed now anyway. That was a long time ago."

"Long time?" laughs Alan.

"Yeah, I'm more mature now."

"It was only three months ago."

"Shut up Alan," snaps Cass.

"Okay Cass, calm down."

"I'm a changed person now."

"I hope you are Cass, that player I saw in Cardiff, had the potential to be world class if he applied himself properly and took the right road in life."

"I'm a different person now Jordan, seeing my best mate Neil Parks signing for Everton made me realise I need to focus on my football and keep my head down, I've grown up a lot in the last three months."

"I've got a great idea, I could write an article on you Cass the headline could be. *'THE BOY WONDER FROM LIVERPOOL FOUND ON THE STREETS OF AMSTERDAM'* that would sell newspapers."

Cass and Alan laugh. "That makes him sound like a pop star not a footballer."

Bob walks into the lounge overhearing about an article with Cass. As he reaches the table he starts pointing at the Welsh lads.

"HEY, there'll be no articles on Cass or on any of my players okay?"

Jordan is shocked and gob smacked. "I told you all scousers are mad Jordy," says Sam. Bob gives Sam a dirty look.

"Shut up Sam, I'm sorry Mate I was just chatting with two of your boys," says Jordan.

"It's okay Bob, they're both from Wales," says Cass.

"They're okay, when I say Cass and as I'm in charge of you on this trip, I decide who's okay. I told your dad I would look after you, so no fucking journalist shit, now get up to the room, both of you and get some sleep. Take your bags up with you."

Alan and Cass look shocked.

Jordan gets up shaking hands with Alan and Cass who in return apologise and get up and leave making their way to the room. Jordan Jacobs approaches Bob, and introduces himself and explains, he's here to report on the Welsh football team and meant no harm.

Bob looks him up and down, and explains he wasn't being rude, but he has young Cassidy's best interests at heart and that they're more than welcome to watch them on Monday, at 12'o clock midday against the Amsterdam Jets.

Jordan shakes Bob's hand. "I would love to be there, without my pencil, I will just be watching as a spectator."

Bob smiles, thanks the Welsh lads and makes his way back to the room.

In the room Alan Jones is on the bed fast asleep snoring. "I can't sleep Bob, I'm going for a walk is that okay?" asks Cass.

Bob bites his lip not sure what to say. "Come on Bob, I'm not a kid."

"Okay, be back before one then and stay out of trouble, just go for a walk," says Bob.

Cass is up and out the room faster than Usain Bolt. He heads out the door towards the front entrance of the hotel, as he gets to the entrance he asks the porter which is the best way to get to the designer shops. The porter points him in the right direction telling Cass it's a 10 minute walk to the shops.

Five minutes into the walk Cass steps out into the road and hears a beep from a passing car, he can't believe what he is seeing, Ginger Lee and Burger pull over smiling.

"Room for one more scouse?" smirks Cass.

"Yeah, get in Cass," says a beaming Burger. Cass jumps in smiling.

"I can't believe you two are here! In Amsterdam, of all the places, that's fucking mad that."

"It's a small world Cass, why are you here?" asks Ginger Lee.

"I'm playing in a football match for the Golden Dock, we're here till Monday night, we get home on Tuesday," says Cass.

"Is right Cass, that's boss that lad," says Burger.

"Why are you both here?" asks Cass.

"We told you last week – we've come away to graft. We're going shopping now Cass," says Ginger Lee.

"That's where I'm going."

"You can come with us if you want, we're only going to one shop, you can do us a favor, if you want," says Ginger Lee.

"Yeah, what's this favor then?" asks Cass.

"Go into the shop before us, pick up a shirt with a bell on, when we walk out the shop, hold the shirt out and let the alarm go off on the shirt. As you walk to the counter, ask for a bigger size, then try the shirt on, give it back to the staff and meet us back at the car," says Ginger.

"Okay, that's no problem, get me two pairs of Dsquared jeans in a 30 and a 32 waist and two Givenchy t-shirts in a medium and a large," says Cass.

"Okay, we will get them for you," says Burger.

Ginger Lee pulls into the car-park and parks the Range-Rover. He points out the shop to Cass.

"Can you see that green shop Cass? It's called *Dam fashion*."

Cass goes into the shop. He looks around seeing two six-foot security guards. He goes to the shirts section of the shop and picks up two shirts. While he's looking at the shirts, Burger and Ginger Lee walk into the shop with lots of bags, as if they have been shopping all day.   Cass walks around the shop for 10 minutes, he glances over at Ginger Lee who nods to Cass to walk towards the security systems with the shirts. Cass gets online with the alarm systems, he notices Ginger Lee and Burger are heading out the door just behind him. Cass who is holding the shirts in his right hand, trips himself up, falling on the floor sending the shirts flying out of his hand, setting off the alarms, as Ginger Lee and Burger whiz past him like two cheetahs, not for even a split second do they look back, they're out of the shop and away out of sight.

The security guards rush to Cass to help him up and ask him if he's okay. One guard picks up the shirts, again setting off the alarms, he puts them on the counter, while the second security guard helps Cass to his feet. He looks out of the shop to make sure Ginger Lee and Burger are out of sight. He brushes himself down, thanks the security guards for their help and heads for the exit of the shop. One of the security guards calls him back.

"What about these shirts son?" enquires the guard.

"It's okay, I'm in too much pain to try them on." As Cass leaves the shop the guards' wave. "See yer mate," smirks Cass. In the car park Ginger Lee and Burger greet Cass like a long lost brother.

"Nice one Cass, you did us proud, at one point Burger nearly got his whistle out to blow for a penalty," laughs Ginger Lee.

Cass has a beaming smile right across his face. "I didn't hear any bells going off from your bags, didn't you get anything?"

Laughing, they show Cass what they've got.

"Fuck me, no way, how did you get all that?"

"We took the bells off in the shop with our magic magnet, you were just a deterrent," says Burger.

"We got all the stuff you asked for," says Ginger Lee proudly. Burger rolls up his sleeve and looks at his Rolex.

"Hey, it's cafe time."

"Do you fancy coming the café with us Cass?" asks Ginger. Cass nods, they all make their way to the café. Ginger Lee sits down in the cafe and starts bonging on a big pipe, Burger joins him whist ordering herbal tea. Cass is confused. He was expecting fish and chips with a can of coke, not a pipe session with Cheech and Chong.

Cass refuses a blast of the pipes and orders a bottle of spring water. Ginger Lee and Burger zone out on the bongs. Cass looks at his watch, its ten to one.

"SHIT!" yells Cass.

"What's up mate?" says a stunned Burger.

"The time, Bob will go mad he said be back at one."

"Don't worry, I'll get you back to your hotel. Where you staying?" asks Ginger Lee.

"The Grand hotel on the border of the red-light district, it's ten to one now."

"Don't worry, I'll get you back on time."

They all get into the Range-Rover. Inside, you can smell the newness of the leather seats. Ginger Lee, who is stoned, drives like Lewis Hamilton taking every bend and corner like a rally driver, he gets to the hotel bang on one. The church bells ring out as he slams his foot down on the brakes. Burger sorts out the clothes for Cass and puts them in a bag for him. They drive off like bank robbers weaving in and out of the parked cars.

Cass makes his way into the hotel lobby where he's met by the team. Bob does not look happy.

Reid Johnson is fuming. "WHERE THE FUCK HAVE YOU BEEN?" he yells.

"Out shopping."

"We have been waiting for you once again."

"I'm back now."

"That's not the point, we have all been worried."

"Worried Why? I'm sixteen I'm not a little kid."

"You just don't get it do yer Cass?"

"I've got you some jeans and a top." Reid grabs the bag and throws it down the lobby.

"I DONT WANT THE FUCKING SHIT, I DONT CARE ABOUT THE FUCKING CLOTHING, I TOLD YOU NOT TO FUCKING DO ANYTHING STUPID AND YOU GO OUT SHOP LIFTING IN A FOREIGN COUNTRY. ARE YOU FUCKING STUPID? YOU'RE GOING DOWN THE WRONG PATH CASS, THE FUCKING WRONG ROAD. GET THE FUCK OUT MY SIGHT CASS, I CANT BE ARSED WITH YOU. YOU WONT LISTEN, I'M TRYING TO SEND YOU DOWN THE RIGHT PATH AND YOU WON'T FUCKING LISTEN."

Reid storms out of the hotel. Bob picks up the bag and hands it back to Cass.

""Put it in your room, hurry up, we're going for a Chinese meal now, give Reid his bits later when he has cooled down, we will wait in the car park for you."

Cass runs up to his room, putting the bag on his big comfy bed and runs down the hotel stairs to the minibus in the car park. Cass goes to get into Fat Joes minibus. Reid Johnson shuts the door on him.

"What do you want? Piss off, get in the other minibus." Cass is a bit taken back as he slowly gets into Scouse Ricco's minibus. Frank Rox shakes his head at Reid Johnson.

"Why did you do that? There was no need for that Reid, you went too far, Cass is only sixteen in a foreign country, he looks up to you, you're his hero, he got that fashion clothing for you so that you would be proud of him."

"All he talks about is our Reid and how good a person you are," says Alan Jones.

"I know, I know but he has so much talent and he has got the potential to be world class, I just don't want him taking the wrong path in life, I'm doing this to teach him a lesson, so he doesn't go down that wrong path, do you think I like being horrible to him, it breaks my heart. He's my cousin but he's as close to me as a brother, I see and treat him like my brother, I'm doing this for him, it upsets me, when I have to moan at him."

In the minibus, Bob sits next to Cass. "Bob, book me a flight home for today."

"A flight? What about the match?"

"I'm not arsed about the match, I want to go home."

"I would be gutted if you went home, you're the reason I'm enjoying playing football again."

"I'm more trouble than I'm worth. People just seem to moan at me Bob."

"Cass, we all think the world of you, we sometimes forget you're only sixteen, because you're so good at football. Reid didn't mean what he said, he just wants the best for you, and he worries about you."

Cass's eyes start to well up. "I understand that but I would still like to go home today."

Bob being captain, puts his arm around Cass. "Cass we're a team, if we have a problem, we sort it out as a team, we stick together. There are lots of people here in Holland that want to watch Brian Cassidy the boy wonder."

"You're global news Cass," says Pat Arrow.

Kevin Bird pokes Cass saying, "You're going nowhere wonder boy, you're my strike partner and I need you." Cass's sad eyes lift.

"You can't go you're a musketeer, all for one and one for all," says Chivers. John Cully looking puzzled, turns to Chivers.

"It's one for all and all for one." Chivers is not amused.

"Does it fucking matter John, you fucking arsehole." Bob looks at Cass and smiles.

"See that Cass, that's proper team spirit." The whole bus bursts out laughing.

The minibuses pull up outside the Chinese restaurant *The Fatty Pig*, which is a twenty-five-minute drive from their hotel. The players get out the minibuses.

Bob whispers into Reid's ear about Cass being upset and wanting a flight home. The players go into the restaurant and sit down on four separate tables, Cass sits with the committee. Reid looks up and sees Cass sitting next to the committee members.

"Hey, Cass what are you doing over there? I've saved you a seat next to me."

"It's okay, I'm good over here."

"Well I'm not okay with it, you're my wing man, now get over here, don't be leaving me next to Frank Rox."

"Nah I'm okay, Frank gives me indigestion."

"Does he Cass? He gives me heartburn when I sit next to him at meal times, that's why I take so many Rennies," says John Paul.

"I could do with some of them John Paul."

"Nah, they're no good for you Cass, on the packet it says they're for heartburn." Cass looks at John Paul and shakes his head as he walks over to sit by Reid.

"Sit down superstar, welcome home," says Reid.

"Thank fuck for that, I can eat now," shouts Alan Jones munching on a pork pie.

The lads all order jugs of lager, except Cass who orders water. Pat Arrow and John Paul are on the brandy

"The food tastes better with the brandy Pat," says John Paul as he sips it down.

"Jib the food, John Paul, I'm drinking the brandy because I'm on a bender and I'm a big fan of Napoleon and Remy Martin," says Pat.

"Hey Pat, didn't that Remi Martin play for Man United?"

"No John Paul, that was his cousin Steve Martin, he was a good laugh that fella."

"No, I can't say I have ever heard of him Pat, his name rings a bell."

"No, you're thinking of Quasimodo, John Paul," says Frank Rox.

"No, I'm not Frank, I'm not thinking nothing."

"That's great then John Paul I'll have a double," says Pat.

"I'm lost me Pat, who won the double? Talking of doubles shall we get another double brandy?"

"Yeah, why not John Paul I prefer the brandy more than the Bells," replies Pat sniggering.

Reid turns to Cass. "Bob said you wanted a flight home, what's that all about, I'm sorry I shouted at you, it's only because I care about you and want the best for you and want you to be the best, I'm so proud of the person you are." Reid offers Cass his hand.

"Mates again." Cass shakes his hand.

"Yeah, mates again." Reid starts laughing.

"Good and I hope them jeans and top fit me." Cass laughs.

"So, do I Reid."

Bob looks over smiling knowing that the team is back together. They are all having chicken and sweet corn soup for their starter. Peter Springsteen burns his nose on the soup forgetting his moustache has been shaved off. Frank Rox calls the waiter.

"Hey, mate have you got pigs feet?" The waiter, confused and puzzled is struggling to understand Frank's accent.

"I'll ask my manager," replies the waiter.

"Trot over and ask him." The whole team laugh their heads off as the waiter comes back with the Chinese manager.

"Hey mate, so you're the manager, have you got pigs feet?" asks Frank Rox.

"No pig's feet, but I've got a size nine boot that will kick you up the arse, if there is any more messing with my waiters," replies the manager. Frank Rox laughs his head off and hugs the manager.

"Quick lads all get piggy, I've got him pinned down," smirks Rox.

The manager laughs, pinching Frank Rox's shoulder muscle, making him wince in pain. The pressure sends Frank to his knees.

"Now you pay double," says the manager as he lets go.

"I want you as my minder," says Rox to the manager. The manager laughs telling them all to enjoy their meal as he heads back into his office. Bob tells them all to eat a decent amount of food if they're going on the ale. Mark Barrow pays the bill and signs his card Harvey Smith. This puzzles Cass every time.

Alan Jones pokes Cass. "That's why his nickname is Wallbanger." Cass is still puzzled.

The manager comes out of his office to say goodbye, giving each player a t-shirt with the restaurant name on it. Alex Sharp is made up.

"Hey, these can be training tops." Ant Hodge looks at Alex Sharp.

"Training tops with the name *the fatty pig* on them are you taking the piss Alex?"

"No, you can all wear them during pre-season training when we run the sandhills in Ainsdale."

"Fuck off Alex, lets enjoy the double we have just won," says John Cully.

"That's gone now, we rebuild now and go again, them medals are gathering dust as we speak." replies Alex.

The lads leave the Chinese restaurant. Frank Rox is pointing at the Chinese manager doing his karate moves. The manager takes off his shoe holding it up to Frank Rox.

Fat Joe takes them to a bar five minutes' walk from the Chinese restaurant. It's now 2.30pm, the afternoon sun is shining. The lads walk into the bar. It's jam packed with lots of beautiful Dutch women. The door is run by Russian ex-military gangsters who are all wearing blue army camouflage outfits, with black Doc Martins boots. They're all at least 6ft 5 inches tall. The drinks are flowing in the bar, the music is blasting and everyone is having a good time. Frank Rox is dancing at the bar like Michael Jackson. All the players are in high spirits, the Russian bouncers are watching, waiting to kick off at the slightest thing. The song 'Come on Eileen' starts playing on the jukebox; all the team form a circle jumping up and down, the Dutch girls join in the circle.

Frank Rox jumps up raising his arm with a clenched fist. "Scousers in the house," yells Rox.

The Russian bouncers don't like this and one of them grabs hold of Frank Rox making him drop his pint of lager.

"Get the fuck off stedhead, the cold war's over soft arse," yells Rox.

The rest of the bouncers rush the area where the players are enjoying themselves. The Russian bouncer pushes Frank Rox knocking him into two Dutch girls.

Reid Johnson grabs the Russian bouncer. "Yer, big ugly twat leave him alone get the fuck off my mate, "Another six-foot eight bouncer grabs Reid by the throat, young Cass sees this and charges over to help him; just as he gets to him, a Russian bouncer blocks his path pushing Cass away, then hits him with a haymaker from behind. Cass doesn't know what has hit him, his legs are wobbling, the bouncer pulls his arm back to finish him off.

Kevin Bird rushes in and tries to push the bouncer away from Cass, all to no avail, the bouncer charges at Cass, so Birdy throws a chair in front of the bouncer, making him trip up before he gets to Cass.

Kevin Chivers charges like a bull, head butting the nearest bouncer to him, sending him backwards onto his fat Russian arse, the Russian bouncers come at them from all directions. Chopper Moon picks up a table and throws it at the bouncers.

"Come on. Let's, have it," yells Chopper. Reid grabs hold of Cass who is in a daze. He gets him out the pub.

John Paul lights his brandy with a match and throws it at the wall, setting the wallpaper on fire, the barman puts the fire out with the water soda syphon.
Pat Arrow turns to John Paul.

"Why, are you wasting brandy?"

"I'm not."

"Yes, you are I've just watched you."

"I hate them Russian bastards Pat, one of the Russian doormen just tried to knock out young Cass." Pat Arrow picks up his brandy, downs it, looks at John Paul.

"That's no excuse to waste the brandy soft-lad."

Pat picks up empty beer bottles, throwing them at the Russians. John Paul joins in with Pat with them both singing, "Rule Britannia, Britannia ruled the world, never ever ever ever will us scousers be tamed."

Fred Kettle and Todd Elliott are throwing pint glasses at the bar staff, the whole bar empties as the team and committee are forced out the door by the Russian bouncers.

Ian Craig is casually sitting down at his table finishing of his pint, tripping up the bouncers as they run past him.

Kevin Chivers, Chopper Moon, Frank Rox and Scouse Ricko, are still trading punches with the Russians in the foyer of the pub. Bob Arrow and Peter Springsteen get Chopper Moon, Kevin Chivers, Frank Rox and Scouse Ricko, out of the pub.

The Russians, who manage to get the team out of the pub, are all cut and bruised. They steam out of the pub armed with baseball bats. The head Russian bouncer named Sergei, goads the players to move closer.

"Feel my bat, English scum."

Chopper Moon grabs hold of the six foot seven inch Russian head doorman by the neck and pulls out his gun, putting it into the chin of Sergei.

"If, you want war, we will give you fucking war," yells Chopper.

Scouse Ricko is in tow with Chopper, pointing at the Russians waving his gun at them like Dirty Harry.

The Russians freeze knowing this is one battle they won't win. Sergei looks at Chopper Moon yelling in a deep Russian accent.

"You win this battle, but we will win the war."

Frank Rox, fuming yells, "The only war you will win is the steroids war, you pumped up water retention Russian twat."

Chopper looks Sergei in the eye and growls, "Au Revoir big boy, till we meet again you little steroid dick prick." The Russians back off retreating back inside the pub.

Fat Joe gathers the players together, getting them back to the minibuses as quick as possible, telling Bob that the Russians run that part of Amsterdam and that they will be wanting revenge.

"Joe take us back to the hotel, I need a meeting with this lot," snarls Bob.

Fat Joe and Scouse Ricko drive to the hotel. Cass is still shaken up in the minibus but smiles when he hears Kevin Bird saved him from serious injury.

They arrive at the hotel with Bob sending them into the lobby for a meeting. Bob sits them all down. "Right lads let me remind you, we're on a football trip, not here to take on Europe in a war."

"Power to the revolution," yells Frank Rox.

"Power to scouse house," laughs Chopper. Bob turns to Chopper Moon shaking his head. "Where the fuck did you get that gun from? We're a football team not gangsters...Thanks anyway, you most probably just saved us from a good hiding, but let's put the guns away from now on."

Chopper stands up. "Bob, I'm only carrying it to protect the team."

"Keep it hidden then, it was like the Wild West before, look at poor Cass, he's sixteen he's just a kid."

"Bob I'm okay, it's not Choppers fault I got a smack."

Fat Joe tells Bob there is a good cafe bar in the red-light district ten minutes away run by scousers with scouse doormen, there'll be no trouble and that they will be looked after and that they can use it as a base.

Fat Joe leads the team to the Cafe Dell Duff bar. It is a ten minute walk away. Reid Johnson walks next to Cass. "What the fuck was you was thinking of charging at the bouncer Cass?"

"I just saw the big Russian grabbing you and wanted to make up for letting you down earlier, so I just charged at him without looking around me, I didn't see that other big Russian who hit me from behind, I wanted to help you."

"Cass, you never let me down, I'm always proud of you, but that was stupid. He was six foot eight, a mad Russian doorman. Thanks for being there for me, but next time just get out of the pub to safety."

"Nah, I would rather take a beating than leave you fighting. We stick together."

Reid laughing looks at Cass with a twinkle in his eyes. "What are you like Cass? What am I going to do with you?"

The players arrive at the *Café Dell Duff*, where they are greeted by head doorman Frankie Robo, who welcomes them into the bar with his thick scouse accent.

"Hello lads welcome to the Café Dell Duff, we only have two rules in here; rule one is only drink what you can handle, rule two is enjoy yourselves."

"Who's that singing mate?" inquires Birdy.

"That's Tony Lacey, our scouse singing sensation." The players split up into groups; half the players go and sit inside the bar, while the other half sit on the tables outside watching the sun shine on the canal.

The scouse singing sensation Tony Lacey is playing the guitar, singing Bob Dylan songs on the stage.

"What else can you play mate?" asks Kevin Bird.

"I can play the banjo also mate," replies Tony Lacey.

"I meant songs soft arse."

"No, I can't play that, I've never heard of that."

"Hey lads who booked the comedian? Have you heard this soft cunt?"

"I'm not a comedian, I'm just the pub singer and DJ mate."

"You're not much of a singer Tony."

"Is that so and you're not very bright mate, have you always been thick?"

"No, I haven't.

"Yes, you have Birdy," laughs Cully.

"Shut up Cully."

"So, when did you start being thick and stupid, is this just a recent thing then that has happened to you?"

"No, I'm not thick. Just sing will yer."

Tony Lacey sitting down on his stool starts strumming his guitar and looks over to the Golden Dock table and winks towards the lads. "This song I'm about to sing reminds me of my good friend Birdy over on the winners table to my right."

Kevin Bird jumps up and down proud that he's getting a song sung about him.

"His old mans a dustman and he looks just like his dad," sings Tony Lacey.

"Brilliant you know me arl fella also Tony. "All the lads piss themselves laughing.

Kevin Bird is dancing like a Wild West apache Indian. Tony Lacey, all six foot of him sings in a broad scouse accent, as he entertains the pub.

Bob and Mills the manager are talking at the bar. Bob is impressed by Tony Lacey.

"Mills, that Lacey the singer is really good."

"Yeah, he's not bad Bob, but he doesn't come cheap,"

"Why, how much does he charge?"

"Four Hundred Euros a night Bob and all the birds he can pull."

"Why, is he a bit of a lady's man Mills?"

"No, the only thing he has pulled since he arrived here, is his hamstring, when he got up too quick"

"How long has he been here then Mills?"

"Four weeks Bob."

"How did you find him?"

"Oh, he knows my wife."

"He's a cracker."

Bob looks over at Mills' wife, a twenty-year old Russian model. She watches Tony Lacey sing with a smile and glint in her eyes like a smitten puppy.

John Paul is at the bar when he smells the sweet smell of cannabis. He sees the manager Mills at the bar smoking a joint.

"Hey mate, where do I get a decent smoke around here?" Mills turns to John Paul.

"Call me Mills. I've got a got smoke here you can have, nice Rocky resin for fifty Euros, what do you want?" asks Mills.

"What do you recommend?" asks John Paul.

"You can have anything you want; Bush, Rocky, Oil, Green, anything you fancy," smiles Mills.

"Hmm, choices, choices, it's like being in a sweet shop, can you get me Rocky based in Oil?"

"Yeah, give me five minutes to get it."

"Can you get me a fifty Euro bag of Green Mills?" asks Ant Hodge.

"Yeah, no problem, I'll be back in five minutes, pay me when I get back." John Paul looks at Fat Joe smiling.

"Hey Joe this is the best bar I've ever been to."

"John Paul welcome to the Dam."

Alex Sharp tells the lads that this is their base, that they can go and visit the sights of Amsterdam, but they must all return to the Cafe Dell Duff. Mills returns, bringing back the packages for John Paul and Ant Hodge.

The players are all relaxed drinking beer in the sun. John Cully goes the bar.

"Hey, Mills have you got any space cake?" Mills introduces John Cully to space cake pork pies.

"Give me two of them pork pies Mills," says John Cully.

"Hot or Cold Cully?"

"Cold please." Mills takes ten Euros of Cully and hands them to him.

"Enjoy them Cully lad."

"Oh, I will Mills, I will enjoy Alan Jones munching on them."

John Cully walks past Alan Jones with the pies on show. "Hey, Cully where did you get them pies?" asks Alan.

"They sell them here Alan, tasty Dutch pork pies."

"I'm starving, I could do with something to eat."

"Have these Alan, here you go." John Cully gives Alan two pork pies. Alan takes a bite smiling at John.

"Hmm they taste good." All the players snigger as Alan is a no nonsense anti-drug man. Frank Robo looks at the Golden Dock lads all chilled out and looks over to Mills and winks. "Mills, these are all good lads, they're more than welcome here."

Chapter 8

A night in the Dam

It's now 5pm and the sun is shining. The Golden Dock lads have been drinking all day. Mills, the manager of the Cafe Dell Duff, brings out meals for all the members of the Golden Dock entourage, giving each member chips with a steak baguette, telling all the lads that if they are drinking then they need food, so the meals are on the house.

A stoned John Paul Anderson smiles at Fat Joe and thanks him again for bringing him to the best place in the Dam, as he chews on his steak baguette, while smoking his joint, sipping brandy. "Joe, man you have brought me to paradise."

"I'm glad you like it John Paul."

"This place is my scene Joe, It's cool man."

"Just chill John Paul."

"Joe I'm fucking stoned man, I should have signed for Ajax as a lad and made the Dam my home."

"Yeah that would have made sense John Paul, you would have been a world class crackhead, says John Cully.

Cass is playing pool. It's five Euros a game, he's unbeaten in twelve games. Four times he has played Kevin Bird, who doubled his stake to ten Euros, he's trying to win the money back off Cass that he had lost on the ferry.

Mills walks over to Cass. "You're very clever you Cass, I have been watching how you suck them in, you let them get drunk while you drink soft drinks, then fleece them all on the pool table... I like your style, in fact while you're here, all your soft drinks are free."

Cass smiles and thanks Mills. Alan Jones is at the bar. "Two more of them Dutch pork pies please."

"The space cake ones?" asks Mills.

"No, the other ones, the Dutch pork pies," says Alan.

John Cully who is playing pool against Cass shouts over to Mills.

"Hey, Mills give him the pies I got before."

"I'll get them now for you Alan," says Mills.

John Cully is just about to snigger when Cass sinks the black ball to knock him off the pool table. Cass smiles at him as he takes his five Euros. Mills comes back with two pies for Alan Jones.

"How much do I owe you for them two?" asks Alan.

"Five Euros each," smiles Mills.

Alan Jones hands over the ten Euros thinking to himself that they're pricey but that must be the right price because they're so tasty.

"Hey, Cass do you fancy going to the hotel with me so I can get more money?" asks Alan. Cass gives up his game on the pool table.

"Yeah, why not, I could do with a walk to stretch my legs."

As Cass and Alan head out the café Dell Duff, John Paul Anderson is walking out with Ian Craig. "Where are you two going?" asks Alan.

"We're going to visit the local totty," beams John Paul. Ian Craig starts smirking.

"I might go Dutch, or I might even go Russian".

"No, don't go Russian, take your time and get your money's worth," laughs Cass.

"I'm going European as I've only got Euros, says John Paul.

They both head towards the south side of the red-light district with John Paul smiling like a man that has found gold at the bottom of the rainbow.

Alan Jones and Cass make their way to the hotel. Alan turns to Cass.

"That is what happens to you when you get fucked off from your club, you become a waste of talent and have to pay for your nuts." Both piss themselves laughing as they enter the hotel foyer.

In the Cafe Dell Duff, Frank Rox approaches Mills. "Hey, Mills would it be okay if I take over as DJ for a couple of hours?"

"No problem Frank go for it lad, rock the house down kid."

Frank gets in the DJ box setting up his iPod on the Cafe Dell Duff laptop, sending out all the cream tunes, the place is rocking, the bar starts filling up with Dutch, German and Swedish girls and Dutch men all wondering who this DJ is rocking the house down.

Alan Jones and Cass make their way back to the Cafe Dell Duff.

"Hey Cass, I know a short cut, follow me champ."

"Lead the way Al."

They turn left at the hotel, leading them down a back alley where all the working girls are at their doors trying to drum up some business. Alan is munching on one of his pork pies.

"Cass, I could do with some brown sauce on this pork pie."

As they get to the end of the alley, an Asian working girl tries to entice them into her room. She speaks very little English. In her Asian accent she speaks to Cass, "You are big strong man; would you like good time?" Cass is shocked.

"No, it's okay, I'm too young, I'm only sixteen." The Asian woman looks Cass up and down.

"You're too young, you just little boy, but your friend okay."

Alan looks over at the room the Asian woman is standing in and has a great idea.

"Cass, my little boy, she might have some brown sauce for my pie."

The Asian woman looking straight at Alan starts licking her lips slowly. "You come in big boy, good time, good time?" Alan goes to her door and looks in the room.

"Hey, love have you got any brown sauce to put on this pie?"

She looks at Alan with beady eyes yelling, "GET OUT! get out, you perverted kinky bastard, you not putting sauce in my brown eye." Alan shows her his pie, making a sauce gesture towards it.

In broken English she yells, "Dirty pervo, you sick bastard leaves me alone, leave me alone." Alan and Cass leg it as fast as they can. Alan, panting shouts, "Hurry up Cass, I think communication was lost in transit somewhere along the way here."

They reach the Cafe Dell Duff. It's booming. Frank Rox has the place rocking. Chopper Moon is enjoying a joint and gets up to go to the toilet. As he gets up, his gun falls out his jacket, he picks it up and slides it back into place and makes his way to the toilet. Frankie Robo, the doorman in the Cafe Dell Duff follows him. Frankie quietly takes him to one side and explains that they don't allow guns in the bar.

"It's for the team's protection Frank, I'm the team marshal." Frankie points out to Chopper that this is a good bar and that he will protect all of them.

"Chopper, can I have the gun please so that I can put it into the safe? You can collect the gun when you leave the bar, at the end of the night."

"Yeah, here you are mate." Chopper hands the gun over to Frankie.

"You know it makes sense son. In this bar, I'll look after all of you, as you're all good lads."

Frankie puts the gun into the safe, which is behind the bar. He gives Chopper a jug of lager on the house for being so understanding.

The place is rocking, the players are in and out of the place, as they go to have a look at the sights of Amsterdam. Frankie Robo gets a call on his mobile from one of the scouse doormen on the other side of the Dam, where the Russians rule with fear.

He tells Frankie Robo that the Russians are looking for the Golden Dock team, armed with shotguns and machine guns, they're all hard core ex-army military, and that to tell them to stay that side of the Dam.

Frankie Robo passes the message onto Bob and Alex Sharp, who warn the players, who are more than happy to stay in the Cafe Dell Duff and to stay in walking distance of the bar when they're out and about checking the sights.

John Paul Anderson and Ian Craig arrive back from their trip. They walk towards the Café Dell Duff, where they are greeted by Pat Arrow, who cracks open two cans of Heineken and hands them to John Paul and Ian Craig.

"How did it go lads?"

"It was great Pat," says John Paul.

"So, did you do the business then, did you shag for England?"

"Yeah, what do you think Pat? I was like a stallion, it was sweet," says John Paul.

"Sweet, did you just say? That's a laugh, you couldn't even get a hard on, shag for England? You couldn't even shag for Accrington Stanley, it's all the lager you've been drinking, it's given the stallion brewer's droop," laughs Ian.

"Brewer's droop, who are they?"

"Alright Pat, stop that, a joke's a joke, stop milking it," sniggers Ian Craig.

"It wasn't the drink soft-lad, it was that smoke I got off Mills, it had something in it," says John Paul.

"It wasn't me who was *soft-lad* was it? Stallion Dick," smirks Ian Craig.

"So, what happened? What did you do?" enquires Pat Arrow.

"I got her to spank me."

"Spank you, spank you?" repeats Pat Arrow.

"Yeah," John Paul whispers. "I wasn't going to waste fifty Euros, was I?"

"What did she do? Sit over here John Paul."

"Go and sit by Pat like a stallion John Paul," smirks Ian Craig.

"Tell me every detail, sit here."

"I can't sit Pat."

"What do you mean, you can't sit." John Paul looking embarrassed stands next to Pat.

"While she was spanking me, she went too hard, she was rough on me, she has bruised my arse. I can't sit down."

"Bruised your arse? Bruised the Italian stallion's arse? What was she, *happy clappy*?" says Pat Arrow laughing.

"Yeah, she bruised my arse and she fucking scratched one of my balls with one of her long nails." Pat Arrow give John Paul another cold Heineken can.

"Why haven't you cracked it open for me Pat."

"That's not to drink that's why, that's to put on the crack of your arse, to bring the bruising out." Ian Craig spits out his drink, laughing his head off.

Peter Springsteen is dancing like a raver in the middle of a group of Dutch women with a bandana on his head. John Arrow looks at Bob and points him into Peter's direction, both simultaneously shake their heads.

Chopper Moon and Kevin Parry go on a walkabout to check out the working girls in the red-light district.

Kevin Bird, Cass, Alan Jones, John Cully, Reid Johnson, Ant Hodge, Todd Elliott, Kevin Chivers, Mark Barrow, Fred Kettle and Alex Sharp are all playing killer darts; it's ten Euros a man, each player having three lives. The moon is shining bright, with a sparkling reflection bouncing off the canal waters.

Frank Rox sees the killer darts game in flow and plays "*The winner takes it all*" in his DJ booth. The Dutch girls love this and start bouncing up and down waving their arms in the air which seems to distract some of the lads while throwing their darts.

Mills walks to the front entrance smoking a joint standing next to Frankie Robo.

"This is the best takings we have had in years. Frank Rox and the lads have filled the place out with their charm. I have never seen it packed like this, it's booming, Frank is booming, look at him on them decks, they love him."

"They sure do Mills, everyone is happy, enjoying themselves. Makes my job easy."

Cass wins the killer darts and Frank Rox turns and plays *"Eye of the Tiger"* on the decks and yells over the mic,   "The Boy Wonder has just won the darts, first one to kiss him gets a free cocktail." He points out Cass. Two blonde Dutch girls run over to him raising his arm kissing him on his cheek. Cass goes bright red and starts pointing at Alex Sharp.

"He's the winner, not me." They both run over to Alex Sharp and start running their hands through his long hair and rubbing his body.

"Hey, Frank did you say feel cock or free cocktail?" sniggers John Cully. Alex smiles and quickly makes a swift exit, over to the committee table, where Bob and John Arrow are seated.

Kevin Bird sits next to Reid Johnson moaning, "Cass has just won one hundred and ten Euros, is there anything he's not good at?" Reid looks at Kevin Bird and quietly says "Yes, he's no good at counting."

"Counting, what do you mean counting?" Kevin Bird says puzzled.

"Kevin, when he won the killer darts, he just put the cash straight into his pocket and he didn't count it, therefore he didn't notice that I didn't put my ten Euro's in the pot," says Reid with a smirk on his face. Kevin Bird is gobsmacked.

"So, Kevin he's no good at counting, so I think I'll go to the bar and have a drink courtesy of Cass, because he's shit at counting," laughs Reid.

Kevin Bird walks away shaking his head saying to himself, "Why didn't I think of that?" Reid goes the bar and orders a pint of shandy.

Ant Hodge and Alan Jones are dancing with two slim blonde Swedish girls. Alan Jones, stoned from the pork pies, thinks he's on *Strictly come dancing,* he's dancing like a matador in slow motion.

Todd Elliott goes to the bar to see Mills. "Mills, can I borrow your bike to go back to the hotel?"

Mills replies, "Yes take it and when you come back, leave it outside by the front of the bar."

As Todd gets on the bike, Mark Barrow runs out of the bar asking if he can get on it with him. They both ride off together, Todd struggles to ride it up over the bridge with Mark Barrow on the back, as they reach the middle of the bridge, they go downhill, it picks up speed. As they near the bottom of the bridge another cyclist pulls out in front of them...Todd can't stop and both bicycles collide.

Todd falls on top of the man, Mark Barrow lands on the man's leg as he falls from the back, the man yells in pain. Todd and Mark pick themselves up and help the man get to his feet. He complains that they were going too fast. Todd, looking puzzled, tells him he was the one who pulled out on them, the man walks away pushing his bicycle limping. Todd Elliott checks his bike, sees that it's okay and pedals it to the hotel making Mark Barrow walk.

In the foyer, Peter Springsteen is pissed. John Arrow and Alex Sharp are holding him up, as they make their way to their rooms. Peter sees Mark Barrow and turns to John shouting. "Ah it's Harvey Wallbanger, I'll have a Wallbanger."

John looks at him with a smirk on his face. "No chance, you have had enough to drink, you can't even stand up." Mark Barrow laughs, turns to Todd Elliott saying.

"That's our manager, what a lightweight, it's only ten o' clock."

Todd and Mark make their way back to the Cafe Dell Duff on the bike. As they reach the bar, they are met by Chopper Moon and Kevin Parry. Chopper has a big smile on his face.

"Why are you looking so happy Chopper?" enquires Mark Barrow.

Chopper, with a big grin says, "We've just been in with one of the brasses. Kevin was getting a blow job, so I opened her drawer in the room, it had three thousand Euros in it, so I slotted it in my pocket and got off leaving Kevin in the room, so he sees me and runs out and follows me with his jeans at his ankles, running down the alley like a penguin."

"Really? Three grand," says Todd.

"Yeah, we just fucked off and have just got back here, that's why I'm smiling, I was thinking of him running like a penguin."

"Oh, so it's not because you just did a three-grand graft?" laughs Mark Barrow.

"Yeah, it's that as well," laughs Chopper.

Todd Elliott parks the bike up and chains it to the Cafe Dell Duff railing, then walks into the bar giving Mills the keys to the lock, thanking him for the use of the bike.

The mood in the Cafe Dell Duff is that of a star shining brightly. In the beer garden, Chopper, Mark Barrow and Kevin Parry are chatting away, when from the side of them, they're approached by four plain clothed men, all 7ft foot tall of stocky build, all with moustaches accompanied by a tiny 5ft slim women, she points at Chopper and Kevin Parry.

"Them two, they're the bastards that robbed me."

The four men approach, showing their badges and grab hold of Chopper and Kevin Parry by the scuff of their necks - introducing themselves as the Dutch vice squad, they start shouting at Chopper and Kevin.

"Where is the money? English scumbags."

"What money? Fucking get off me," screams Chopper.

Mark Barrow rushes into the Cafe Dell Duff, to get the lads out to help Chopper and Parry. Frank Rox storms out of the DJ booth, picking up a chair, he heads towards the door with Reid Johnson, Kevin Chivers, Fred Kettle and Ian Craig in tow, they reach the door fuming, but head doorman Frankie Robo locks the doors, blocking their path out of the bar.

"Fuck off Frank, let us out to help them," barks Chivers.

"Open them doors mate," yells Ian Craig.

"All calm down, that's the police with them, the vice squad. They take no shit, they run the red light district, they will just arrest you and let you rot in jail. They make up their own rules, they will close this bar down and take our licence off us, so all of you just calm down, there is nothing you can do to help Chopper and Parry," says Frankie Robo.

Chopper and Kevin Parry are still acting daft, pretending that they have never seen the girl before and don't know what they're talking about, the police take no messing and take their guns out, sticking them into Chopper Moon and Kevin Parry's necks demanding the money.

"Throw them into the canal and let the English pigs freeze,"

"You can't do that mate," says Parry.

"We can do what we want, we are the law and in ten seconds, if the money is not handed over, both of you will be getting a fifty volt shot into your necks from my electric shock gun."

The police go into Chopper Moons jacket and pull out three thousand Euros in a bundle, they also take two hundred Euros out of his trouser pocket.

"Hey, soft-lad you have got your money back, that money from my trousers is my own money, I had two hundred Euros." The police man punches Chopper in the face.

"Let's say that two hundred is your fine then, dickhead English pig."

Chopper looks the Dutch policeman in the eye. "You're not a policeman you're just a bully, now get the fuck off me shithead."

"I'm the law son, now fucking shut up, otherwise I will arrest you and let you rot in jail."

Kevin Parry has four hundred Euros taken off him. "That's my own money, you've got your money back off my mate."

The policeman kicks Parry up the arse. "Shut up, English idiot or I will throw you in the canal, horrible man."

Parry shakes his head. The working girl approaches him and spits in his face. "You, little dick English bastard."

"Fuck off you, yer dirty bitch," The vice policeman smacks Parry knocking him onto his arse. The police walk off with the working girl getting into the unmarked police Volvo car.

Chopper helps Kevin Parry up as the police drive away. "What has just happened there Kev? That was heavy shit, I didn't recognise the bird with her clothes on."

"She spat at me, it was her who was supposed to make me spit," says Parry.

They both laugh as Chopper touches his bruised cheek. "I feel like I've been mugged."

"You feel like you've been mugged. I was mugged, they took four hundred Euros off me, that was my own money," complains Parry.

"Oh, shut up," yells Chopper. "You win some, you lose some, at least we live to fight another day."

Frankie Robo unlocks the Cafe Dell Duff doors, as Chopper and Parry make their way back into the bar. Frankie Robo takes Chopper and Parry to one side explaining that he had to lock the doors and that the lads were all trying to get out to help them, but that they were the police, who have the most power in Holland and take no shit.

Chopper looks Frankie in the eye shaking his hand. "Frankie, I see the madness in your theory and that in reality you were just looking after the lads."

Frankie Robo reminds Chopper about the gun and that by him taking it off him and putting it into the bar safe, that he has just saved him from doing at least ten years in a Dutch jail. Chopper smiles and thanks Frankie Robo and goes to the bar and buys him a cold bottle of water. "This drink is on me, you're a top man, who had my back,"

Frankie smiles thanking Chopper. "Just remember, be careful out on them streets Chopper."

John Paul Anderson gets one of the Swedish girls up to dance, he has the moves and the rhythm, all the lads cheer him. Alan Jones get the other Swedish girl up to dance, but he's more geek than chic on the dance floor. Bob stands in the DJ box and announces on the mic that all players have to be at the breakfast bar, in the morning at ten o' clock. Slurring his words, he tells them to enjoy the rest of the night.

Ian Craig walks Bob out of the Café Dell Duff. As he reaches the doorway, he passes Cass. "Hey, Cass you're our boy wonder and the boy wonder can forget about drinking and you take the right path to be the best of the best." Cass smiles at Bob.

"Whatever, skipper get to bed you're drunk." Bob smiles, shaking Frankie Robo's hand on his way out.

Alan Jones goes to the bar and orders four more Dutch pies. Mills shakes his head.

"No, Alan you have might have had enough pies for today." Alan looks puzzled.

"They're only pies, Mills I'm not on a diet."

"They're not just pies, they're specials pies, that you can't buy in U.K." says Mills.

"I know they're special Mills, they taste lovely, they make me feel good when I'm eating them, so four more please," says Alan. Mills goes in the back and comes back with four pies handing them to Alan.

"That's twenty Euros please Alan," says Mills. Alan smiles and smells the pies as he hands over the twenty Euros and thanks Mills. Cass turns to Alan.

"You're mad you, take it easy with them, you will get addicted." Alan walks away laughing.

"Shut up Cass, how can you get addicted to pies?"

"Easy, they're laced with cannabis, you fucking big daft muppet." Alan is out of earshot of young Cassidy's reply and is non-the wiser.

Frank Rox steps out of the DJ booth, the crowd all cheer him, Frank takes a bow shouting, "Frank Rox is in the house."

The crowd cheer shouting, "Frank, Frank, Frank." Raising his arms, he salutes the crowd. Mills gives Frank a hug and gives him one hundred Euros for his nights work.

"You rocked the place Frank, you fucking rocked the place down, the punters loved you," says Mills with a smile as big as his takings which have trebled during the night.

Frank Rox rocked the house down. It's now midnight, the bar has emptied now Frank has stopped the music.

The two Swedish girls introduce themselves as Erika and Tam. They're both air hostesses and have got a few days stay in Amsterdam, courtesy of their employees, they have enjoyed the lads company, they thank them for their hospitality, they say goodbye as they make their way back to their hotel, they're going for a few drinks in their hotel bar.

Fat Joe gathers all the lads together. "Get in the minibus lads, I will take you all back to the hotel."

John Cully says, "It's only a ten minute walk Joe, why do we need a lift?" Fat Joe looks at all the players, looks back at John Cully.

"John in just two minutes you lot could start world war three, so all squeeze into the minibus." The lads make their way to the minibus. Mills and Frankie Robo come out to shake their hands. The lads all thank them for a great night out.

Mills and Frankie Robo both reply simultaneously, "The pleasure has been all ours."

Fat Joe drives off and in Three minutes flat the lads are back at their hotel. They all get out of the minibus and make their way into the building.

Alan Jones, Cass, Ant Hodge, Kevin Bird, John Cully, Pat Arrow and John Paul Anderson all make their way to the hotel bar. The rest of the lads all turn in for the night.

Fat Joe makes his way to his room with Scouse Ricko in tow. "Hey Lads, try to keep out of trouble."

"Don't worry Joe, we will behave," says Cully. Joe shakes his head and turns to Scouse Ricko. "I don't think that word is in their vocabulary."

"Don't worry Joe, even they can't get into trouble in here."

"Ricko, don't under estimate them fuckers they could start a war on a deserted island."

In the bar Cass sees the Welshmen Jordan and Sam and introduces them to all of the lads. Pat Arrow looks them up and down and turns to Jordan.

"We're here to conquer Europe son, not Wales, we conquered Wales in Frith on the beaches when we were kids."

"Yeah Pat, our base was the Robin Hood camp," laughs Kevin Bird.

Kevin Chivers walks into the bar and takes a full ice bucket off the bar. He waves to the lads and heads off back to his room. John Paul asks Pat Arrow what is that all about with Kevin Chivers and the ice bucket. Pat shrugs his shoulders.

"I aint got a clue, it might be to clean his ten pence's, to keep them shiny."

"His pockets aren't big enough, he must need the bucket for them," laughs John Paul.

Ant Hodge is at the bar ordering six pints of lager and a blackcurrant and soda water for Cass. Erika and Tam, the two Swedish girls who were dancing with the lads in the Cafe Dell Duff walk into the bar and catch Ant Hodge's eye. "What, are you two doing here?" asks Ant.

"We're staying here," laughs Tam.

"So are we," yells John Cully.

"Would you both like a drink?" asks Ant.

"Yes, please we will have two cocktails," replies Tam.

"Get over here then," shouts John Cully. Erika and Tam walk over to Ant Hodge.

"What cocktails would you like girls?

"Sex on the beach," they say in tandem, gigging.

"Yeah, sex on the beach, the three of us," smirks John Cully

"That's just your luck Cully, two Swedish beauties wanting sex on the beach with you in Holland and there are no beaches, it just borders with other countries," laughs Kevin Bird.

"It has beaches soft arse, what did you think the ferry passed, when we were going into Rotterdam harbour? We sailed passed Dutch beaches, duh Kevin Bird, fucking brains of Britain," snarls John Cully.

"Oh yeah, I forgot about them," laughs Kevin Bird. The girls join the lads at their table as the barman brings over the drinks.

"Enjoy your drinks lads," says the barman.

"Hey, hang on mate, are you a scouser?" asks Cully.

"Yeah, what give it away?" asks the barman with a smile.

"Your accent, yer daft twat," replies Cully.

"Hey, I might be a twat, but I'm far from daft, so watch your mouth, fat head," replies the barman with a smile. John Cully is stunned and rooted to the spot.

"Is right mate, you tell him, proper scouser you, you have just terrorised Cully, you have just put him on his toes," laughs Alan Jones.

"I'm Birdy, what's your name mate?"

"Ste, Ste Grant, pleased to meet you Birdy."

"You were like the smiling assassin then Ste."

"It's the scouse in me Birdy."

"It's full of scousers this Amsterdam, it's like little Liverpool," says Cass.

"That's why they call it Little Liverpool," says Ste Grant the barman. John Cully shakes Ste Grant's hand.

"No, hard feeling Ste, pleased to meet you."

"Likewise, Cully lad."

"Is that why Liverpool people leave Liverpool, cos it's a shit hole?" asks Sam from Wales.

"No, it's not Taffy, we're all proud of our city, Liverpool people are the salt of the earth," snarls Cully.

"Hey, Welsh boy. Liverpool is the capital of comedy, the people are known for their sense of humour even the miserable grumpy bastards like to have a laugh," says Pat Arrow.

"Yeah, and it was capital of culture in 2008," says Ant Hodge.

"Scousers have always travelled the world, we are known for our itchy feet, it's to do with the docks. We were the main Shipping port years ago, scousers used to go out for the paper and jump a ship to America," says Pat Arrow.

"So, that's where the saying, *I have been longer on a message*' comes from," says John Paul. All the lads look at John Paul shaking their heads.

"It's rumoured that the Italian sailor Christopher Columbus' grandad was from Liverpool and it was him who gave him the map to find America," says Kevin Bird.

"Bullshit" says Sam.

"No, I think he's telling the truth, I'm sure I learnt that in History at school," says John Paul.

"Sam, scousers have the best fashion in clothing, Liverpool was rumoured to have the first fashion shop ever opened by that other Italian explorer Marco Polo," says Birdy.

"Oh, fuck off, now you're taking the piss," replies Sam.

"No, I'm not, his uncle was a scouser, who ran the shop for him while he went to explore China, he used his own brand... He's even rumoured to have opened the first Chinese chippy on his return, but I'm not one hundred per cent sure on that cos it was in the thirteenth century."

"No, I think your right, Birdy. I learnt about that in my history class," says John Paul.

"Hey, John Paul, did Albert Einstein teach you for history?" smirks Cass.

"I can't remember Cass, his name rings a bell, hmm Mr Einstein, no he wasn't' the history teacher, I think he was my French teacher, his name sounds French doesn't it?"

Cass turns to Jordan and whispers. "I think John Paul went to the University of Bullshitters, he should be on *University Challenge*."

"I think Sam could compete against him representing the University of Dumbnuts with him trying to diss Liverpool whilst he is in the company of pure genuine scousers. I bet he's gutted he opened his mouth now," Jordan whispers Back. Ste Grant has heard enough, he makes his way back to the bar giggling.

Pat Arrow swigs his pint in one go and wishes everyone a goodnight, as he makes his way to his hotel room. Jordan Jacobs tells the players how good the hotel swimming pool is, with its Jacuzzi. Alan Jones jumps up. "Let's go for a swim, who's up for it?

"I'm up for it," John Paul says.

"Me too," says Ant Hodge. John Cully asks the Swedish girls do they fancy a swim.

The Swedish girls nod. "We will ask our four work mates if they fancy a swim also," says Tam.

Kevin Bird jumps up. "Count me in then, let's go and get changed now."

"Cass do you fancy a swim?" asks Ant.

"I might do in a bit, I'm staying here for a bit talking to Jordan and Sam.

"Okay," says Ant.

"On your way up bring twelve bottles of Champagne to the pool with you Cass," shouts Birdy.

"Yeah, okay," says Cass, "pay for it with what soft-lad?"

"Put it on the bill, room 324, Bob's room," shouts Ant Hodge as he exits out of the bar.

The girls finish their cocktails and leave the bar. Cass is left with the Welsh lads Sam and Jordan.

Alan Jones is the first out the room in just his shorts and his hairy body with his t-shirt in his hand. John Cully is next out. "Why are you wearing a mohair jumper Alan?"

"It's what all real men wear Cully." John Paul, Kevin Bird and Ant Hodge follow behind as they all get in the lift.

"What floor?" asks Kevin Bird.

"Eighth floor Kev, it's on the top floor of the hotel," says Ant Hodge. Kevin Bird presses the eighth-floor shouting "Up, up and away to infinity and beyond." Alan Jones looks at everyone in the lift and notices no one has brought a towel.

"No one has got a towel," says Alan Jones.

"It's okay, we can all dry ourselves on your hairy back," laughs Cully.

The lift stops on the eighth floor, they all march out of the lift and head towards the swimming pool. Ant Hodge opens the swimming pool door and sees clean towels.

"We have towels lads," says Ant Hodge. The lads all take a fresh clean towel, it's one in the morning and the pool is empty. Alan Jones jumps in the water doing a bomb, he splashes all the lads at the side of the pool, as he surfaces his shorts have fallen down. He floats, showing his big hairy arse. Kevin Bird laughs pointing at Alan's arse.

"Now, that is a pie arse." Alan throws his shorts out of the pool. "Hey lads I'm skinny dipping." The lads all follow suit, throwing their shorts onto the sunbeds at the side of the pool and jump into the water naked, the lads are enjoying themselves in the water.

Tam and Erika walk into the swimming pool in gold bikinis followed by their four friends. The lads look up from the water in awe of the six beautiful Swedish ladies. The girls notice that all the lads are naked in the pool.

"Why are you lot naked?" asks Tam.

"We're skinny dipping," shouts Alan Jones.

"Oh, is that right," says Erika.

The girls gather together and chat amongst themselves. Erika emerges from the group and takes off her bikini, she stands naked proud of her body. She stands tall telling the lads. "In Sweden, we're very liberated and being nude is a way of life." The rest of the girls strip off, standing naked at the side of the pool, the lad's eyes pop out like that of a crazy frog.

Ant Hodge looks at John Paul Anderson and whispers. "John Paul, what a sight that is, five natural blondes and a black bush."

"I love a bit of black bush," replies John Paul.

Ant Hodge shaking his head whispers, "John Paul, you can't smoke that black bush."

"I know that Ant, but I would give it a good go."

They both laugh with their eyes firmly fixed on the naked bodies of the Swedish girls. The girls all jump in the water holding hands.

"Tidal wave," yells John Cully. Kevin Bird stands up in the shallow end and looks down, horrified. "I think I'd better stay in the deep part, no way can I stay in the shallow end, this rocket is about to launch..."

John Cully grabs a ball from the side of the pool. "Anyone for handball?" He throws the ball up into the air knocking it with his hand to Tam. "Let's play ball, Tam."

"Hmm, I will play with your balls, big boy."

She jumps up out of the water, her firm breasts bouncing as she whacks the ball back towards Cully as her bum wobbles as she turns in the air. John Cully turns to Ant Hodge and whispers. "I think this is going to be a good game."

"It will be if you pass the ball back to them greedy arse." Cully throws the ball to Ash.

The girls play keep ball, Cully goes over to retrieve it back, Ash, the black-haired Swede passes it to Tam. John Cully stands behind Tam and catches the ball with both hands, with his arms stretched out.

"Hey, be careful big boy, your arm has just wacked my arse." Cully whispers in her ear, "I caught the ball in front of you with my arms held up that wasn't my arm."

"No way, big boy, do it again." Cass walks in with twelve bottles of Champagne, he can't believe what he's seeing. Ant Hodge jumps out the pool.

"Nice one Cass, let's have our Champers in the Jacuzzi." All the lads and girls get out the pool naked and climb into the Jacuzzi. Cass is still in a state of shock.

Ant Hodge opens four bottles of Champagne, popping the corks into the swimming pool, the lads and girls swig the Champagne out of the bottles. Alan Jones points to Cass. "See him girls, if that lad takes the right path in life, he will end up a world class footballer."

"Yeah, not only world class, he could be the best player in the world," says Ant Hodge.

The girls, impressed by this, invite young Cass into the Jacuzzi. "Join us champ," says Tam. Cass, without hesitation, takes off his trainers and jumps in still wearing his shorts and t-shirt, he sits in between Tam and Ash, with their firm breasts in his face. Cass looks up at the lads, takes a drink from his bottled water.

"I feel like George Best, I don't know if this is the right path I'm meant to take but it sure feels good."

Chapter 9

The Boss Rocks the House Down

It's Sunday, 8am in Amsterdam on this fine sunny morning. John Paul Anderson is snoring in the bath tub, Cass is asleep on the sofa. Kevin Bird and Ant Hodge are sharing the queen bed while Alan Jones and John Cully share the other queen size bed.

Kevin Chivers with his hand still in the ice bucket wakes up and looks around the room and politely asks, "Why is everyone in this room?"

"I'm here for the camaraderie," Cass says smiling.

"Are you really Cass?"

"Yeah, and because of Bob Arrow's snoring."

"Yeah Chiv, Cass is spot on with that remark about Bob, he farts as well. It's that bad it lifts up my duvet covers, they're that loud," pipes up Alan Jones.

John Paul Anderson gets out of the bath and walks into the room in a Grand Hotel housecoat. He turns to John Cully. "Fuck me Cully that was some night, did that really happen?"

"It sure did John Paul, it sure did." John Paul yawns and stretches his arms back.

"That bath tub was so comfy it was like sleeping in a water bed."

"That's what happens when you fill the bath up with water soft-lad."

"Cully, I only filled the bath to warm up my bed."

"You're mad you John Paul."

"No, I'm not, I emptied the water before I went to sleep and used the hotel housecoat as my blanket so I didn't get my toes stuck in the bath taps."

John Cully looks over to Chivers and whispers, "Give me Strength."

Alan Jones walks over to the mini fridge taking out a Dutch pork pie. As he takes a bite, he looks towards Cully. "That really did happen but for some reason my night was blurred." Cass sits up onto the sofa and smiles.

"That was every sixteen years old kids dream that last night."

"Cass," shouts Ant Hodge. "What happened last night was every man's dream."

"Why, what happened?" asks Kevin Chivers.

"We can't tell you Kev, you know the saying, what happens in Vegas stays in Vegas," Kevin Bird says, smiling, pleased with himself.

"That's bollocks, tell me what happened last night," yells Chivers with his hand still in the ice bucket.

"Chivers, why is your hand in that ice bucket?" asks Ant Hodge, changing the subject.

Chivers takes his hand out the ice bucket showing the lads his swollen hand.

"I've broke my hand when I was punching them Russians yesterday, that's why it's in the ice bucket."

"Will you be able to play in the match Kev?" asks Kevin Bird.

"What do you think soft arse? I can't even move it, never mind be able to catch a ball with it."

"That's fucking great that is, now we haven't got a goalkeeper for our biggest match in Europe," snarls Alan Jones.

"Does Bob know about your hand?" asks Cully.

"No Cully, he doesn't know, I'll tell him at breakfast."

"Why is it always Bob, Bob, Bob," asks Cass "Why isn't it 'have you told Peter Springsteen' as he's the manager?"

"Cass, it's because Bob is Mr Golden Dock, it's his team, he makes all the decisions. Peter is the manager only in name and title because Bob is still playing in the team otherwise he'd be the manager." points out Alan Jones.

Ant Hodge goes into the mini bar fridge and gets out seven small bottles of bottled spring water passing them round to each player reminding them that they're playing a football match tomorrow, so they will have to take it easy on the ale today and try and keep themselves fresh for the match.

John Paul Anderson is building a joint. "I agree with you Ant, think and act like professionals hey." The lads all look at him and shake their head in disbelief. There is a knock on the door.

"Oh shit, I hope it's not the Swedes coming back for more action," laughs Ant.

"Don't they know that we have a match tomorrow and we have a no sex rule the day before a match," rants Alan Jones.

"I'm okay," bellows Kevin Chivers. "I'm injured I'll take the lot of them, open the door." Cass gets up to open the door. It's Pat Arrow.

"Good morning lads did you have a good time last night, what happened?"

"We can't say Pat, you know the saying when in Rome do as the Romans do," replies Kevin Bird.

"Well, you're not in Rome dickhead and you're certainly not a fucking Roman, so what happened last night?" John Cully stands up looking Pat in the eye.

"Pat, last night was a mystery of pure delight centred on clouds of sky blue descent."
Pat looks puzzled. "So, what does that mean soft-lad?"

"It means Pat in quick and short terms, mind your own fucking business."

"Pat. If you don't mind me asking, what's the real reason you have knocked this early?" asks Ant Hodge.

"Well I'm going to the shops to get some English newspapers, I thought I'd ask you ugly bastards if any of you wanted one."

"English newspapers, it's only our third day here Pat and you're homesick already. What happened to you and John Paul conquering Europe and setting up home here?" asks Kevin Chivers.

"Well, it's like this Kev, we are going to conquer Europe and I know it's the third day but I've got assets to check for when I'm back home in England."

"What assets Pat? You haven't got a pot to piss in never mind assets, have you won the lottery while we have been away?" Kevin Bird asks.

"Don't be stupid soft-lad, I need to check the Euro rate back in England, it's in the papers for when I change my money back home, you know, to get the best price."

Kevin Chivers smiles at Pat. "We're on holiday, you're supposed to spend all your money Pat and enjoy yourself."

"Chivers, he's the only fella I know that takes a fiver out his pocket at the bar and puts two fivers back in his pocket at the same time, Pat's that tight, at school he used to peel oranges in his pocket," laughs John Cully.

"I'm not tight," says Pat. "I'm just careful."

"Yeah, careful going the bar to buy a pint," laughs John Cully.

"Pat, I heard you're that tight, you use to squeak when you walked and you recorded the squeak and tried to sell it on I-tunes," says Kevin Chivers laughing.

"Listen, I only knocked to see if anyone wanted papers not to get the piss taken out of me."

"We're not taking the piss Pat," laughs Ant Hodge. "We're just asking what happened about you conquering Europe because I know your comrade John Paul Anderson conquered Sweden last night."

"Well there you go," says Pat. "That shows you lot, I'm not homesick when one of my generals has conquered Sweden, now who wants a paper?"

"I do Pat," say Cass. "There is nothing better than reading the sport section while eating your breakfast."

"Nothing better Cass, not even last night?" smirks John Cully.

"Well last night was an exception Johnny boy," laughs young Cass.

Pat leaves the room saying "I'll just buy you all a paper and you can pay me later."

Cass and Alan Jones leave the lads and make their way to their own room. As they enter the room Bob is brushing his teeth in the bathroom.

"Have you two been out all night?"

"No Bob, we got up early to go for a run."

"Don't lie to me Jonesy, where did you sleep last night?"

"We stayed in Kevin Chivers room," replies Alan Jones.

"Well, make sure you're both washed and dressed and downstairs for breakfast at ten," shouts Bob.

"Okay dad," replies Cass.

"Yes sir," says Alan Jones.

Downstairs in the foyer, the players are gathering. Fat Joe is pacing up and down at the entrance of the breakfast bar. "Hurry up Bob," shouts Fat Joe. "Who are we waiting for?"

"Pipe down Joe, for fucks sake," yells Scouse Ricko. "Yer think you've never been fed."

"Shut up Ricko you know breakfast is my favourite meal of the day."

"That's because you have ten breakfasts a day fat arse." Bob does a head count.

"Right everyone is here, make sure you all have a good meal, because we're only booked in here for bed and breakfast.

"Nice speech Bob, now can we eat?" yells Fat Joe.

The lads make their way into the lounge and get food before returning to their seats. It's a buffet breakfast set up.

Fat Joe arrives at the table with 12 rounds of toast piled on the top of his plate. "I love my toast."

Kevin Chivers looks at Joe's plate amazed and turns to Frank Rox. "Look at Joe's plate, is he going mountain climbing?"

"Hey, Joe have you taken up mountain climbing?" asks Frank.

"No Frank, but I have always fancied climbing Everest, I dream of conquering it"

"Joe, first you will have to conquer that plate of toast because not many could climb over that."

"When I was a kid me ma was from Scotty Road and she always said Joe never go to work on an empty stomach."

"Yeah, Joe that maybe so, but all that on your plate would have fed all of Scotty Road with a bit left over for the sailors who had just got off the ships when your ma was a kid," laughs Frank Rox.

"I had a few stocky uncles who were sailors," Joe says with a smirk.

Pat Arrow gives everyone a newspaper charging every player five Euros.

"Five Euros for one paper? Our paper lad doesn't charge me that much for a week's papers back home," moans Kevin Bird.

"Yeah, the pounds down to the Euro here so shut up and pay up, dickhead," rants Pat.

All the lads pay Pat who walks away with a handsome profit. "Money money money," smirks Pat. John Cully shakes his head.

"No wonder you went the shop for the papers, yer a fucking right tight arse."

Pat, laughing says, "Yeah it's a tight arse now because all my pockets are full, bulging out with money, it's making my jeans tight."

"You make me laugh, you must be the oldest paperboy in Europe."

Pat looks up and shouts, "Echo, Echo," over to John Cully. Bob is sitting eating his breakfast when his mobile phone rings.

"Hello, Bob speaking, who is this?"

"Hiya Bob, it's Ted Hike, we're in a bit of pickle here. The referee that was going to take charge of the match was in a pedal bicycle accident last night. Two fellas on a bike crashed into him damaging his knee. He's said he can't referee the match because he can't walk, so the match is in doubt."

"What will we do Ted?"

"I'm not sure, but we really need this match to happen Bob."

"So do we Ted, the players are all up for it. We want to be the champion of champions."

"I'm going to make some calls Bob."

Bob tells the players what Ted has just told him. Todd Elliott and Mark Barrow sink down into their seats saying nothing. Cass points to the Welsh lads Jordan and Sam.

"Hey Bob, why don't you ask Sam? He's a qualified referee in the Welsh league."

Bob phones Ted Hike back and tells him he might have found a referee and that he will ring him back as soon as he has more information. Bob and Cass go over and ask Sam.

"Hey Welshie, will you referee the match between us and the Amsterdam Jets? Otherwise the match will be cancelled."

Sam looks up and says "No."

Jordan Jacobs thinks quickly on his feet because he's so desperate to watch the boy wonder Brian Cassidy play in the football match. "Sam, you might as well, it will be a good warm up for you and we were going to watch the match anyway, it would be such a shame for it to be cancelled when such a good referee as yourself is available." Sam nodding to himself looks up.

"Okay, I'll Referee the match for the scouse tearaways."

"Nice one Welshie," beams Bob. "We will pick you up and take you with us in the team's minibus." Bob phones Ted Hike to tell him the good news, explaining to him it was young Cass who told him about the referee. Ted Hike thanks Bob and arranges to meet him and the team tonight in the Dutch pub The Orange Oak at 6pm and that Fat Joe and Scouse Ricko have the directions before he puts the phone down, he asks what size young Cass is in football boots and in a tracksuit. Bob tells him large top and a size eight in football boots.

Bob tells the lads there is a match tomorrow so today should be a rest day and at teatime they will have a few beers with the match sponsor Ted Hike. John Paul Anderson raises his glass, "I agree with you all the way Bob, cheers," as he drinks a double vodka and coke during breakfast. The players all exit the dining area and go to their rooms to freshen up before they are taken on a tour of the Johan Cruyff arena stadium, home of the mighty Ajax of Amsterdam.

Fat Joe and Scouse Ricko are in the hotel car park cleaning the minibuses.

"They're a bunch of scruffy bastard's," moans Fat Joe. "Look at the state of the minibus, they're not eating anything in the minibus anymore," as Joe cleans under the seat he finds a full bottle of Jack Daniels.

"Pigs they are Joe. Fucking loveable pigs."

"Look Ricko, a full bottle of Jack Daniels, they have more money than sense."

"Are you putting that in the bin Joe?"

"No way, fuck that, that's for us when these lot have gone home, them greedy bastards will just waste it." As Scouse Ricko is cleaning under the seat he finds a bottle.

"Hey Joe," shouts Scouse Ricko. "We're in luck. I've just found an unopened bottle of coke."

"We're sorted now Ricko, Jack Daniels and coke for us two my dear friend," smirks Fat Joe. Scouse Ricko hands the coke to Joe who bags it up and puts it with the bottle of Jack Daniel's in a safe place in the minibus.

"Away the lads."

"Yer, I would drive them scruffy bastards away to the tip Joe."

"Tell me about it Ricko, this bus is like a location for that kid's program Stig of the Dump."

In the hotel Kevin Bird, Cass, Reid Johnson and Todd Elliott are all in the entertainment room dressed and ready to go. There is a pool table draped in an orange cloth.

"Hey Cass, fancy a game, best out of five for a hundred Euros?" asks Kevin bird.

"No thank you Kev," replies young Cass.

"Come on Cass give me a chance to win my money back," Kevin Bird says picking up two cues.

"Kevin just leave it will yer, it's going to spoil the team spirit if he keeps winning your money," snaps Reid.

"No, it won't Reid, come on Cass, one hundred Euros, the best out of five." Cass looks at Reid and shrugs his shoulders. Reid nods at Cass.

"Go on then Cass take his money and teach him a lesson."

Kevin Bird sets the balls up and breaks, Cass is in no mood to let Kevin Bird off the hook and 18 minutes later he puts the black ball in the left bottom pocket to make it three to zero.

Cass looks at Kevin Bird straight faced and says, "Now let that be a lesson to you, stop gambling your money when you play me, I'm too good for you, you're not on my level Birdy."

Kevin Bird hands over the one hundred Euros but Cass refuses his money.

"Keep your money Birdman, I value our friendship more than your money, so stop trying to beat me." Cass walks away whistling the tune of *Every Loser Wins*.

Bob gathers all the players in the foyer giving them all a chicken salad baguette, a bottle of spring water and an apple, banana and an orange in a brown paper bag.

"What's that?" asks Kevin Chivers as he takes it off Bob.

"It's a packed lunch, I got the hotel kitchen staff to make it up for us for the trip to the stadium, but more to the point what have you done to your hand Kevin?"

"I think, I've broken it Bob, I can't move it."

"Well that's you fucked for the match isn't it Kev?" moans Bob.

"Have you seen this Peter?" yells Bob. "Chivers won't be playing in tomorrow's match, he's broken his hand." Peter heads straight to the bar, orders a double whisky on the rocks, drinks it in one swig, looks at Bob and smiles.

"That's better, now where was we, oh yeah Chivers out, hmmm, don't worry Bob we can put Kevin Bird in goal and Todd Elliott up front in Birdy's place, problem solved," says Peter as he orders another double whisky on the rocks.

Fat Joe notices the paper bags as the lads make their way to the minibuses.

"Bob what are the bags for?" Bob hands one to Joe.

"Enjoy Joe, it's your packed lunch."

"Oh, fuck off Bob, no food, it's just took us an hour cleaning the shit them scruffy bastards left behind from yesterday." The players all look stunned. No way is Fat Joe refusing food.

"Bob are you serious feeding the monkey's?" moans Fat Joe.

"We have to eat Joe."

"Ricko guess what? Bob has only gone and given the monkeys a packed lunch,"

"Is he fucking kidding Joe?" moans Scouse Ricko.

"No, the monkeys are getting fed on the way to the stadium."

"What's with calling us monkeys Joe?" asks Kevin Bird.

"Well," says Fat Joe. "let me think, hmm you're all fucking wild, you're all out of control and you're all good at leaving a mess and shitting the place up and he's fucking giving you all bananas, so yes, that's my fucking monkey theory." Kevin Bird looks at Joe and crunches up his chin.

"Hmm yeah, I think you've got a point with that Joe."

Birdy jumps on the bonnet of the minibus and crouches down like a monkey with his arms swinging then jumps down grunting as he gets into his seat. The players get in the minibuses making monkey noises and Frank Rox swings in the gap of the sliding doors holding on to the roof with one arm with his banana in his other hand. The minibuses drive away and the lads in Fat Joe's bus all take out their bananas simultaneous and chew on them while making grunting noises at him.

Fat Joe laughs and gets on his walkie talkie to Scouse Ricko and while he's laughing, he tells him that he has a bunch of cheeky monkeys on his bus.

"That's nothing Joe, I've got a bunch of clever monkeys in my bus, one of them is smoking a joint and another is drinking Jack Daniels and coke."

Ian Craig shouts from the back of the minibus. "If we're all monkey's Joe, I must be a baboon the ones with the dangling red arses because my piles are playing up."

"I'm a gorilla then," yells Frank Rox banging his chest with his hands. "I'm King Kong hard as fuck but even King Kong who climbed the Empire State building and was quite agile could not have climbed Joe's breakfast plate this morning."

The minibuses pull into the car park outside the stadium, it has shops, restaurants and beer houses next to the stadium, the players get out of the minibuses while Bob goes to the front desk to get information about the tours.

Fat Joe and Scouse Ricko get out of their minibuses and check the back seats. They're like shit heaps, they both look at each other shaking their heads. Bob walks back, does a head count telling them its fourteen Euros per person.

"What about Cass?" asks Mark Barrow. "He's only a kid it must be cheaper for him?"

"Cass is sixteen, even the boy wonder has to pay fourteen Euros for this seventy-five-minute tour but the good news is that we have an English speaking guide named Willem Hardy to show us around," beams Bob.

"No way, not Willie Hardy," screams Cully.

"Why, do you know him?"

"I don't know him Bob but I know his brother Ivor, he's the hard man of the Dam."

The players all snigger and are trying not to laugh in front of Bob.

"Ivor Hardy," says Bob.

"Have you Bob? Is that because you're in a football stadium? Most men get them in the red light district, have you taken a Viagra knowing you'll be walking out onto the Ajax pitch?"

"Shut up Cully, yer gobshite."

"Has it got free WI-FI?" asks Ian Craig.

"Yeah, it has," replies Bob.

"That's good, I can do some work while we're doing the tour," says Todd Elliott.

"It's Sunday, Mr Moneybags don't you have a day off?" asks Fred Kettle.

"No Fred, it's first up, best dressed in my walk of life."

Fred nods, "Yeah I know what you mean Todd, I had to be up early today or Frank Rox would have worn all of my best clobber." Todd looks at Fred and nods his head at him with a fake smile. Ian Craig gets out his tablet and checks for the Wi-Fi connection so he can go on the racing page to check out the first horse race in England.

Willem Hardy arrives, the first stop is the dressing rooms where the leather seats look amazing. Kevin Chivers sits in the seat.

"This seat is boss, if it was windy, cold and raining before the match then no way would I leave this comfy seat to play football."

"That's because you play in goal and you don't run around," states Ant Hodge.

"You do enough running for both of us Ant that's why," laughs Kevin Chivers. "I'm just there to tidy up the mistakes made by Bob."

"The only mistake I make every game is letting Peter pick you as the goalkeeper," Bob says with a smirk on his face feeling pleased with himself.

The players leave the dressing room and make their way down the tunnel towards the pitch, the guide Willem Hardy tells them politely to stay off the pitch. Frank Rox stops and sits on the home team's seats. The guide politely asks him to refrain from sitting in that designated area.

"What do you mean mate? I'm always on the bench for the famous Golden Dock, if you move me from here I won't know where I'm supposed to go." The players piss themselves laughing. Frank Rox gets up out of the dugout and runs to catch up with the team shouting to Peter Springsteen, "Gaffer, I'm warming up, are you sending me on?"

Peter Springsteen shouts "Yeah Frank, strip off, you're up front," as he takes a swig of brandy and coke from a plastic coke bottle. Frank Rox strips down to his boxer shorts and runs on the outside of the pitch.

"Peter, get me on I'm fit and ready." Peter looks up at Frank and gulps down the remainder of the coke.

Sitting in the bottom tier of the empty stadium, the players admire the architectural structure. Willem Hardy, the guide moves them on to the trophy room. Some of the players start to get bored as the guide is talking about the history of Ajax, he's over talked by the voice of John Paul Anderson. Bob looks at John Paul giving him the stare of a cowboy who is about to draw for his gun.

"John Paul, be quiet and you might learn something."

"Bob are you winding me up? I'm a red, Liverpool is my team that's all I'm interested in. I was bought up on the kop singing 'You'll never walk alone'. I discovered my football there."

"Yeah, and you discovered and got hooked on that shit you smoke and snort in nightclubs, otherwise this man might have been talking about you being a star that had graced their stadium. Instead you're here with us, so shut up and listen and have some respect."

"I'm still only interested in the reds Bob no disrespect to Ollie Hardy, Ajax is Ollie's team, Liverpool is my team."

Ian Craig shakes his head. "We're in Ajax's trophy room and you're talking about the red shite."

"Yeah, well you can't talk about the blues trophy room can you Ian because there are no trophies in it," laughs John Paul.

"There is plenty in our trophy room, so talk sense soft-lad and they were won by scousers playing in Everton's royal blue jersey, that's why all blues fans are from the city. Most are proper scousers because they support the peoples club,"

"Ian did you just say the peoples club? That's a laugh bitter blues club more like," laughs Kevin Chivers.

"Shut up Chivers we're proper scousers," shouts Cully. "Not like the red shite, on sky sports the other night ten Liverpool fans were interviewed, eight of them were from Norway the other two were fucking cockney reds."

"That's because we have got a worldwide fan base and they interview the Norwegian reds because they speak better Queens English than scousers," says Todd Elliott with a grin like a Cheshire cat. The guide has now stopped chatting and is engrossed in the scouse banter. Bob attempts to calm the situation down by reminding the players that they're in a foreign country and that they should take in some of the cultures.

Alan Jones, laughing in between bites of his beloved pork pie looks at Bob with a wry grin. "Bob, I've been here three days and in all that time I've seen more scousers here than in Liverpool and that all the houses have vases with tulips in them and that everyone rides a bicycle smoking pot, while the girls need to invest in a set of blinds because they're all sitting in the windows in their underwear, while the men all walk around in long macs with moustaches, while some try to sell oxo cubes to gullible tourists, so shove your culture up your arse." Bob walks away fuming shaking his head.

"Fat Joe was right, you lot are a fucking bunch of clueless monkeys."

"We know that Bob, and with you being our captain the monkey's leader, that makes you the chief monkey," laughs Kevin Chivers.

"That rhymes that, Monkey Bob Chief Monkey sounds like the Kaiser Chiefs," says John Paul. The players all look at John Paul Shaking their heads.

"That's some fucking weed he's smoking," says Todd.

"You can say that again Todd, he thinks Bobs an Indian now", remarks Cully.

"Well if Bobs an Indian he's a fucking space cowboy." Alex Sharp walks with Bob.

"Do yer still want to bag that team spirit, Bobby boy?"

"Of course, Alex I'm just firing them up for tomorrow's match," says Bob with a grin.

The players follow the guide into the press room. Pat Arrow jumps into the top seat at the press table. "Attention, attention, we have called you to this press conference today to announce the sacking of Peter Springsteen. With immediate effect the board wish him well."

Peter Springsteen, standing near the back of the press room raises his arm saying "I'll drink to that" as he takes out a new bottle of brandy and coke from his coat pocket.

"The board puts his sacking down to not playing his best team like myself," says Pat Arrow.

"I can understand the board's decision, he never played me either," yells Frank Rox.

Kevin Chivers laughing, shouts, "No, that's why he was manager of the year because he didn't play the shite players like you two."

Pat speaking into the mic says, "Golden Dock have also released Kevin Chivers because he's a clueless gobshite." The players burst out laughing, the guide Willem Hardy thanks them for their co-operation during the tour as he shows them the exit.

On the way back to the hotel in the minibuses all the players clean up their mess leaving both minibuses spotless.

Fat Joe gets out his minibus, he looks over to Scouse Ricko smiling "I told you monkeys could be trained Ricko."

Scouse Ricko, smiling says, "They're not that well trained, their leader is having a piss at the side of your bus." Fat Joe looks behind to see the manager Peter Springsteen having a pee at the side of his bus.

"Sorry Joe, this monkey is not potty trained yet. I was bursting, it's all that coke in the brandy."

"It's okay Peter just don't piss in the petrol cap that piss would turn into rocket fuel and the busses have only got little engines."

"You taking the piss Joe?"

"No Peter, I'm certainly not but I think the side of the minibus has though."

The players go to their rooms for a rest until 5.30 when they're getting picked up to meet Ted Hike. Peter Springsteen and John Arrow stay in the hotel bar drinking, talking about tomorrow's match. Bob joins Peter and John in the bar ordering himself a pint of blackcurrant and soda water as Peter sinks yet another double brandy and coke.

The Dutch clock hits 5pm, the cuckoo bird makes its hourly visit as it cuckoos, the big grandfather's clock chimes away making a big blissful noise.

Bob rings the player's rooms reminding them to be at the hotel foyer for half past five. First down is Frank Rox and Fred Kettle. They're both arseing around trying to trip each other up Frank catches Fred Kettle on the shin bone. Fred goes down onto one knees holding his shin.

"Be careful, I'm playing in the match tomorrow."

"Fuck off Fred," laughs Frank Rox. "We're here to conquer Europe not throw the game, you can't even walk straight never mind kick a ball mate."

"Oh, fuck off Frank, I'm better than you, that's why you're substitute."

"Yeah, I'm substitute for the best team in the Liverpool Sunday league, even John Paul Anderson is sub in this team and he's played for Everton."

"Frank, your arse is full of wood splinters you spend that much time on the bench."

"At least my arse gets on the bench Fred, your fat arse watches from the touchline."

"So, does yours soft-lad, you never get on Frank, you never get a game."

"At least I can kick a ball Fred, your strongest foot is your right hand, you're that bad with both of your feet."

"What's that supposed to mean?" Fred Kettle says puzzled.

Frank looking Fred up and down says, "It means you're a load of wank Fred, that you're shit." Fred walks away.

"Fuck off Frank, you're shit."

The rest of the players make their way to the hotel foyer and board the Mercedes minibuses and head towards their meeting with Ted Hike. The minibuses pull into the car park of a Steak House, they are greeted by a smiling 5ft 9 slim built middle-aged man.

Fat Joe and Scouse Ricko lock up their minibuses.

"Hello boys, you both okay?"

"Yeah boss everything is fine," say Joe and Ricko together.

Ted introduces himself to the team leading them through the double doors of the Steak House telling all of them that this meal is on him. Inside the Steak House they're met by Max and Ronnie.

The players all order their meals each ordering steak and chips with a pint of lager, except for young Cass who has an orange Fanta with ice. There is loads of banter in the steak house. Ted tells the lads that they will be playing for two trophies, a trophy for the winners and a trophy for the fair team award and that the Amsterdam Jets are a top team in not only Amsterdam, they're also champions of the Netherlands Sunday football national cup.

Frank Rox stands up next to Ted Hike. "Ted we're here to conquer all that is put before us, we believe that we're the best Sunday league team in Europe and as you're a fellow scouser we will turn up and hammer any team put in front of us, so Ted watch us play and you will see that we're the best and that we will never be defeated."

"Son, can I ask you your name?"

"Frank Rox."

"Well Frank Rox, if your team have the same beliefs as you then your lot would beat Real Madrid." With this all the team start banging on the table with their knives and forks chanting.

"GOLDEN DOCK, GOLDEN DOCK, GOLDEN DOCK."

Max and Ronnie look at Ted shaking their heads. "I told you they're fucking mad Ted, they're all fucking nutters."

"Max, they're just young men finding themselves in life."

"Teddy is a Scouser," comes the cries from the Golden Dock Players.

Ted Hike smiles and stands up shouting, "Fellow scousers, I say this from the bottom of my heart with all seriousness, with that team spirit Golden Dock will never be beaten. I'm proud to be in your company on this historic night, standing beside you as you prepare to go into battle as you vie to be the best of the best and me being side by side you in your time of becoming champion of champions feeds me with great joy, now let the greatness in your souls shine through your bodies as of tomorrow on the playing fields of the Dutch capital you will achieve greatness."

The players all rise to their feet chanting;

"TED HIKE, TED HIKE, TED HIKE,"

"LONG LIVE TEDDY, LONG LIVE TEDDY."

"TEDDY AS OUR CHAIRMAN."

Ted smiles, saying "I would love to be your chairman if I was still on the shores of Mother England."

Peter Springsteen, smiling, looks at John Arrow saying, "That would be a good idea, Ted as our Chairman. Imagine all the duty-free brandy he could bring back with him."

John Arrow says, "Never mind the brandy, imagine the clubs financial muscle with Ted as our chairman, I could stop selling the teams lucky number tickets in the pub after the matches." Ted Hike stands up to address the players as they finish their meals.

"Tonight, is my treat you lot won't have to put your hands in your pockets for anything."

The lads all stand up shouting, "TEDDY, TEDDY, TEDDY."

Peter Springsteen turns to John Arrow and whispers, "Looks like I'm on brandy all night Johnny boy, courtesy of our good friend uncle Ted."

"No coke then Peter?

"Nah fuck that shit right off," replies Peter. "Drugs are for mugs," he says smiling.

Ted tells the lads he's taking them to a little old-fashioned pub just outside Amsterdam where there is a friendly atmosphere, where even they can't find trouble.

Max turns to Ted saying, "Them bunch of Lonnie's could find trouble in an empty house."

"Yeah, they might Max, but they will be in that house together causing trouble with no one in the house and they will still be side by side."

Max looking puzzled says, "Yeah Ted, you have got a point there."

Bob leads the players out and they all jump in the minibuses. Max and Ronnie get a lift of Ted Hike in his chauffeur driven Bentley. They head towards the Windmill pub. It's a little old fashioned Dutch ale house.

As they enter the pub there are six old Dutch men inside. The landlady has got sixties music blasting out of an iPod speaker situated behind the bar. There is a pool table in the pub. Ted Hike gives the landlady four hundred Euros for drinks and snacks and tells her to tell him when it runs out.

Kevin Chivers stands next to Ted Hike at the bar. As he's looking around he notices there are only six grumpy old men in the pub.

"Is this time the equivalent of the Dutch happy hour Ted?"

"Happy hour in here are you fucking kidding? It looks like happy hour is banned," smirks Frank Rox.

Ted smiles saying, "Every hour at their age is a happy hour, at least in here you will have a nice peaceful relaxing night before tomorrow's match." Max and Ronnie are at the bar discussing the match with Ted, Bob, Alex Sharp and Kevin Chivers. Bob is telling them at tomorrow's game they will see a world class player in the making. Ted Hike is excited at the mention of the game.

"I'm really looking forward to watching young Cassidy play, I've heard so much about him."

"Well you're honoured Ted because tomorrow will be young Cassidy's last game for Golden Dock. When he's gets home on Tuesday, there'll be a queue a mile long around the block of his council house with all league clubs wanting to sign him, it makes us all so sad Ted that he's leaving, but at the same time we want what's best for him, so none of us ever mention it. We want him to get a chance in life to better himself, he's such a lovely lad, we will miss him," says Bob holding back the tears.

"That reminds me," says Ted. "I've got something for young Cassidy in my car."

Ted Hike leaves the pub retuning a couple of minutes later with two bags, he calls over Cass and introduces himself.

"Hello Brian, I'm Ted, I've heard all about you."

"Hello Mr Hike, all good I hope, call me Cass"

"Yeah, it was all good and you can call me Ted, you calling me Mr Hike makes me sound like a school teacher." Scouse Ricko, Fat Joe and Max and Ronnie overhear this reply from Ted and burst out laughing. Ted Hike gives them a quick glare and they all stop laughing and drink their drinks quietly.

"Okay, Ted it is then Mr Hike," says young Cass with a smirk on his face.

Ted laughs and hands Brian two bags. "I got these for you Cass because you sorted the referee out for me and it saved me a lot of time and effort finding a new referee."

"Thanks Ted."

"I only wish I knew who crashed into the poor man I had to referee the match," says Ted Hike. "I would string them up by their bollocks." Mark Barrow and Todd Elliott who were in earshot of that comment look at each other then down at their drinks saying nothing.

Cass pulls out a green hooded Hugo Boss tracksuit out of one of the bags.

"Ted, nice one it's my size."

Ted replies, "That was lucky then wasn't it," and smiles and winks at Bob.

Cass opens the other bag and pulls out a pair of black leather New Balance football boots, size eight with Brian Cassidy boy wonder stitched in gold cotton into the side of each football boot. Young Cassidy is over the moon.

"Ted thank you, I don't know what to say, you got the size right again, thank you Ted, you're a diamond geezer Ted you really are."

"It's just pure luck that they're your size, just make sure you win them cups and take them home and score a goal with your new boots," says Ted with a glint in his eye.

Peter Springsteen is at the bar drinking brandy telling Ted Hike that there are lots of injuries so don't expect too much as they are playing the Dutch champions. Frank Rox is not amused at Peter Springsteen comments. "Hey, Peter shut up! We can and will beat anyone." Peter orders a double brandy at the bar.

"Cheers Ted, I need this."

"I need a winning team Peter."

"Ted, don't worry my team will deliver."

"They best had Peter, otherwise I will hold you responsible." Peter's eyes widen as he hears that last comment.

"Hey love, fill that up, make it a treble."

Poppy, the landlady hands Peter his treble brandy and turns the tunes up higher playing rock and roll songs. Peter starts dancing like a man who has problems.
Kevin Bird joins Springsteen, they're both dancing at the bar. Ted Hike finishes his drink and says goodbye to all the lads as he's leaving he looks to Fat Joe.

"Hey, Joe make sure they're on their best behaviour, don't keep them out too late."

"Okay boss, we will get them back to the hotel before 11 pm."

Ted Hike walks out with Max and Ronnie, they all get into his Bentley and are driven away into the distance through the tulips of Amsterdam.

In the doorway a middle aged Dutch man walks into the pub heading towards the bar shouting in Dutch to Poppy as he orders a pint. Poppy just smiles at him as she gives him a pint of Heineken lager. He takes off his scruffy leather jacket and places it onto the bar stool. The players are now all in a party mood Peter Springsteen is rocking the house down dancing like a born-again teenager.

Kevin Chivers is on the fruit machine complaining about it eating his Euros. Poppy plays *'Born in the U.S.A.'* by Bruce Springsteen. It sends Peter Springsteen wild he jumps onto the pool table and rocks on one leg playing air guitar, Poppy smiles and raises up the tune. Kevin Bird joins Springsteen on the pool table rocking the house down.

Chopper Moon, Frank Rox, Ant Hodge and John Paul Anderson are outside at the front of the pub smoking joints, as *'Born in the U.S.A.'* finishes Poppy replays it putting it on repeat smiling as the lads put some much-needed life into this old-fashioned ale house. Young Cass joins Peter Springsteen and Kevin Bird on the pool table.

Peter Springsteen wraps his bandana around his head. He's now the boss of rock and roll as Poppy turns the tunes higher a smiling Peter Springsteen swings on the lights over the pool table which are connected to the pubs false ceiling. The six grumpy old men cheer as Peter Springsteen rocks the house down. As he swings on the lights the celling collapses sending Peter into Kevin Bird who knocks into Cass who flies off the back off the pool table, his fall is broken by Kevin Chivers who bangs his head on the fruit machine. Kevin Bird falls onto a table, the legs snap leaving him flat out on the floor. Peter Springsteen follows, falling onto Kevin Bird standing on his hand in the process.

As he lands there is a big cracking noise, the false ceiling and pool table lights falls on them. They look up as a big hole in the pub ceiling appears. Poppy is still smiling with the song still playing on repeat. The middle aged Dutch man is not happy, he pulls out a gun pointing it in the player's direction.

"English Pigs you have five seconds to get out my Pub before I shoot you all" The players make a hasty exit followed by the six grumpy Dutch men.

"What's going on?" asks Frank Rox. Mark Barrow explains about the Dutch man pulling out a gun at them. Frank is fuming.

"He did what?" yells Frank. Chopper Moon runs into the pub shouting. "Hey bully boy take a shot me," as he points his gun at the Dutch man. The Dutch man sees Chopper with his gun and runs behind the bar. Chopper fires his gun missing the Dutch man by miles hitting the last orders bell. The Dutch man runs into the back of the pub and opens the door escaping into the darkness of the night.

Peter Springsteen who is well and truly pissed hears the noise of the gun being fired. He turns to Alex Sharp, "If I knew Chopper could shoot like that I would play him up front for us."

Alex shaking his head says, "Fuck off Peter, this is serious." Chopper Moon walks out the pub like a cowboy with piles. "Did you get the horrible twat?" asks Frank.

"No, the bastard got away the shithouse legged it out the back door."

Frank Rox is fuming. He starts kicking the pubs square French windows, he kicks one piece breaking the glass. As he drags his foot out he rips open the bottom of his leg on a jagged piece of glass that was still stuck in the window. There is blood everywhere.

Bob takes off his jacket wrapping it around Franks open cut, strapping it tightly applying pressure to the wound to keep the blood flow under control.

Bob picks up Frank putting him into Fat Joes minibus, telling him to get Frank to a hospital right away. As Fat Joe pulls away the police sirens can be heard in the distance. They're getting nearer to the pub. During all the commotion Cass left his bags in the pub. He goes into the pub to retrieve them. As the blue lights get nearer the six Dutch grumpy old men scatter into the mist of the night. Scouse Ricko tells everyone to pile into his minibus and packs everyone in and pulls off. No one can see who's in the minibus as they're all on top of each other. There is a tight squeeze.

In the pub Cass collects his bags. Poppy looks over and smiles at Cass, she still has the music blasting even though the pub is completely empty. Cass walks back outside to find no one is there, the minibus has left without him. The police sirens are blasting the blue lights are flashing in the distance. Cass can see the five armoured police vans that are racing towards him, he's in a place he's not familiar with, stranded with nowhere to run. He's in Shit Street.

Just as Cass is looking towards a night in the police cells Ginger Lee and Burger pull up outside the pub. "Hurry up Cass get in," yells Ginger Lee. Cass jumps in and Ginger Lee speeds off taking a sharp right turn just before the police armoured vehicles pull up outside an empty pub.

"What are you two doing here," asks Cass. "You have just saved me from going to prison for a long time."

Burger laughs saying. "Our hotel is just two minutes away, we were just going to fill up the Range Rover with diesel as we're going to Germany in the morning and we saw you like a cub lost from its pride."

Cass explains what happened to Ginger Lee and Burger. Ginger Lee laughing says, "They can't send you to prison for falling off a pool table Cass."

"They could," laughs Cass. "They all left me, I was snookered." The three of them burst out laughing as they safely make their way to Cassidy's hotel.

In the minibus. Scouse Ricko scratches his head shouting. "What the fuck has just happened there, how do I explain that to Ted?" he pulls into the hotel car park everyone piles out of the minibus they're all stretching off as it was jammed packed in the minibus. Peter Springsteen is so pissed John Arrow and Alex Sharp hold him up and start carrying him into the hotel.

"Where is Cass?" yells Reid. He starts to look around and can't see Cass.

"Where the fuck is Cass has anyone seen him?" yells Reid again. He runs around the minibus panicking. "You stupid bastards, you have left Cass at the pub!" yells Reid.

Peter Springsteen looks at Scouse Ricko and shouts. "We have to go back for Cass."

Scouse Ricko says, "We can't, it's a half hour journey to the pub. It'll be crawling with Dutch police. We can't go back."

The whole team yell together, "Yes, we can, he's one of us, we're not leaving him behind, we're a team we leave no one behind."

Bob, close to tears yells. "He's fucking sixteen years of age in a strange country and he hasn't got a clue where he is, now get them fucking keys in the minibus and take me back to that fucking pub."

Reid shouts. "I'm going. He's my cousin, I can't stay here while he's at that pub all alone." Peter Springsteen staggers towards the minibus. "I'm coming too I'm the manager."

"So am I then," shouts Alan Jones. "He's my roomie."

"I can't drive back lads, think about it," says Scouse Ricko pleading with them.

"I will drive the bus," yells Ian Craig.

"You can't you're pissed."

"I can Ricko, if I get a pull off the police I will only get banned here in Holland not in the U.K., Cass is more important."

"No, I will drive, let's go." The rest of the players all jump in the minibus.

"We're a team, we leave nobody behind, we all stick together, we can look down the streets for him, the more of us the better," yells Todd. Alex Sharp stays behind at the hotel in case there is any news. In the minibus Cully is sitting next to Ian Craig.

"You're okay you Ian, I was wrong about you."

"No Cully, I'm still a cunt. I just want to get Cass so I can get some sleep."

"You can't kid me Ian, you're a good lad, you're still shit at footie though."

"I wasn't wrong about you, you're still a bus driver but now I think you would make a good coach," says Birdy with a drunken smirk on his face.

Scouse Ricko speeds out of the hotel car park, Ginger Lee pulls in front of him. Scouse Ricko beeps his horn pointing at Ginger Lee to get out the way. Ginger Lee laughs and points to Cass shouting.

"Is this who you're looking for?"

Scouse Ricko reverses into the hotel car park and the players get out the minibus. Bob grabs hold off Cass giving him a big bear hug.

"Alright Bob, take it easy, yer will mess my hair up."

"I don't care Cass, at this moment I'm so happy seeing you, it's like I've won the lottery." Reid shakes the hands of Ginger Lee and Burger thanking them for bringing back Cass safely. The players thank Ginger Lee and Burger. Bob invites Ginger Lee and Burger into the hotel for a drink, he tells them to leave the car in the hotel and books them into the penthouse suite for the night, courtesy of Max and Ronnie and thanks them once again.

Reid hugs Cass asking him what happened. Cass tells him he went back in for his bags and when he came out no-one was there and that the police were yards away from him when Ginger Lee picked him up in the Range Rover and that he sped away taking a sharp right turn getting him away from the pub and out of the sight of the oncoming police cars.

Cass close to tears, tells Reid he was really scared. Reid tells him it's okay to be scared you're only human and shows him his trademark right handed clenched fist saying. "This will only make you a stronger person," as he taps him on the chin with his clenched fist.

The player's all have one drink with Ginger Lee and Burger and then Bob reminds everyone that they all have to meet at nine o clock in the morning at the breakfast diner and then he sends everyone to their rooms to get some sleep before the big match tomorrow.

On his way out, Bob hands Burger fifty Euros saying. "You and Lee have a drink on us and you are both more than welcome to come and watch the Golden Dock in their champion of champions match."

Chapter 10

Golden Dock march on

The sun is shining, it's the 1st of June and it's match day. This is the day Golden Dock hope to conquer Europe. In the breakfast room, the smell of the bacon is filtering through to the players who have a nine-o clock breakfast call. Bob is first down in his Golden Dock tracksuit that Todd Elliott bought for the team. Ginger Lee and Burger are walking out of the breakfast room.

"Morning lads, are you both looking forward to watching the game today?"

"Morning Bob," replies Ginger Lee. "Thanks for the room last night."

"We're not going to be able to watch the match Bob," says Burger.

"Why not Burger?"

"We have to go to work."

"Can't work wait lads? It's history in the making today."

"No Bob, we're setting off for Germany, it's a long drive. We like to leave first thing. You know the saying *first up best dressed*, well that's how us two roll, early birds catching the best worms and all that shit. We've had breakfast, so wish all the lads good luck from us in today's match," mutters Ginger Lee as he fills his pockets with the sachets of milk, butters, sauces, teabags, cups, sugar, jams and fruits from the breakfast bar.

Bob stares at Ginger and Burger in disbelief as their pockets bulge with half of the hotels stock. "Do you really need all that Ginger?"

"It's for the journey to Germany Bob."

"Why, has Germany run out of food? Are they on rations over there?"

"No, Bob it's for us," laughs Burger.

"Burger, you two won't use all them."

"We know that Bob, we bag them up. We do it in every café we go in and when we're home we sell them to Arthur, he buys them for his café."

Burger and Ginger Lee bid Bob farewell and drive off towards Germany on their next adventure.

Bob is down for breakfast first to make sure everything is in place for the players. It will be a light breakfast as it's a 12 noon kick off.

Jordan and Sam, the two Welsh lads are at their breakfast table eating Corn Flakes. Bob gives them both the thumbs up, letting Sam know that they will be leaving the hotel at 10.30 am so they can be picked up outside in the carpark. Both give Bob the thumbs up back.

The players filter into the breakfast room, there is a sombre mood in the camp... They sit at the table reflecting the previous night's events. Chopper Moon and Fred Kettle enter the breakfast room to give an update on Frank Rox.

"Frank is still in hospital. He needs an operation on his Achilles tendon which he lacerated on a piece of broken glass. He will be in hospital for at least three days," says Chopper Moon.

"So, won't he be watching us today?" asks Kevin Bird.

"No, not a chance," says Fred Kettle.

"He's in too much pain," says Chopper.

"We're going to the hospital in a bit to see him," says Fred.

"What time you going?" Bob asks.

"We're going straight after breakfast," says Chopper Moon.

"That's good," says Alex Sharp. "Now both of you sit down and get something to eat before you go."

The players are eating breakfast as Ted Hike pulls into the hotel car park in his Bentley. The players can see him from the breakfast room windows. Fat Joe looks at Scouse Ricko on seeing Ted Hike.

"Fuck me, Ted doesn't look happy Ricko," mutters Joe.

"Shit, he looks well pissed off."

Ted Hike walks into the breakfast room and makes his way over to the players, his face like thunder. He stands next to Bob, picking a sausage off his plate. He looks at Scouse Ricko and gives him a dirty look.

"Well, you lot have only done the impossible and managed to cause trouble in an empty pub." He looks at Chopper Moon. "Have you got it lad?" Chopper nods at Ted. "Go and get me it son."

"I have it here Mr Hike."

"Hand it over to me then son. Your days of John Wayne are over."

Chopper Moon hands the gun to Ted. "I'm sorry Mr Hike."

"You don't have to say sorry to me son, I don't blame you. I blame that gobshite over there." Ted points to Scouse Ricko. Ted puts his hand on Bobs shoulder and looks at him straight faced.

"Bob, the match is off."

"Why is that Ted? The whole reason we're here is to be the champion of champions."

The players look really disappointed, they can't believe what they have just heard.

"Well, me, Max and Ronnie thought about it and the three of us went to the zoo this morning and got fifteen monkeys to take your places. We felt that in the real world the fifteen monkeys would be easier to control. Less hassle."

The players look at Ted and groan as he bursts out laughing.

"Aww, I got you all there, yer gang of knobheads," Ted says, laughing as he munches on the sausage from Bob's plate.

Bob looks up at him saying. "Ted, we won't let you down on the football pitch."

Ted looking at the team says, "You bunch of fuckers have not let me down, I've never laughed so much in my life when I went to see Poppy this morning."

"What do yer mean Ted?" asks Bob.

"I went to see her before I came here. She was still in a trance this morning. She didn't blame you lot, she blamed the drunken Dutch idiot."

"What about the collapsed ceiling Ted?" asks Kevin Bird.

"Shut up Birdy," whispers Peter Springsteen.

"Oh, the rock and roll man swinging on the lights do you mean Birdy?" asks Ted.

"Yeah," says Birdy who gets a sly kick to his ankle from Peter Springsteen.

"It's okay, she going to claim on the insurance and get all new decor in the pub. She told the police that the drunk Dutch man shot the celling," laughs Ted Hike. "And don't worry about Frank Rox, we will take care of him. He will stay with Joe when he comes out of hospital for a few days until he's fit to fly home."

"Chopper didn't hit the celling Ted, he hit the closing time bell," says Kevin Bird.

Chopper gives Birdy a look that could cut him into two.

"I know," beams Ted. "But Chopper is that bad a shot he hit the last orders bell that ricocheted into the ceiling above the pool table, so everything is sweet."

"How can we thank you Ted?" asks Bob.

"You can't Bob, just go out there today and win."

The players finish their breakfast and go to their rooms to brush their teeth and freshen up. There is still a quiet mood in the camp.

Chopper Moon and Fred Kettle are going the hospital to see Frank Rox. On the way out Ted Hike shouts asking them if they are going to see Frank.

"Yeah, Mr Hike," replies Chopper.

"Get in my car, I'll drop you off." They get in the back of the Bentley; the chauffeur opens the door for them. Ted Hike gets in the Bentley clapping his hands.

"Away we go Marco," shouts Ted. "Let's take Butch Cassidy and the Sundance Kid to see Billy the Kid in hospital." Chopper and Fred Kettle look at Ted laughing.

It's twenty past ten and Bob reminds the players it's time to leave for the match. The players gather in the foyer in their new Golden Dock blue and green tracksuits. There is a negative mood in the camp. Bob notices this and tries to gee them up, but all the players are down and are missing Frank Rox. The lads get in the minibuses and head towards the stadium. It's a twenty minute drive. The two Welsh lads get in Fat Joes minibus with Bob.

Pat Arrow shouts, "Hey Taffy, no mistakes today or when we get home we will rob all your sheep."

Sam, looking puzzled says, "I haven't got sheep. I live in Cardiff but I do have red cards so watch what your chatting little Pat."

Alan Jones looks at Pat and says, "Little Pat, you have just been terrorised by a Welsh man."

Pat, not amused tells Alan to fuck off.

Bob Arrow looks at Alex Sharp saying, "That's our team sprit Alex, we need to snap them out of this mood. It's like a dark cloud has ascended over us."

The minibuses make their way to the stadium car park. It's a little non-league stadium that Amsterdam Jets call home. As the players make their way to the dressing room, there is no banter or chat amongst them. Their mood is flat as they seek to be champion of champions.

Sam the Welsh referee has a walk on the pitch. He's doing a pitch inspection.

The Amsterdam Jet players are in the stadium. They eye up the Golden Dock players as they make their way to the dressing room. Some of them stare as they pass each other. The Amsterdam Jets mascot, Tony the Tiger, growls at them.

Kevin Bird pretends to be scared and jumps back saying, "Shit, it's Tony the Pussy," the players half-heartily laugh as their mood is still dampened by the absence of Frank Rox. They make their way into the dressing room where they sit in silence. It's that quiet you could hear a pin drop.

"I have never heard a dressing room so quiet, you'd think we had been robbed of our sense of humour, snap out of it," yells Peter Springsteen.

"Snap out of it?" yells Reid Johnson. "This was Franks dream to conquer Europe and he's not here with us."

"Well conquer Europe then," yells Peter Springsteen. "Let's go out there today and make him proud."

"It's not the same without Frank," yells Kevin Bird.

"He didn't play that much," bellows Kevin Chivers. "But he was always here for us willing us on."

"Yeah, that's what Frank was good at," says Cass. "He generated our team spirit."

"He was our twelfth man," yells Alan Jones.

"Yeah, that means he was sub Alan," sniggers Cully.

"No, he's more than a sub he was our lucky charm."

"Yeah, still means he's a sub," mutters Cully under his breath.

"Go and have a walk on the pitch," says Peter Springsteen. "Get a feel of it." The players walk out looking glum with their faces down. Peter looks at Bob who shrugs his shoulders.

On the pitch young Cass talks to the Welsh journalist Jordan Jacobs who is reminding Cass that it's up to him - Brian Cassidy - how far he goes in football, that's it's the path he takes that decides his fate in life.

Cass smiles at Jordan. "Me scoring the winner in the world cup final for England like in my dream, is the path I want to take Jordan."

"That's good Cass, I hope I get to write about it," smiles Jordan.

"Me too," laughs Cass. "Make sure you give me a nine in the match report."

Chopper Moon and Fred Kettle arrive at the stadium and head straight into the dressing room to report back to Peter and Bob.

Peter Springsteen walks towards the dugout in the stadium and shouts all the players to come back into the dressing room. As they pass, the Amsterdam Jets mascot Tony the Tiger is making wanker gestures towards them. The players ignore this and filter into the dressing room, sitting down quietly.

"Right lads, I have a message from the one and only Frank Rox." He gets his phone out of his pocket, stands in front of the players and calls Frank Rox on *Facetime*.

Frank Rox answers, laying in his hospital bed his ankle in plaster. The players sit quietly and watch and listen to what Frank Rox has to say.

"HELLO LADS YOU ALL OKAY? I'M A BIT CONFUSED HOW I ENDED UP IN HERE, WHO PUT THAT PANE OF GLASS IN THAT PUB WINDOW? I WASNT EVEN DRUNK. WELL ANYWAY DONT WORRY ABOUT ME, I'M OKAY, I HAVE MY OP LATER SO I'M SORRY I CAN'T BE THERE WITH YOU TO CONQUER EUROPE. DON'T WORRY ABOUT ME. IN ABOUT FIVE MINUTES I'VE GOT TWO NURSES IN UNIFORMS, BOTH AMAZINGLY BEAUTIFUL, GIVING ME A BED BATH. THEY'RE GOING DUTCH, SO I'LL BE OKAY... I'VE TO THANK TED HIKE, HE VISITED ME LAST NIGHT AND GOT ME SEEN TO STRAIGHT AWAY AND GOT ME MY OWN PRIVATE ROOM AND GOT THE TOP SPECIALIST AND SURGEON TO SORT MY LEG OUT. TED IS A TOP MAN, CASS WAS RIGHT WHEN HE SAID HE WAS A DIAMOND GEEZER, HE'S A GEM, HE REALLY IS. SO REID, CASS, ANT, CULLY, BIRDY, AND THE REST OF YOU LOT ALL GET YOUR SHIT TOGETHER AND STOP MOPING AROUND THINKING OF ME. GET OUT THERE AND KICK SHIT OUT OF THESE DUTCH BASTARDS AND LET'S CONQUER EUROPE. CHIVERS, GET THEM UP FOR IT, I'M OKAY. MAKE SURE YOU HAVE MY SHIRT WITH MY NAME ON THE BACK HANGING UP IN THE DRESSING ROOM AND DONT LET FRED KETTLE WEAR IT. NOW GET OUT THERE AND THINK OF WINNING, AND SHOW THESE BASTARDS WE RULE THE WORLD WITH OUR PASSION AND HUNGER. LET OUR TEAM SPIRIT SHOW THEM WHO IS THE BEST, WE FEAR NO ONE, I'VE SET UP A TUNE FOR YOU LOT ON MY IPOD. BOB WILL PLAY IT TWO MINUTES BEFORE YOU GO OUT TO KICK THIER DUTCH ARSES, NOW GET OUT THERE AND WIN WITH THE STYLE AND CLASS YOU WERE ALL BORN WITH. I'VE TO GO NOW, MY NURSES ARE HERE TO GIVE ME MY BED BATH... FRANK ROX IS SIGNING OUT WITH ONE MESSAGE, GOLDEN DOCK GET OUT THERE TODAY AND FUCKING KICK ARSE, BRING THE TROPHY BACK HOME TO THE LAND OF FOOTBALL. GO OUT AND WIN BECAUSE WE WILL NEVER BE DEFEATED."

The players stand up and roar like lions.

"FRANK ROX, FRANK ROX, FRANK ROX!!!"

The noise is deafening as the stadium shakes. Frank Rox gives a thumb up as two nurses close the curtains around his bed. Peter Springsteen switches the phone off. The mood is lifted.

Bob turns to Alex Sharp, "That team spirit is pure gold."

Peter stands up to name the team. "Right lads, let's get ready to kick arse, the team is: Kevin Bird in goal."

"I'm not in goal," replies Kevin. "How can I play in goal when you broke my two fingers last night when you fell off the pool table and stood on them? I'll go sub and play if I'm needed."

"Fuck me," says Peter. "We're in shit-street now, no Chivers, no Birdy, what the fuck do we do now?"

"I'll go in goal," says Pat Arrow.

"Oh, behave Pat this is not the time to joke."

"I'm not joking, I'm serious."

"What, all five foot six of you Pat?

"I'm five foot six and a half."

"Oh well that's okay then, why didn't you mention that half an inch earlier, I feel much better now Pat."

"Don't take the piss, Peter."

"Taking the piss? It's full-sized goals Pat, not five a side goals," snaps Peter.

"Yeah and what like," says Pat. "Have you got a better option?"

"No, I have no options Pat not unless some of Doddies Diddy men are free."

"There you go then, throw me over the keeper's jersey."

Peter throws Pat the keeper's jersey. "Right it's Pat in goal. Back four is Bob, Alan Jones Ian Craig and Mark Barrow. In midfield it's Reid, Ant Hodge, John Cully and John Paul and up front it's Cass and Todd Elliott. Subs are Birdy, Parry, Fred Kettle and Chopper Moon. Now go and get changed and let's win and conquer Europe for Frank Rox.

The Dressing room is rocking as the players get changed into their new blue kit, with their names on the back and team number below.

Bob remarks, "We will be the smartest team in Holland."

Todd Elliott has got his name on the number eleven jersey.

"How come you have number eleven Todd?" asks Birdy. "You're usually sub."

"Don't be stupid all your life Birdy, have a day off, look at my number, that's a starter not a substitute."

Birdy, looking puzzled looks at Peter Springsteen, "He's usually sub."

"For fucks sake, shut up Birdy, Todd bought the kit, he can be whatever number he wants to be but it doesn't mean he will always start."

"I heard that," shouts Todd Elliott.

"Good," says Peter. "Now get out there out and show me your good enough to play from the start all the time Todd."

Pat Arrow puts the goalkeeper's jersey on. It's three sizes too big. It's like a dress on him. Bob looks at him and tells him to tuck the jersey into his shorts, which are too big and up over his waist.

"Fuck me, when did we sign Billy Casper? The skinny lad that was in that film *Kes*," shouts John Paul.

"Shut up John Paul or I'll whip you with my sleeves." They are twice the length of his arms. Peter Springsteen looks at Pat Arrow and just stands and shakes his head.

The players are ready to go out. Bob is ready to play the tune Frank Rox told him to play from his iPod. He has it set to full volume, he presses play and 'Stand and Deliver' blasts out of the iPod.

Peter Springsteen jumps up and down. "It's Adam and the Ants!" He puts Vaseline and black boot polish across his cheeks and starts dancing jumping up and down like an Indian Sioux warrior shouting, "Stand and Deliver, it's your money or your Life." All the players follow Peter and dance, jumping up and down in a circle roaring out;

"STAND AND DELIVER, IT'S YOUR MONEY OR YOUR LIFE."

Birdy turns to Chivers and asks, "Who the fuck is Adam Ant?"

"Fuck knows," shouts Chivers. "But it's your money or your life, so you best deliver."

The players are now ready to go out and conquer Europe. In the dressing room everyone is hyped up. Bob leads the Golden Dock players out like a pack of wolves ready for the fight; they're now ready to march on and fulfil their destiny to be one of Europe's elite...

Chapter 11

The Russian Invasion

As the Golden Dock players reach the pitch, the Amsterdam Jets are wearing the same colours. Sam the Welsh referee calls the two managers together explaining that they can't play in the same colours. Peter tells Reni, the Amsterdam Jets manager, that they can lend their spare green and white hoops kit. Reni shouts his players back into the dressing room to change into the spare kit.

John Arrow runs to the minibus to get the kit and passes it into the home team's dressing room.

Golden Dock are on the pitch warming up, kicking footballs around. Ted Hike is on the touchline with Max and Ronnie, while Mills the manager of the Cafe Del Duff has turned up to watch the match with Frankie Robo. Fat Joe is egging on Scouse Ricko to ask Bob for a game.

"Hey, Bob is there a kit for me and Joe?"

Bob smiles and shouts sarcastically, "Yeah Ricko, you do know that this is a football match not a darts match? Best coming back when you're both ten stone lighter."

Fat Joe smirking shouts, "Is that a defo no then Bob?"

"I think so Joe."

Fat Joe laughing shouts, "Thank fuck for that Bob. I can eat these cheese-burgers now then," He pulls two out of his jacket pocket.

As the players are warming up on the pitch waiting for the Amsterdam Jets, five white transit vans pull into the stadium parking bays. A strong-handed mob of Russians led by head doorman Sergei march into the stadium armed with shotguns, hammers, machetes, crossbows, and baseball bats. They merge at the far end of the stadium next to the corner flag, forty men deep. They're all over 6ft 5.

The Golden Dock players stop their warm up and gather together in the centre circle as they watch the movements of the Russians.

Kevin Bird whispers, "Fuck me, we really are at war, we're going to have to conquer Europe without weapons, while the Russians have the full whack. They're only missing a tank."

"Don't worry, we can throw your smelly socks at them Birdy, that will take a few of them out," laughs Ant Hodge.

Ted Hike sees the Russians and goes to confront them, all five foot nine of this slim built middle-aged man. He's followed by Max, Ronnie, Mills and Frank Robo, Fat Joe and Scouse Ricko.

Scouse Ricko turns to Fat Joe, "Fuck me Joe, what a time for me to leave my gun in the minibus."

"Let's get ready to rumble Ricko lad."

The players walk towards Ted Hike and stand behind him as he walks up to Sergei. Ted looks him in the eye. The forty plus Russians have hatred in their eyes, they're here to win the war and inflict damage on the players with their weapons. Ted strains his neck as he looks up at the six-foot eight Russian head man Sergei.

"Can I help you?" asks Ted staring at the Russian mob.

"No, I don't think you can, we're here to destroy them bastards," yells Sergei as he points at the Golden Dock players.

"Well, then we have a problem," says Ted. "Because they're here as guests of mine."

Sergei, steaming pouts, "I've no problem with you or any other people in this stadium besides them English bastards." He points again at the players. "But if you or any others try to stop us, we will destroy and damage anything in our way."

"Ted, tell them Russian wankers that we're not scared of them," yells Kevin Chivers.

"Yeah, tell them to put their weapons down Ted, tell them we will fight them man to man, Queensbury rules," screams Kevin Bird.

"We can take them," yells Chopper Moon.

Cass looks at Reid and sniggers, "It's lucky we're the fastest runners in the team."

"Cass even with our pace we can't outrun bullets."

"Fuck it then Reid, looks like its plan B then."

"What's plan B Cass?"

"Fuck knows Reid, I was relying on you," laughs Cass.

Sergei looks Ted in the eye and snarls, "Little man, do you know who I am?"

Ted straight faced replies, "Why don't you know your own name because you see I know my name. I'm Ted Hike, so why don't you be a good little boy and phone your boss and ask him does he know who I am?"

Sergei phones his boss and talks to him in Russian. He's taken back a bit at what he has just heard. He puts the phone down and smiles at Ted.

"Mr Hike, I'm sorry if I speak out of turn, please except my sincere apology."

"It's not me you want to apologise too, it's that sixteen-year-old boy," He turns and points at young Cass. "One of your henchmen punched him the other night nearly knocking his head off."

"No way, he more than sixteen Mr Hike? He a man, he built like a bull," says Sergei.

"Yes way, he's sixteen and not only that, he's also a Boy Wonder, a boy who has the potential to be world class. He could become one of the best footballers in the world, so why don't you and your pack of hyenas go put your weapons back in your vans and come back and witness a future world football player of the year."

Sergei nods at Ted then turns to his comrades saying something to them in Russian. He leads them back to the car park to clear themselves of their weapons. They return to the side of the corner flag and wait like angry bears to watch the match between Golden Dock and the Amsterdam Jets.

Tony the Tiger leads out the Amsterdam Jets in Golden Docks green kit making a middle finger gesture to the Golden Dock bench.

Amsterdam Jets have two scousers in their team; 35-year-old Paul Fizzy who is 6ft 4 with ginger hair, he's their captain. He played professional football in the English Premier league. He's their ball playing centre half. The other scouser is Jamie Dunne who imports flowers and fresh fruit; he's their midfield dynamo, aged twenty-five. He's the engine in the Dutch team.

Welsh Sam blows his whistle, bringing the two captains together to toss the coin to get the game underway, Bob wins the toss and decides to kick off. Paul Fizzy smiles at Bob.

"That's the only thing you will win today little man."

Bob smiles back, "Is that right, yer big ginger prick."

John Paul kicks the ball to Ant Hodge. The match is underway.

Pat Arrow is standing in goal like a boy in men's clothing. His kit is three sizes too big on him.

Golden Dock attack. Ant Hodge sprays the ball out wide to Reid Johnson who crosses the ball into the box. Paul Fizzy out jumps Brian Cassidy, heading the ball to his Amsterdam Jets team mate. Paul Fizzy taunts Brian Cassidy.

"You don't jump very high do you son? You would have struggled to fit the Liverpool Echo between the grass and your jumping feet there." Cass looks at Fizzy, thinking *cheeky twat* but ignores him and goes to retrieve the ball.

The Dutch team have a great chance to score. Their six-foot skin-headed Dutch striker is clear through on goal with only Pat Arrow to beat. Pat comes off his line and bravely dives at the feet of the towering Dutch skinhead, smothering the ball into his hands and chest. Peter Springsteen looks at Kevin Chivers on the bench and laughs.

"Chivers here's your p45, I've found myself a new keeper."

Chivers laughing says, "You're kidding aint yer? He was slow out."

"Slow? Don't be silly, he was like Usain Bolt then."

"Fuck off Peter, the only *Bolt* Pat resembles is Frankenstein's Bolt."

Cass gets a short pass from Pat Arrow in the right back position, but he's closed down so he flicks the ball up and heads it back to him in goal. As he turns to run into position, the Dutch skinhead striker kicks him in the arse as Cass passes him. Quick as a flash, Reid Johnson has the Dutch striker by the throat strangling him with both of his hands. The two teams pile in pushing and shoving each other. Sam the Welsh referee blows his whistle to calm things down. He gives the Dutch number nine and Reid Johnson a warning. Tony the Tiger is running up and down the line doing cartwheels.

Golden Dock have a corner. Todd Elliot takes a short one to Cass who is on the edge of the six-yard box. As Cass goes towards the ball to receive it, Paul Fizzy puts his studs down the back of Cassidy's Achilles tendon sending him to the floor. Paul Fizzy stands in front of Cass and retrieves the ball sending it down the right wing. Paul Fizzy leans over young Cass who is on the ground in pain.

"Hey son, where I come from we play like men not boys, I shit out players like you."

Cass gets to his feet limping. The Dutch team have a chance, their tricky right winger cuts inside smacking the ball into the far-right corner of the goal. Pat Arrow leaps into the air turning the ball around the post. From the resulting corner Alan Jones wins the header and sends Ant Hodge free, Ant looks up and sees Cass tightly marked by Paul Fizzy, he plays the ball into Brian Cassidy's feet ….

Cass flicks the ball around Paul Fizzy and as he turns elbows him in the solar plexus sending the giant centre-half to the floor gasping for his breath. He strikes the ball from the half way line where it sails over the goalkeeper who is yards off his line into the back of an empty net.

Cass grabs the grounded gasping giant centre-half Paul Fizzy by his armpit hair and whispers in his ear, "Where I come from revenge is sweet and I piss all over players like you." Cass runs off towards his teammates, standing on the hand of Paul Fizzy on his way.

It's one nil to the Golden Dock.

The Amsterdam Jets kick-off. Their stocky centre-midfielder gets the ball played to his feet. Young Cass slides in winning the ball, sending the Dutch man onto his arse. The stocky Dutch midfielder jumps up and stands on Cassidy's ankle. He darts away towards the ball but he runs into Reid Johnson path, who has seen what he has just done to young Cass.

Reid Johnson runs straight into the stocky Dutch midfielder butting him on the bridge of his nose. The Dutch midfielder falls to the ground, his nose full of blood pointing towards the North West.

Tony the Tiger is on the touchline with his hands in the air cursing the Golden Dock players.

Sam the referee blows his whistle so the managers can attend to the injured players. As Alex Sharp is seeing to young Cass, John Paul is gulping down the drinking water. He's blowing for tugs; the last few days are catching up with him. He's in no fit state to play football.

Sam restarts the match with a drop ball in the centre circle. Young Cass and Amsterdam Jets Jamie Dunne contest the drop ball. Cass wins and goes on a run, he dances past two Dutch players with ease. Running down the by-line, he knocks the ball in front of himself going through the gears motoring down the wing. The leggy centre-half Paul Fizzy moves towards Cass and slides towards the ball with his long legs stretched. As he's about to touch the moving ball, Cass puts his studs on the top of it and drags the ball back sending Paul Fizzy into the corner flag, ten feet ahead of the ball sending him into no man's land.

Cass smiles shouting, "See you later Ginger," as he passes the ball across the penalty area into the path of the incoming Todd Elliott, who passes the ball into an empty net. He runs away towards the dugout, standing in front of the manager and turns his back to Kevin Bird, pointing with both his thumbs showing him the number 11 on his jersey as the players mob him.

Peter Springsteen turns to Kevin Bird saying, "I think he's letting you know why he's wearing the number eleven shirt."

Kevin Bird shakes his head saying, "He only had to kick the ball into an empty net, my nan could have scored that and she's eighty-nine. It was Brian Cassidy who did all the work for that goal."

Two-nil to Golden Dock.

The Jets kick off. Jamie Dunne hits a shot from the half way line, Pat Arrow grasps the ball out of the air like a golden eagle catching its prey. Pat throws the ball out to John Paul who goes on a run. He beats four players then pulls up, out of gas. The ball runs out of play, John Paul bends over, his hands on his knees grasping for breath in these hot humid conditions. He puts up a hand telling Peter Springsteen to make a change.

Peter looks at the bench. He sees three injured players and Fred Kettle and Chopper Moon who look more like netball players than footballers.

"Get your tracksuit off Fred you're going on, go and play left back. Tell Mark Barrow I said move into midfield in John Pauls place," instructs Peter Springsteen.

"Okay, Peter I will make you proud of me."

"Never mind making me proud just get on the fucking pitch."

"I like your style Peter. I can see your method in your kidology there with you not giving Fred a confidence boost, seeing as he's never kicked a ball in his life or has never played football in his life. I see what you're doing there," says Birdy sarcastically.

"Shut up Birdy, it's your fault we have shit subs, you and your broken hand."

As John Paul walks off, Tony the Tiger runs onto the pitch getting into his face shouting, "Get off dickhead, you're shit."

John Paul looks at Tony the Tiger telling him to fuck off. As he passes him, the mascot kicks John Paul playfully up the arse. This makes him see red as he's kicked him in the bruised area so he turns and smacks Tony the Tiger in the mouth sending him reeling backwards to the ground. John Paul jumps on the mascot unleashing a barrage of blows. The players and management team have to drag him off Tony the Tiger. Pat Arrow goes into the back of his goal grabbing his goalkeeper's bag and runs over to John Paul and gets a can of Carling out of it cracking it open before handing it to John Paul.

"Calm down John Paul get that down your neck."

John Paul takes a swig of Carling and thanks Pat as he makes his way to the dugout.

Fred Kettle runs onto the pitch and stands next to Alan Jones. "Hey Alan, what's the offside rule?"

Alan, shaking his head replies, "Fred don't worry about the offside rule, just kick the ball up the field as hard as you can."

Cass is on the ball... He beats two players as he runs towards Paul fizzy doing an Ossie Ardiles flick over his head and then whizzes past him and plays the ball out to Reid Johnson who shoots with his trademark clenched right fist, (he clenches it when he's about to shoot). The ball hits the woodwork bouncing over the line and back into play, it's at the goal end where the Russians are standing. Sam the Welsh referee looks then waves play on.

Todd Elliott runs to Sam protesting. "That ball was behind the line it should be a goal."

Sam smiles at him, "Play on, I couldn't be sure it was all over the line."

"Sam, it was miles over the line."

"Todd, it's a pity one of them Russians in the corner wasn't a linesman because he could have given a goal like his grandad did in the sixty-six-world cup final," says Sam with a grin as wide as the Welsh valleys.

Todd being patriotic replies, "That's typical Welsh shit that Sam, we won the world cup fair and square just like that was a goal, fair and square."

Sam jogs away. "Get on with the game son before I book you for being English."

Amsterdam Jets press forward. Their tricky Dutch right-winger gets the ball down the right by-line and knocks it across the goal towards the back-post. Fred Kettle goes to kick it clear but spoons the ball back towards his own goal. Its heading for the bottom corner until Pat Arrow makes a world class stop, saving it with his right hand, knocking it around the post.

"I said kick it forward Fred, not fucking backwards."

"Sorry Alan, it was a miskick."

"That's okay then Fred cos you're a fucking misfit, how the fuck did you get to play today?"

"Jack Daniel's and brandy Alan."

"I will be needing a bottle of brandy if you do anymore of them miskicks."

In the corner, two of the Russians are talking to Sergei. They leave the ground via the stadium car park. Young Cass notices this and says to Todd, "Did you see that Todd? Two of the Russians have just left the Stadium. Do you think they're going for more men?"

"I don't know Cass, I thought it was all sorted."

The Jets have a free kick ten yards outside the penalty area central to the goal. Paul Fizzy smacks the ball over the wall. It's swerving, heading towards the top right corner of the goal like a scud missile. Somehow, Pat Arrow managers to tip it over the bar for another world class save.

Peter Springsteen standing next to Kevin Chivers says, "Kev, I can't believe the saves Pat has made, he's like Pickford."

"Yeah like *Pickford removals*."

"No, he won't be moving anywhere."

Smiling, Chivers replies, "Yeah, he has done well, he will make a good understudy."

Sam the Welsh referee looks at his watch and blows up for half time. The players make their way to the dressing room.

Golden Dock head in two nil up at half time.

The players are in the dressing room. They sit down while Peter Springsteen talks to the team. He turns to Bob and points to Pat. "Where did he learn to make saves like that?"

"I don't know, I've never ever seen our Pat in goal ever. As a kid he was a good saver but that was his money from his paper round."

"Well done Pat you're doing great mate," pipes up John Paul Anderson. Fred kettle is drinking water from the plastic bottles like it is going out of fashion

"Take it easy Fred, there'll be a water draught the way your guzzling that down," bellows Kevin Chivers.

"What are you Fred, a camel?" laughs John Cully.

"No, its hot out on that pitch, I haven't run that much in my life since I was getting chased by plod," says Fred as he wolfs down more water.

"You've only kicked it once Fred and that was a miskick," laughs Kevin Bird.

"I know," replies Fred. "I'm running trying to keep up with the offside rule."

The player's all laugh as Fred ducks his head into the team's water bucket.

Peter Springsteen sends them out telling them to do the same again in the second half reminding them that they will return to the dressing room as champions of Europe. The players run out of the dressing room roaring like lions going for the kill.

The Amsterdam Jets kick off the second half.

Jamie Dunne the Jets' all action midfielder goes on a run with the ball. He beats John Cully and glides past Fred Kettle and strikes the ball hard and low into the near post. Pat Arrow dives making yet another world class save. He throws the ball to Fred Kettle's feet who quickly passes it to Alan Jones two feet away from him. Fred Kettle can run no more. He waves to the bench to be taken off but they all think it's funny to wave back to him. The bench piss themselves laughing, there is a happy mood on the side-lines.

The game is flowing in the Golden Docks' favour.

Alan Jones plays the ball to Ant Hodge who plays it into Reid Johnson who side foots it to young Cass who runs at goal forty yards out. He does a step over whilst running towards Paul Fizzy, Cass nutmegs and goes past him. Paul Fizzy turns and lashes out, kicking Cass sending him tumbling over clutching hold of his ankle.

Sam the Welsh referee blows for a foul and books Paul Fizzy.

Paul Fizzy stands over young Cass shouting, "That's what happens to players that showboat, leave your showboating on the training ground Dickhead." Cass gets up. He places the ball down from thirty-five yards out and steps up whacking the ball over the wall. It sails into the top right corner of the net. Three nil to the Golden Dock.

Cass runs over to Paul Fizzy shouting, "Sail your boat on that, yer ginger cunt," as he's mobbed by his teammates. Before the game resumes, Golden Dock make a substitution. Fred Kettle limps off like a cowboy. Fred is panting for his breath. Kevin Parry replaces him filling in at left-back.

Fred Kettle lies on the floor next to the bench saying, "Never again."

Kevin Bird, laughing says, "You were only on twenty minutes, you only kicked the ball twice."

"Twenty minutes each half," whispers Fred. "I'm shattered."

Paul Fizzy is on the ball running with it. As he strides into the Golden Docks half Reid Johnson flies into Paul Fizzy with a two-footed knee-high tackle. He didn't even try to win the ball. Fizzy goes down in a lot of pain.

Reid stands over him shouting, "You kick the kid again and I'll do your other knee," Sam blows his whistle calling over Reid to book him. As Reid is getting booked, Alan Jones goes behind Fizzy and kicks him in the bottom of the back and yells, "If you kick young Cass again I'll rip your fucking head off ginger and spit in the hole."

As Fizzy sits up Ant Hodge approaches him and stamps on his right hand yelling, "Kick my mate again and I'll break your hands." With twenty minutes to go Reid Johnson is on a run with the ball, he's on the edge of the area. Cass is waiting for a pass off him then he notices Reid making his trademark clenched right fist. Cass runs into space taking the Dutch centre-half with him, Reid uses the free space to move into the box and cracks the ball high into the net.

Four nil to the Golden Dock.

The Golden Dock start to play one touch football, passing and moving. The Amsterdam Jets players are chasing thin air. Ted Hike is smiling on the touchline enjoying the game. The two Russian's return with a green canvas bag. It's about six feet long.

Cass watches the Russians as they return with the canvas bag. He turns to Todd Elliott saying, "Hey, Todd they've returned with a rocket launcher."

Todd smiling says, "It might be for that Fizzy the Jets ginger centre-half. He will need a rocket up his arse, if he gets in a one to one with me."

Time is ticking down… John Cully signals to the bench that he needs to come off. Peter Springsteen looks at the bench, there is no one fit to go on, he turns to Chopper Moon.

"Have your ever-played football Chopper?"

"Of course, I have soft-lad. I was the PlayStation 2014 world cup champion."

"I mean real football lad," moans Peter Springsteen.

"Nah," replies Chopper. "But it's just the same isn't it?"

"Yeah, it's just the same Chopper, now get out there and pretend you're on the PlayStation."

John Cully walks off giving Chopper a high-five as he runs on the pitch for his first ever football match. He runs to Ant Hodge.

"Hey, Ant where do I stand?"

"Stand on your feet Chopper," replies Ant Hodge who runs to mark a Dutch player. Chopper more confused, stands on the centre circle none the wiser. Cass has the ball at his feet. He goes on a run, he beats five Dutch players and is left one on one with the keeper, he stares at the keeper shuffling his feet before rounding the keeper and putting the ball into an empty net.

Five nil to the Golden Dock.

With just one minute left to play Jamie Dunne the Amsterdam Jets scouser is on the edge of the penalty box. He is running with the ball. Chopper Moon sees him and tackles Jamie just outside the box. They say tackled but it was more like a rugby tackle. Sam the Welsh referee points to the penalty spot.

Pat Arrow races out of his goal furious with the decision. "That foul was out of the area Sam, it's a free kick, not a penalty," fumes Pat.

"I'm the referee, I call the shots. It's a penalty Pat, now get back in your goal."

"Penalty my arse," fumes Pat as he makes his way back to his goal.

Jamie Dunne steps up, he drills the ball hard into the far-right bottom corner, Pat dives knocking the ball onto the inside of the post, it rebounds hitting him on the back and goes into the back of the net.

Five-one five to the Golden Dock.

Sam Llewellyn the Welsh referee blows the final whistle, the game is over.

Pat runs over to Sam manhandling him shouting, "It was never a penalty yer Welsh prick."

Sam stands his ground shouting. "Go away Pat, it wasn't even a close decision, your player rugby tackled their player. It's football not rugby. I know that more than most as I'm a Welsh rugby man, it's the worst foul I've ever seen as a referee. He dived with both arms around the player's ankle."

"Fuck off, yer Welsh sheep shagger, wanker," fumes Pat.

"Come on Now Pat, get it right, I'm either a sheep shagger or a wanker, I can't be both," says Sam. "I'm the referee and my decisions are final."

John Paul pulls Pat away from Sam. He's carrying two cans of Carling. He cracks open a can, handing it to him saying, "Drink that my friend and calm down, we all make mistakes, you were world class today."

Pat takes a swig out of the can and smiles, "Why have you bought two cans?" John Paul cracks open the other can swigs it looks at Pat and says, "It was a thirty-yard sprint to you from the touchline, that's the most I've ran today, so I knew I would need a refreshment."

They both start laughing walking away with their arms around each other's shoulder. Paul Fizzy shakes Cass's hand saying, "Well done kid, you were brilliant today, I've played in the Premier league for ten years against meatheads and none of them did what you did to me today. You have got the talent kid, get out there and set the football world alight. I was impressed with you today, you were on a different level."

Cass thanks Fizzy and walks towards Reid Johnson in the centre circle. The Russians come onto the pitch shouting. "истинный воин, истинный воин, истинный воин".

They're heading towards young Cass, the whole team gather together. Reid Johnson stands in front of him to protect him.

"Fuck me," says Cass. "They have got that rocket launcher in their bag, they're going to blast us with it."

"Don't be fucking stupid Cass," says Reid. "If it was a rocket launcher, they would fire it from a distance, not walk towards us and fire it."

"It might be a short distance rocket."

"What? Stop being daft, a rocket is a rocket," snaps Reid.

"Yeah, they're new you can buy them three for twenty quid on the QVC channel."

"Stop talking shit Cass."

"I'm shitting myself, never mind talking shit."

"Me too. It's squeaky bum time here not knowing what's coming next," says John Paul. Ted Hike sees them walking towards Cass and walks and stands next to him. The Russians are standing tall shouting louder and louder.

Jordan Jacobs stands next to Reid. Cass notices Jordan standing by Reid. "Jordan this is our fight, you go and save yourself mate."

Jordan smiling says, "Cass I'm a journalist you get the best story on the front line."

"истинный воин" the Russians chant as they approach the Golden Dock team. The players stand toe to toe ready for battle. Ted stands at the front of them all, the Russians are smiling as they get nearer.

"Fuck me. It's the smiling assassins," says Birdy.

"I'll make them smile on the other side of their faces," whispers Fred Kettle.

"Speak up Fred, they can't hear you," sniggers Chopper.

"They can't understand English anyway, the daft husky bastards," yells Chivers.

"Yes, we can my English friends, we embrace you in peace, the cold war is over, we greet you as fellow patriots," says Sergei.

The Golden Dock players and Russians come together, all the Russians embrace the players with open arms.

"Well done you really are a *Boy Wonder*, you're a boy in a man's body," says Sergei as shakes the hand of young Cass. He picks him up giving him a bear hug.

Cass smiles back at Sergei. "You sixteen, you are a boy, but play football like a giant, you are a man in my eyes."

"Thanks mate, but I still can't vote or drink alcohol," replies Cass.

"I would like your jersey, your top with your name on. I want to frame it and put it in my bar, on the wall to show people in my bar that we have a football jersey that was worn by a world class footballer." Cass looks at Ted Hike for approval. Ted Hike smiles at Cass giving him the thumbs up. Cass takes his Golden Dock jersey off and hands it to Sergei.

"So, is the war over Sergei?" asks Birdy.

"Yes, the war is over my friend. You and all your team are welcome in my bar anytime and won't ever have to pay for a drink again," says Sergei, he smiles looking at Cass. "Soft drinks only for you *Boy Wonder*." He points to Chopper saying, "You can have a job with me anytime mad English man."

"Ta mate, is it double pay at weekends?"

"Double pay and you can fight all weekend alongside me, my friend."

Chopper laughs giving Sergei a fist up sign.

Sergei opens the bag and pulls out the Red Russian football kit with "истинный воин" on the front. He gives it to Bob. "My friend a gift to your team from Russia with love."

"Thank you, Sergei we will wear it with pride."

"What does "истинный воин mean?" asks Birdy.

Sergei says, "It what we shout to you when we approached you, it means true warriors in Russian. We have a full kit for your team to wear when you play your football. You have shown us that you are all true warriors, we came here today to win the war, but we have witnessed your team spirit and realised when you lot were in bar you were sticking together as a team because you have such a strong bond and we are honoured to be your comrades. The cold war is over."

Ivanhoe, the Russian who hit Cass in the fight in the pub approaches Cass. He picks Cass up hugs him and apologises saying, "I'm sorry, you're a true warrior. I hit you with my best shot and you took it."

Cass smiles as he gets bear hugged, "I took it? That's a bit rich, after you hit me I could see three of everything."

"Back in Russia I was Ivanhoe Orgil. Super heavyweight champion three years in a row. I knocked out every fighter I fought. So I know you are tough man, never mind a boy and to show you I'm sorry for my actions, I present you with this solid gold chain with a gold boxing gloves pendant."

Cass accepts the gold chain and shakes Ivanhoe's hand. "Thank you Ivanhoe there is no hard feelings, I guess you were only doing your job."

The Russians shake every one of the player's hands, hugging them, then they leave the pitch happy. Sergei looks at Ted Hike and nods. Ted winks back at Sergei and gives him the thumbs up. As Sergei passes Cass he tells him he will treasure the football Jersey for ever and it will be on show in his bar to remind him of the day he went to a football match to destroy Englishmen, but came away proud to be allies with them without a punch being thrown and to witness the boy who played like a world class footballer.

Sergei ruffles Cass's hair as he leaves the pitch saying, "Sixteen, they make them big and powerful in England."

As the Russians disappear into the back streets Peter Springsteen pipes up, "Well now the Russian invasion is over and the cold war is over, let's get our trophies." Reid looks down at the kit bag and turns to Cass, "fucking rocket launcher, hey Cass?"

Laughing he says, "Shut up Reid, let's go get our medals and the cup."

The players go and receive their medals. They get a bronze medal on a ribbon with winners stamped on it. The cup is solid sliver. It's shaped like a vase with a rock-hard ten-inch marble base. They receive that cup for winning the match. The Golden Dock also win a cup for the fair play award, it's like the champions league trophy but has a ten-inch marble base attached to it.

The players walk back towards the dressing room with the cups in happy sprits, they're singing, throwing Champagne over each other as they pour it into the cups.

Bob gives Cass a bottle of water. "You drink that Cass it's better than drinking Champagne."

"Is that right Bob? So why did I just see you blast open a bottle of Champers, drink it then pour it over your head like a Champagne Charlie."

"That's cos, it's as close as I will get to being a superstar that's why, but you're a real superstar so get that water down your neck and shut up."

Jordan Jacobs pulls young Cass to one side. "Cass you were world class today, I knew you were good, but never in a million years did I expect that performance from you today, you exceeded all my expectations and more... You have to promise me you will take the right path in life and fulfil your true potential."

"Thanks Jordan I will do my best to be that player people see when I'm on the pitch enjoying myself." Cass goes into the dressing room.

"That win was for Frank," yells Cass.

"Hear, hear Cass," yell the players, "long live Frank."

Bob plays 'We are the champions' on Frank's iPod. Kevin Chivers videos the lads singing champions of Europe with the two cups and sends the video to Frank Rox. The celebrations are cut short by Peter Springsteen who tells the players to get a quick shower and get back to the hotel for a quick lunch and to pack their stuff for the return journey home. Ted Hike comes into the dressing room shaking all the player's hands with a smile the size of the Great Wall of China, he pats Bob on the head.

"Well done captain marvel you did good for an old man."

Bob smiles, "Now, now Ted, leave the old out of it. I'm still a young lad."

Ted picks up Pat Arrow. "You were outstanding today, you saved everything they threw at you."

Smiling, Pat says, "Yeah Ted I saved all the shots, but you saved the day by standing up to the Russians."

Ted smiles, "Oh that was nothing, it shows little men like you and me are not easy pushovers Pat and anyway I was not letting anything get in the way of me watching the Boy Wonder." Ted grabs young Cass in a head lock smiling, "Cass today I witnessed history, I saw the future *ballon de arc* player of the year in the making."

Cass smiling says, "I hope I don't let you down Ted."

With a smirk on his face Ted says, "Somehow, I don't think you will let me down Cass."

Max and Ronnie walk into the dressing room, pick up the two cups and tell Bob that they will take care of the cups and will bring them to the Rotterdam port in a few hours' time.

Bob is a bit miffed and looks at Ted Hike who assures him that it's okay and that Max and Ronnie will look after the cups, that they're safe in their hands.

Mills and Frankie Robo both come into the dressing room to congratulate the players and to wish them a safe journey home. Mills tells them anytime they come back to the Dam that they are always welcome at the Cafe Del Duff with open arms.

"Mills have you got any of them pies in stock?" asks Alan Jones.

"Alan they're special pies, they're not normal pies."

"I know," says Alan. "They're amazing pies, best I have ever had."

Mills is about to tell Alan that the pies are laced with cannabis. John Cully looks at Mills shaking his head whispering, "Say nothing he will kill me. I'll make sure he doesn't buy anymore."

The Jets manager passes the kit back into the Golden Docks dressing room thanking them for the match.

The players get into the minibuses and head back to the hotel. John Cully tells Alan Jones that Mills told him to tell him the bar is closed until tonight and that there are no pies in the bar, that they're out of stock.

It's now four in the afternoon, they're back at the hotel. Bob tells the players to freshen up, as they leave in one hour so get everything ready for the journey home. Cass and Alan Jones go out to the shops for last minute presents. Cass buys his mum an Apple I-phone with his winnings from the pool and darts tournaments. He buys his dad an Ajax football jersey and a Hugo boss t-shirt.

As they're passing a porn shop Alan Jones says, "Let's just pop in here for a second Cass." Alan picks up the porn magazines looking at them saying, "look at them Cass, they're hard-core porn." He hands Cass two magazines. Alan Jones laughing says, "I'll buy a few of them and sneak them into Bobs bag for when he gets checked at customs."

Cass inquisitively opens up one of the magazines and looks in it. As he does there is a tap on the shop window, it's only Chelsea. Cass looks at Chelsea and panics and throws the mags out of his hands only for them to hit the shop window landing at his feet.

"Oh, what have you got there hey? You dirty boy, do I see dirty magazines?"

Cass goes bright red stuttering, "Th th... they're not mer mer mine, I'm just holding them for Alan."

Chelsea laughing, "So that's what you came to Amsterdam for, hey Cass, you pervert."

"Chelsea have you seen the women in these mags they all have fannies like a wizard's sleeve."

"So why are you looking at them?"

"Of all the people for me to see at this moment and you turn up, they're not mine, honest. I came to the shops to buy me mum and dad a present and Alan dragged me in here, now like a magician, he's disappeared."

Chelsea laughing says, "I believe you Cass, millions wouldn't."

Chelsea steps into the shop, giving Cass a kiss before leaving, saying, "I'm going to board my coach, we're going to Rotterdam port now." Cass waves goodbye to Chelsea as she runs up the street.

Alan Jones reappears. "Where have you been Alan?" asks Cass.

"I've been in the back room via that black door over there," as Alan point towards the black door. "There's proper porn in that room, do you fancy a look?"

"No thanks," replies Cass. "I was just caught looking at your mags by Chelsea, the girl I met on the ferry."

"No way," laughs Alan. "What are the chances of that happening?"

"It's not funny. I felt like a right knobhead."

Alan pays for the magazines and they both leave the shop and head towards the hotel. As they reach the hotel, Alan tells Cass he has forgot something, that he will meet him in the hotel room.

Cass is greeted in the hotel lobby door by Jordan Jacobs and Sam Llewellyn. He shakes their hands and thanks Sam for refereeing the match and agrees with him that it was a penalty and that he made the right decision.

Sam laughs saying, "I don't think Pat was happy,"

"Forget Pat, you two just enjoy your time in the Dam."

"We will now the scousers are leaving," says Sam tongue in cheek.

Cass laughs and says his goodbyes as he goes to pack his bags for the journey home.

Alan goes to the Cafe Del Duff on the off chance of getting some of them amazing pies. Mills is not in the bar. Benny, the head barman is standing in for Mills.

Alan asks Benny if there are any pies for sale. Benny nods saying, "Yeah we have loads of them," Alan asks for twenty-five pies. Benny puts them into a thermal bag so they can stay fresh for a few days. Alan thanks him and pays him, munching on one of the pies. He returns to the hotel and puts his thermal bag inside his holdall and slips the porn mags at the bottom of Bob's bag.

The players all head to the minibuses for their return journey to the port of Rotterdam.

The manager of the hotel runs out shouting, "Mr Bob Arrow your bill." Bob is confused because he paid money upfront for their stay in the hotel.

"I've paid Mr Kroll."

"No, no, no, you have a five hundred Euro Champagne bill that was put on your room."

Bob, fuming shouts, "Who fucking bought the Champagne." John Paul, Ant Hodge, Alan Jones and Kevin Bird all point at Cass.

Bob looks at Cass saying, "Explain Cass?"

"It wasn't me Bob, well it was me but they all told me too. It was for them, I was drinking water. They were trying to impress the Swedish birds."

"Now, now, Cass," says John Cully. "What happens in pool 101 stays in pool 101."

The players all start laughing. Ant Hodge shouts over to Bob, "Just fucking pay it Bob, it's not your money, it's Max and Ronnie's money, pay the bill. We're champions of Europe Bob, champions of Europe." Bob pays the bill thanking the manager shouting, "Golden Dock the champions of Europe." The minibuses head off to Rotterdam to make the return journey to the mother land of Great Britain.

Chapter 12

The Cups sail home

The clouds in the port of Rotterdam have gone grey. It's 5.55pm. The two black Mercedes minibuses pull into the departure car park of the Dutch port. Fat Joe gets out of the minibus. His eyes are welled up as he takes out the kitbags. Scouse Ricko stands alongside him, he's squinting trying to hold back the tears.

Fat Joe hugs all the players, tears flow down his face as he says goodbye. Rubbing his eyes he mutters, "I'll miss you bunch of crazy bastards and don't you lot worry, I'll look after Frank Rox until he's fit to come home."

Scouse Ricko puts on his sunglasses to hide the tears.

"Why have you put your sunglasses on macho man the clouds are grey Ricko? It's going to rain, there is no sun out." yells Pat Arrow from the side of the minibus.

"It's the bright light Pat," replies Scouse Ricko.

"Yeah is that right?" replies Pat.

"Of course, it is Pat. I can't wait to see the back of you lot. You lot are nothing but trouble." Welling up, Scouse Ricko mutters. "You crazy fuckers are all a pain in the arse."

Max and Ronnie pull up in a taxi in their Golden Dock tracksuits. As they get out of the taxi they are carrying the cups. The players are stunned seeing Max and Ronnie in the Golden Dock tracksuits. Max lifts the cup shouting. "CHAMPIONS" the players look at each other.

Max and Ronnie nod to Fat Joe who passes them the dirty playing kits in the kit bags. "We will carry these for you Bob," says Max.

Ronnie chants, "Champions of Europe Bob!"

"Yeah, I don't remember you playing Ronnie, you or little legs Max," mutters Bob under his breath.

"We're your kit men today Bob, we will both show you how proud we are of you lot."

Bob shocked turns to Alex Sharp, "I've seen it all now Alex, what's their game?"

"Fucks knows," replies Alex. "At least we don't have to carry them smelly kits."

The players head towards the departure lounge. Tears roll down Fat Joe's face openly as he waves the players off. Scouse Ricko is holding back his own emotions behind his sunglasses. As the players disappear into the distance, tears flow down his cheeks beyond his sunglasses like a waterfall. He turns to Fat Joe and chokes, "I will miss them bastards, the spirit they carried together is installed in my heart forever."

Fat Joe sobbing mutters, "I know where you're coming from Ricko son, I'll miss them, they were all heroes in my book." He wipes his tears. "Now wipe them tears away and let's get out of here before we get parking tickets, we're supposed to be tough guys not dickheads crying over a team of legends."

"That's just what they were Joe, a gang of legends that will never be forgotten," replies Scouse Ricko.

"That lot would have put their lives on the line for us, unlike the usual horrible bastards we mingle with."

"I know Joe, we mingle with scum. I suppose it's part of the job, the company we work with."

"Your words have never been so true Ricko, that's why the memory of looking after them will never leave me."

Joe and Scouse Ricko reminisce about their time with the wild crazy fuckers with smiles on their faces as they jump into their minibuses to head back to the big house in The Hague.

Bob heads towards the booking office to confirm that they have the same cabins as their outward journey. The ferry ticket officer checks Bobs return paperwork and hands him the keys to the cabins. Bob gathers the players, telling them they're in the same rooms that they were in on their inward journey.

"Hey Bob, will our cabin still have four bunks in the cabin even though there is now three of us with Frank Rox still being in Holland?" enquires Chopper.

"Yeah," replies Bob.

"Get in there," yells Chopper. "We've got a spare bunk for all our bags."

It's now half past six in the evening. People are boarding the ferry, it sets sail at 9pm Dutch time and is due to arrive in Hull harbour at 8am English time. The players are going through passport control. They pass through except Peter Springsteen. The Dutch passport officer is not satisfied.

"Your different person sir to the man on the passport? The man in passport is much older with moustache?"

"No, that's me," replies Peter.

"No, no, no I see my supervisor. I'm not satisfied," says the Dutch passport officer.

Kevin Bird laughing shouts, "He was mugged mate, someone robbed his whiskers. Let him pass, he's the rock and roll king."

The passport officer is not amused. He gives Kevin Bird a dirty look and gestures to him to move along. His supervisor passes Peter Springsteen through to allow him to catch up to the rest of the team. They reach the customs area where a strong mob of forty plus drunken Jocks are singing 'Bonnie Scotland' making nuisances of themselves.

John Paul Anderson, Kevin Bird and Pat Arrow join in the singing with the Scottish drunks jumping up and down with them as they sing 'Scotland the brave.' The Scottish lads offer the three players a swig of whisky from their bottles. Kevin Bird and Pat Arrow decline but John Paul Anderson accepts taking a good swig. Bob looks over, his face is steaming.

"Hey, you three, get over here, get away from the Scottish party, they will get you into trouble."

Kevin, Pat and John Paul walk back to the team

"We were only having a sing song," protests Kevin Bird.

"I don't care," yells Bob.

"Oh, wind your neck in Bob," moans John Paul. "We're only having a laugh."

"Never mind, you're only having a laugh. That lot will be lucky to be able to board the ferry they're that drunk, and you three gobshites are bang in the middle of them, bouncing up and down singing," rants Bob.

"Okay point taken," replies Kevin Bird.

John Paul mutters to Pat, "What's his problem? We had a free drink and a good sing song going Pat."

"I know. It was Birdy singing out of tune that upset him I think."

Ant Hodge turns to Cass as he points at the Jocks. "Would you like to play for their team, *the hoops* Cass? Their fans are so passionate."

"Yeah, they're very passionate fans Ant," replies Cass. "I was on trial there last summer for two weeks. They wanted to me sign schoolboy forms but my dad wouldn't let me sign for anyone, he just let me go for the experience, to challenge myself against the best Scotland had to offer."

"How did you do against Scotland's finest?" asks Ant.

"I must have done okay," replies Cass. "They wanted me to sign for them."

"I expected nothing less from you Cass, you're the best player I have ever seen play football."

"To be honest Ant it was easy. I was too strong for the kids of my age, so they put me with their under 18's and I was too strong for them too. I was only fifteen, I want to play in a stronger league than the Scottish league. The Celts are a top club, it's just the league. It's a bit weak Ant I want to play in the Premier."

"Well, if you get your head down and follow the right path Cass, that will be the league you will play in, your future is in your own hands. You have the talent to reach the top," beams Ant Hodge.

"Thanks Ant, I appreciate your advice."

The players pass through customs. Three Dutch customs officers are pointing at Kevin Bird, Pat Arrow and John Paul Anderson as they pass.

The players board the ferry where Cass and Chelsea exchange cabin numbers as they pass each other. Bob tells the players to meet at the restaurant at ten o clock so that they can all have an evening meal together. The ferry sets sail at 9pm so all the players make their way to their cabins to relax and freshen up. Max and Ronnie make their way to their cabin with the two trophies tightly gripped in their hands with the kit bags over their shoulders.

Cass is in Bob's cabin. "Hey, Bob will it be okay if I put my bags in Chelsea's cabin? I'll be staying up all night with her, we'll be going through the passport control together so it makes sense."

Bob looks at Cass with a smile on his face, "Yes Cass, that will be okay but do it after the evening meal so we all have something to eat as a team and don't be late off the ferry with Chelsea. If you can do that for me everything will be okay." Cass nods and thanks Bob

The ferry motors whizz around. It's 9pm, it blasts its horns as it sails out of the harbour.

Cass is talking to Bob about signing professional forms in the cabin. Bob asks him his plans for next season. Cass explains there has been lots of interest but none of the clubs have been in touch and that his best mate Neil Parks has signed for the Blues.

"Don't worry Cass, you will soon be signed by a big club, if you take the right path, you'll be fine."

Cass smiles at Bob. "I really hope so Bob. It's my dream to be a professional footballer. I feel I've fallen behind not signing schoolboy's forms, my dad wouldn't let me... He said it's not worth it, but they coach them kids from a young age fitting them in with the team's system."

"Cass, you have natural talent that no coach could teach, no matter who you sign for you will fit into their system. The two years you have spent with us will set you up for the future, it will have taught you how to handle playing against men, it will toughen you up for the professional leagues."

"Thanks Bob. I have enjoyed the last two years playing for the Golden Dock."

"Cass in the two years you have been playing for the Golden Dock you have been a pleasure to watch. You have done things with the ball that amazes me week in week out. You're like a wizard with the ball and like a magician the way you glide pass players."

Cass thanks Bob once again as he leaves to see his cousin Reid Johnson.

John Paul Anderson and Pat Arrow are on the top deck of the ferry, drinking cans of Carling Black Label, counting windmills as they pass the sandbanks off the coast land of Holland. Peter Springsteen and John Arrow are drinking brandy and coke in the bar as they discuss today's match. Mark Barrow Kevin Parry and John Cully are having a power nap.

Cass goes to see Chelsea before he meets up with his cousin Reid. He knocks at Chelsea's cabin where she answers without any make-up on.

"Wow, you have natural beauty Chelsea."

"Shut up Cass," laughs Chelsea. "I can't talk right now."

They arrange to meet up after 12 midnight so Cass can have his evening meal with the rest of the players whilst Chelsea freshens up. Cass gives her a kiss then makes his way to Reid Johnson's cabin. Cass knocks on the door. He's greeted by a smiling Reid.

"Come on in champ," beams Reid. "Cass, you did me proud today. You were amazing."

Smiling, Cass replies, "You made me proud too, the only people you didn't fight when you were sticking up for me was that old man and his dog. I'm glad you had my back Reid."

Kevin Chivers and Alan Jones are in the arcade, the magnet is out drawing the ten pence pieces towards its magnetic force as the ferry bobs up and down on the waves of the North Sea. The ferry glides through the choppy waters as meal time arrives.

The players make their way to the restaurant. It's ten-o clock with the moonlit sky reflecting off the dark murky sea waters. Bob is at the entrance of the door greeting all the players as they arrive for their champions of Europe meal. Max and Ronnie arrive still in their Golden Dock tracksuits with the two trophies. They sit down on their own table placing the cups on the top of the table not letting them out of their sight.

"Look at them pair of wankers in our tracksuits," snarls Cully.

"I know it makes me sick. Them horrible bastards trying to be connected to our team," replies Chivers.

Alan Jones and Todd Elliott go over to the cups to pick them up. As Todd lifts the cup above his head Max and Ronnie start shouting, "Put them fucking trophies down!" They snatch the cups off Todd and Alan placing them back on the tables.

Max shouts, "Leave the fucking cups alone, don't fucking touch them." Alan annoyed shouts, "What's your fucking problem mate, they're our cups, we won them, so why can't we touch them?"

Max gets in Alan's face shouting, "Touch them again and I'll smash you up." Bob notices the commotion and walks over. "What's up?" asks Bob.

"It's them muppets," yells Alan Jones, pointing at Max and Ronnie. "They won't let us pick up the cups."

Bob looks at Max and Ronnie asking, "Is that right Ronnie?"

Ronnie looks at Bob with red misty eyes shouting, "Who do you think you are Bob? Talking to me like you're talking to a daft schoolkid. I'll fucking knock you out, you fucking prick."

"No, you won't bell end," yells Kevin Chivers. "You won't fucking knock any one out. I don't give a shit who you are, to me you're a ten a penny gangster, I'll punch you all over this ferry."

"Shut up soft-lad," snarls Max. "How are you going to do that with your good hand broken?"

"I could smack both your arses with my weaker hand, yer pair of tosspots."

Peter Springsteen steps in waving his white handkerchief over his head. "Hey Ronnie why can't the lads touch the cups? They did win them after all."

"If you all calm down I will explain why," replies Ronnie.

"It's you and little legs kicking off not us," yells Chopper.

"JUST LISTEN!" yells Ronnie. "We have been asked to make sure the cups stay undamaged, you only have the cups for ten months, then another team gets to play for them. We picked your team because you won the league and the Sean Quinn challenge cup, you did the double. That's why you were invited to play for these cups, but you only keep the cups for ten months, then they go back."

"That's a load of bollocks," yells Bob. "It's the first I've heard of that."

"That's how it is Bob," replies Max. "So why don't we all have something to eat before the cups get damaged."

"I hate that horrible little patronising man," whispers Alex to Bob.

The players make their way to their tables and sit eating their food in a mood that could cut the steaks just by looking at them. Alan Jones goes to the buffet bar and gets chips, gravy and two steak and kidney pies. He sits down next to Peter Springsteen saying, "Look I got two meat pies so you're not confused, like you were with my fish pie."

Peter with his serious face on looks at Alan and replies, "I'm more confused about them with our cups, they're a pair of horrible twats."

Alan munching on his pie replies, "Forget about them Peter go get yourself a couple of pies, they're delicious," as he licks his lips.

Bob is still in shock with Ronnie threatening to knock him out. Ant Hodge puts his arm around Bob saying, "Don't worry about that wanker Bob, we stick together as a team and as our skipper, if he touches you, he has to go through all of us."

Bob smiles and replies, "I know that Ant, no one could ever question our team spirit, he's just a bully and I've got no time for bullies. He's a fucking tosser, him and his mate."

Max and Ronnie finish their tea. Ronnie approaches Bob.

"Bob I'm sorry for having a go at you, I apologise for threatening to knock you out, it's down to me having a headache."

"It's okay Ronnie, forget about it, it's gone now but no one told us the cups would only be ours for ten months."

"Yeah, that how it rolls Bob, that's why we keep them with us until you lot get back to base." Max calls Ronnie over, they both leave the dining room with the cups in tow.

"We should nickname that Ronnie *the plug*," says Mark Barrow.

"Why's that Marko?" asks Kevin Bird. "Do you mean after that ugly goofy cunt from the Beano comic?"

"No soft-lad, it's because his mood switches all the time and you put plugs in switches." replies Mark Barrow.

"I thought you put them in plug sockets?"

"No, don't be stupid they're all the same thing, you plug in and switch on, Dick-brain," replies Barrow.

"I would love to plug the big horrible twat," pipes up Chopper Moon.

"Let's just forget about them now," says Alex Sharp. "Let's just enjoy the journey home. By the way, why do they call you Chopper? What's your real name?"

"Well he certainly didn't inherit that name from the legendary Ron Chopper Harris, the way he tackled that lad today," laughs Bob.

"Ron Chopper Harris who played for Chelsea back in the day Bob," smirks Chivers.

"Spot on Chivers lad," replies Bob.

"I'm called Chopper cos I have got a big chopper Bob."

"You wish," laughs Fred Kettle.

"Why didn't they nickname you Donkey Moon then?" smirks Birdy.

"Tell them the truth Chopper, you got that nickname cos as a kid you chopped up wood and sold it around the houses for firewood."

"Shut up Fred, you plank."

"Bob his real name is Alex." spurts Fred Kettle.

"Alex is a girl's name," splutters Birdy.

"Stop talking shit Birdy! Alexandra the Great was no bird, that's who I was named after yer fucking delusional juvenile delinquent."

"Alexandra the Great was Alexander III of Macedon who was king of the ancient Greek kingdom of Macedon and was a member of the Argead dynasty. He was born in Pella in 356 BC and was king at the age of twenty creating one of the largest empires of the ancient world by the age of thirty, stretching from Greece to north-western India," spurts Kevin Chivers.

Half pissed Pat Arrow and John Paul stand up saying, "We'll both drink to that, cheers."

"Chivers you're like a walking Wikipedia Google box of shit," laughs Birdy.

"No Birdy, It's called having a masters in History, unlike you who never went to school you thick fuckwit. People should read more books and educate themselves."

The players finish their meals and make their way to the duty-free shop except for Reid Johnson who goes to his cabin for a power nap. In the duty-free shop, the Scottish football posse are all pissed. They're bouncing up and down singing football songs, picking up the scotch whiskey and opening bottles in the shop swigging from them, then putting them back onto the shelf.

The Golden Dock players are messing at the front of the counter spraying the aftershave testers. The manageress who has her name 'Ceri' displayed on here badge, is serving on the front counter. Kevin Bird sprays her with a perfume tester and turns to her singing;

"OH CERI, YOU SMELL SO BEAUTIFUL WILL YOU MARRY ME?"

Ceri, laughing replies. "Piss off scouse. I bet you have a girl in every port."

"No Ceri my fair lady, my eyes belong only to you," replies Kevin Bird as he goes down on one knee with his right hand on his heart.

"Oh scouse you charmer, get real. I've got a shop to run."

Ceri takes her keys out of her pocket to put the perfume testers in the cabinets out of reach. Over in the far corner one of the Jocks knocks over a bottle of Jack Daniels, smashing it as it falls onto more bottles below. Ceri goes over to investigate, leaving her keys on the table behind the counter. Quick as a flash Mark Barrow spots the keys.

"Hey Birdy, lean over and block the closed-circuit camera, stand in front of Cass."

"Will do. Is that okay Marco?"

"That's fucking spot on lad, Cass lean over the counter pass me them keys," whispers Mark Barrow.

Cass looks both ways, leans over and gets the keys and passes them behind to Mark Barrow who goes to the display cabinet on the shop floor again getting Kevin Bird to block out the closed-circuit camera. Mark Barrow fumbles with the keys until he finds the cabinet key where the Rolex watches are on display. He opens it and as quick as a flash takes out two fifteen-thousand-pounds Rolex diamond encrusted watches. Carefully checking the shop floor, he locks the cabinet just as Ceri makes her way back to the counter. Mark passes Cass the keys who places them back behind the counter as Kevin Bird blocks the closed-circuit camera with his huge skinny frame.

Ceri, the shop manageress is back at the counter moaning about the Jock lads to her colleague who is at the far end of the counter, when she sees her keys. "Oh, my word, I'm so dizzy at times, I left my keys on the table. It's lucky I had my scousers in shining armour protecting my counter."

"So, you're a dizzy blonde hey Ceri? Just my type, just like my wife," says Kevin Bird.

Laughing, Ant Hodge says, "That's a classic that soft arse, what a boss chat up line that was Birdy, yer best hope she's a swinger or you're fucked mate."

Ceri looks at Kevin Bird, "Wife hey big balls? Your charm is believable but your bullshit can be smelt a mile away, so take your scouse arse out my shop and have a safe journey home to your wife."

All the players walk out of the shop laughing at Kevin Bird.

Kevin Chivers slaps Birdy on the head saying, "You're fucking thick Birdy, you're not even married, you were in there as well."

Birdy, smiling says, "Aww never mind, there's plenty more fish in the sea, especially when you're on a ferry in the middle of the North-Sea," Birdy jumps up and does a little jig as he follows the rest of the players walking to their cabins. Mark Barrow hands Cass one of the Rolex watches and winks at him and says, "That's your share Cass."

Cass heads to his cabin, gets his bags and heads towards Chelsea's cabin. On his way he sees Kevin Parry.

"Where you going Cass?"

"I'm taking my bags to Chelsea's cabin and leaving them there till the morning Kev."

Kevin Parry goes into his bag and throws Cass a Coco Channel perfume. "Here you go Cass, that's for you to give to Chelsea. Make a good impression, in fact my friend you can have the whole bag, there is six boxes of Golden Virginia tobacco in it, you can have the lot. It's my way of saying sorry for what happened in The Hague."

Cass thanks Kevin Parry and heads towards Chelsea's cabin, where he's greeted by a beautiful beaming smile from Chelsea. Her long dark hair is shining like a model from a shampoo advert, she looks stunning. Cass gives Chelsea the Coco Channel perfume. She's shocked and ecstatic at the same time, she tries to pick Cass up but can't budge him, so she just gives him a big hug.

The ferry is sailing through the night as the choppy sea waves whistle out in the dark sea sky.

Cass and Chelsea have a stroll around the ferry on the open air top deck. Pat Arrow and John Paul Anderson are sitting on the bench with the sea breeze hitting them in their faces as they sing, "SHOW ME THE WAY TO GO HOME, I'M TIRED AND I WANT TO GO TO BED, FOR A WANK, I HAD A LITTLE DRINK OVER AN HOUR AGO AND IT'S GONE RIGHT TO MY HEAD," They're both drinking cans of Carling Black Label. They see Cass and Chelsea and give them both the thumbs up and start singing, "THE LOVE BOAT. IT'S EXCITING

AND NEW, CASS HAS FALLEN IN LOVE AND WE WILL DRINK TO THAT TOO," as they gulp the Carling down their necks.

Cass laughs and shouts, "Yer pair of drunken bastards."

"We just like a drink Cass," laughs John Paul.

Cass and Chelsea's next stop is the ferry's arcade games room. Kevin Chivers has his magnet working its magic on the ten pence drop machines. Alan Jones and Ant Hodge are on the pin-ball machines concentrating like pinball wizards. Ian Craig is on the fruit machine but it doesn't look like he's winning as he keeps kicking the bottom of the fruit machine. Todd Elliott is making do with the free Wi-Fi connection as he catches up with his company's workload on his laptop. Kevin Bird is playing Kevin Parry at pool, they're all oblivious to Cass and Chelsea in the room so they both sneak out and head for the bar.

The sea breeze cuts through the ferry's steel as the waves clatter into the stern.

Reid Johnson is fast asleep in his bunk. He failed to resurface after his power nap deciding to catch up on sleep he missed on the club's tour of Holland.

Max and Ronnie sleep with the cups in their bunks never letting them out of their sight guarding them like a lion guarding its pride.

Cass and Chelsea walk into the bar. Bob, Peter Springsteen, Alex Sharp and John Arrow are seated in the corner, discussing the incoming football season. They see Cass and wave.

Peter Springsteen shouts, "Water only Cass." Young Cass looks over at the committee members showing them the middle finger and laughs shouting, "sit on that fuckers." Chelsea goes the bar.

The night sky is awash with shooting stars as the night air gets colder and colder.

Cass and Chelsea finish their drinks and go to the top deck watching the stars and the moon as the ferry sails to Hull. They chat all night long till the dark night makes way for the rising sun. It lights up the sea. They have chatted all night into the early hours of the morning. They're made up in each other's company. Cass makes a pact with Chelsea, they both lock index fingers saying that they will always only be a phone call away no matter where they are in the world. They seal their pact with a kiss, then both make their way to Chelsea's cabin to get their bags, then they head to the bridge so they can exit the ferry as it cruises into Hull harbour.

The clouds have gone dark as the morning light fades behind them. They look into each other's eyes as they exchange phone numbers. Cass writes his home phone number on Chelsea's hand as they wait patiently to exit the ferry.

Chapter 13

The calm before the storm

As the ferry moors into the calm waters of the Hull docks, there are dark grey clouds gathering. Cass is the first off the gang plank with Chelsea in tow. They head towards the passport control pass-point. Young Cass is struggling carrying his bags. Chelsea notices this and takes his duty-free bags off him that have the Rolex watch and Tobacco in. She looks at him, "I can't watch you struggle. I'll carry these bags for you." They smile at each other with not a care in the world. As they reach passport control, there are four suited men standing, watching every movement. As Cass shows his passport, the officer takes a look at then signals to the suited men. Cass and Chelsea are separated. Cass is taken away and is being led off by two of the suited men. He realises Chelsea has his bags and turns to her and shouts;

"Chelsea me - ."

Chelsea interrupts Cass in mid flow of his sentence, "- I know, I love you too, I'll ring you," and winks at him as she's ushered towards customs control in the opposite direction.

Cass is led away by the two custom officers into a big empty room. There are rows of tables either side. He's led to the tables at the far end of the room and told to wait. The two suited men leave and lock the door behind them, leaving Cass alone in the big square room. Cass looks around; it has three exits. All the doors are locked.

Alan Jones who was 30 yards behind Cass as he headed towards passport control has seen what happened to Cass and has double backed to tell the rest of the players. The team are bunched up by the toilets at the top of the walkway. Alan tells them what he has just seen.

Mark Barrow asks Alan, "Was it just Cass?"

"Yeah," replies Alan.

"SHIT," says Mark Barrow. "They'll be after the watches me and Cass have. I'll have to get rid of mine in the bogs."

"What watches?" pipes up Reid.

"The Rolex's, the watches we got from the duty-free last night," replies Mark Barrow.

"What are you talking about?" snarls Reid. "I was asleep all night, what fucking Rolex watches?" Mark Barrow tells Reid how they got the watches from the duty-free shop.

Reid fuming starts punching Mark Barrow. He hits him with two right hooks, a left upper-cut and two big haymakers to his head knocking him on his arse. Reid is shouting, "Are you fucking soft, he'll be nicked now, his life ruined, you fucking tit."

Reid is grabbed away, he volleys Mark Barrow in the face shouting, "Why involve Cass? He'll be fucked now, you fucking dickhead, I'm going to rip your fucking head off."

Mark Barrow gets up and runs to the toilets to get rid of the watch. Reid is restrained by the players.

Bob asks Reid what has happened. Mark Barrow goes into the toilet cubicle and lifts up the cisterns lid and places the diamond encrusted Rolex watch into the cistern and closes the lid back into place. He goes to the sinks and washes the blood from his face with cold water. As he's swilling his face, Bob kicks open the toilets door heading towards Mark Barrow and grabs him by the throat lifting him off both feet and carries him into the walkway. The rest of the players have gathered as he chokes Mark Barrow.

"If anything happens to young Cass, I'll fucking take your last breath."

Bob releases his grip sending Mark Barrow to the floor choking and gasping for his breath. He mumbles, "I'll take the rap for Cass, I'll say it's mine, I'll say I made him carry it and that the watch is mine."

Chopper Moon standing over Mark Barrow says, "They will still nick him you gobshite and if they do I'll fucking slice you up, you fucking muppet."

Alex Sharp jumps in saying, "Everyone calm down, let's just go through passport control. Let's see what happens and we'll deal with it then."

The players make their way towards passport control. Reid Johnson is sweating profusely as he walks, he's so worried about his cousin Brian Cassidy. As each member of the Golden Dock show their passports, the guards take their passports and look towards the suited men who in return lead each player away to the big square room where Cass is being held. Reid Johnson shows his passport. The guard takes it and gives the suited men a thumb up. Reid is led away to a different room all by himself.

Ronnie and Max walk through passport control in their Golden Dock tracksuits, carrying a cup each plus the smelly kits.

The players enter the room. Cass is pleased to see them. Bob goes straight to him. "Are you okay Cass? Give me the watch, I'll carry it for you. You're not getting nicked for it, you have too much of a bright future ahead of you. I keep telling you that you have to take the right path."

Mark Barrow goes straight to Cass. "Give me that watch Cass, I'm to blame, I'm not having you getting nicked, place it in my pocket now whilst no one is looking." Mark Barrow opens his jacket pocket.

Cass looks at both Bob and Mark and smiles.

"The pair of you need to calm down, I haven't got the watch or anything else as a matter of fact. Chelsea was carrying my duty-free bags because I was struggling and I didn't have time to get it back off her because they separated us and lead me to this room and locked the doors behind me."

Bob and Mark both burst out laughing, Cass looks at them and notices the swelling and cuts on Mark Barrow's neck and face.

"What are you both laughing at?" asks Cass. "What have you done to your face and neck Mark?"

"Oh, it's nothing," quips Mark.

"He just had a misunderstanding with two nutters, but it's been solved now." laughs Bob.

"It sure has Bob," laughs Mark as they hug each other and make up.

On overhearing the conversation, Kevin Parry whispers to young Cass, "Did the duty-free bag have the tobacco and perfume in too Cass?"

"Yeah," replies Cass. "It's sweet."

"Thank fuck for that," Kevin Parry whispers under his breath. "I wouldn't want them two nutters having a misunderstanding with me now, would I?" he walks away talking to himself.

As the players are gathering in the corner, the Scottish party are put in the opposite side. They enter singing 'William Wallace Freedom.'

Reid Johnson is in a tiny separate room with three suited custom officers.

"Why have you bought me in here?" enquires Reid.

"We noticed how much you was perspiring son," replies the suited officer.

"I'm not your son, so is it a crime to sweat now?"

"What are you hiding?" asks the teacher-looking customs officer, as the little fat customs officer searches his bags.

"I'm not hiding nothing you fucking bell end."

"Why are you perspiring so much?" replies the customs officer.

"It must be to do with my job in Iceland, packing the fridges, so when I'm not in the shop any warm weather makes me sweat."

"So, what will I find in these bags?" asks the fat customs officer.

"Nothing, search my bags fatty, see what you can find."

"We're going to search more than your bags son," replies the teacher-looking customs officer as they lead him into the next room to do a strip search on him.

During the search, Reid looks at the custom officer snarling, "Is this why you took this job? To strip search men, why don't you get a real job?"

"We do these searches so no pieces of shit enter the U.K. uninvited," replies the fat customs officer with a smirk on his face.

"You're funny you fatty, why aren't you a comedian? You already have the look of one of them fat comedians." Reid is clean. He's taken back into the tiny room.

"So, what are you hiding son?" asks the fat customs officer.

"I'm not your son fatty."

"Let's cut the insults, just tell us what you're hiding?"

"You tell me Sherlock. You've given me a full body search and searched my bags, doesn't that give you your conclusion with you being *'detective I-know- fuck-all'*? I'm hiding nothing!"

"So, why are you sweating?" asks the teacher-looking officer.

"Because it's hot, numb-nuts."

"I don't believe that, us three are not sweating and we're wearing suits," the fat customs officer says as he stands over Reid.

"Well that has surprised me," replies Reid. "I'm astonished, especially with you being a fat cunt, you might not be sweating but you stink of B.O. fatty so move them pits away from me before I put in a complaint of G.B.H to my nostrils, you smelly horrible fat man."

"You're a nasty little perspiring man, aren't you son?" says the bearded customs officer.

"No, I'm not nasty nor am I your son hairy chin man, I'm sweating because it's hot, it must be my Eskimo blood I've got in me from my Eskimo grandad."

"Don't be funny, or you'll be arrested and detained," yells the fat customs officer.

"Arrested for what?" snaps Reid. "Arrested for sweating and having to listen to your shit?"

"No, for being a mouthy prick," yells the fat customs officer.

"Well arrest me then fatty," yells Reid. "It should read well in the newspapers; *SCOUSER ARRESTED FOR SWEATING IN A HEATWAVE*."

The three suited customs officers chat amongst themselves looking Reid up and down. The fat customs officer walks over to him handing him his passport, "Get your bags and clear off, you're free to go."

"About fucking time," replies Reid. "You're all fucking muppets, strip searching me for fuck all."

The teacher-looking customs officer ushers Reid out towards the exit door, "we have a job to do, and we're only doing our job."

"Whatever." replies Reid. "Do a job on fatty, buy him a deodorant for his smelly pits."

"You're free to go, enjoy your day."

"Don't worry I will," replies Reid as he walks out the exit door.

The three suited men make their way into the big room, where the rest of the Golden Dock players are being kept waiting. They head towards the Golden Dock players and explain that their bags will be searched. They are told to form a line where they will be searched on the long row of tables, three at a time, and that when they are cleared to go, the customs officer at the end of the table will return their passports. There are four customs officer's at the exit door at the side of the tables. The Scottish group are checked the same way as the Golden Dock players. The first three to get searched are Bob, John Arrow and Peter Springsteen. Their bags are searched by three different customs officers.

"Excuse me sir, can I ask why we are being treated this way?" Bob politely asks the teacher-looking customs officer.

The customs officer looks at Bob straight faced and replies, "It's just routine sir."

"Routine my arse," snaps Peter Springsteen. "That's a load of bollocks."

The fat looking customs officer who is searching Peter's bags looks him in the eye, "If you have nothing to hide sir, you will have nothing to worry about, will you?" as he makes a thorough search of his two bags.

"Whilst you're doing that thorough search, see if you can find my moustache at the bottom of my bag," sniggers Peter.

John Arrow pipes up, "This is a disgrace," as the bearded customs officer searches his bags. The officer looks up at him and says. "It's only a disgrace, if you're all completely innocent sir."

"What is that supposed to mean?" asks John Arrow.

"It means what it says sir, only time will decide what the outcome will be," says the bearded customs officer with a smarmy look on his face.

"How long will this take?" asks Bob.

"Only as long as it takes you to explain these magazines," replies the teacher- looking customs officer as he pulls the porn magazines out of Bob's bag,

"What magazines?"

"These porn magazines sir," replies the customs officer as he points to the magazines.

Bob looks at Alan Jones who's laughing behind him, he snarls him giving him an icy stare. "It's not a crime is it?"

"No sir, you're free to go, perverts that way."

Bob, Peter Springsteen and John Arrow are cleared to go. They get their passports from the customs officer at the end of the table and proceed out of the doors, making their way to the car park. They reach the open doors, the clouds are grey, there is little light in the sky. It's 9am and there is a storm brewing.

Bob is greeted by Reid Johnson who is pacing up and down by John Arrows parked car.

"Where's Cass? What's happened to him?" asks Reid nervously as he bites his fingernails.

"Don't worry," replies Bob. "He's okay that girl Kelsie took his duty-free bags off him with all his stuff in."

"Kelsie? Who the fuck is Kelsie?" asks Reid.

"The girl with the Brown Hair."

"Do you mean Chelsea?"

"Yeah that's her, the girl who he met on the ferry."

"Where is he now?"

"They're in a big room getting searched," replies Bob. "They won't be long."

"I won't settle till Cass is out of that room," Reid says as he paces up and down.

Next to get searched are Max and Ronnie, both holding a cup. Just before they move to the tables, Max shoves the kit bag with the new Russian kit in it into Kevin Bird's chest giving him a stern look telling him to carry the kit. Kevin Bird reluctantly agrees and takes the Russian kit bag with him as his bags are searched.

In the waiting queue John Cully calls Ant Hodge over, "Have you got some clear hair gel and Vaseline in your bag Ant?"

He looks in his bag and pulls out the clear air gel and Vaseline and gives it to Cully who squeezes the gel into the crotch of his black Armani boxer shorts and mixes it with Vaseline and adds milk to it. He spreads it inside the crotch of his boxer shorts until it's thick and slimy with an off-white colour.

Laughing Alan Jones pulls out a brown sauce sachet and gives it to Ant Hodge who squeezes it into his jock strap at the back end and adds it with the gel and Vaseline, mixing it into a dollop, so it's thick and brown.

Kevin Bird is at the desk bored, getting his bags checked. The fat customs officer asks him about the Russian kit in the kit bag. Max butts in, "That's our third kit, we took three kits for the tournament we played in."

Kevin Bird looks baffled as he wonders where this tournament was.

The bearded customs officer is searching Max's bags. "So how many games did you play then?" enquires the fat customs officer.

"Five," replies Max before Birdy's lips could move.

"Five football matches, is that why these kits stink?" asks the bearded customs officer to Max.

"Yeah sorry about that." says Max. "It's just smelly socks and shorts with jerseys full of spit, snot and Vaseline."

"It's lucky we're wearing these gloves," says the teacher-looking customs officer as he searches Ronnie's bags.

"We're used to handing the smelly kits," says Ronnie. "We're the kit men for the team, they're usually caked in mud. We'll get home and take them to the laundrette and wash and dry them, getting them ready for the next match."

Kevin Bird is standing at the tables confused and bewildered as Max and Ronnie reel out the bullshit.

"Why have you got two big cups like that?" enquires the bearded customs officer.

"One is for winning the group stage of the tournament," says Max. "The other one is for winning the tournament outright."

Kevin Bird looks at Max and Ronnie amazed by the lies and starts making Pinocchio signs with his nose. Ronnie gives him an icy cold stare so Kevin just zips up his bags. The fat customs officer waves Kevin through and shows him where to get his passport. As Max and Ronnie are walking away they're stopped by the bearded customs officer.

"Can we have a picture with the cup?"

Max looks at Ronnie, "Yeah, no problem mate," says Ronnie as he puts them on the table.

"Can we hold them, as you take pictures?" asks the fat customs officer.

"Yes, no problem," replies Ronnie. "They're only cheap cups, made to look good, they could fall to pieces at any moment."

The bearded customs officer hands Ronnie his camera phone for him to take the picture. The bearded customs officer and the fat customs officer each hold a cup each as the teacher-looking customs officer stands behind them. Ronnie takes the picture and hands back the phone, then he goes to the table to retrieve the cups.

"They're very heavy for sliver cups," says the bearded customs officer.

"Why is that?" asks the fat customs officer.

"It's because they're so big and made of solid cheap marble bases," replies Max.

"They look expensive," says the teacher looking customs officer.

"They're just made to look good, they're not even worth a fiver in scrap," says Ronnie.

The three customs officers look at each other and allow Max and Ronnie to pass showing them where to pick up their passports.

Next to the tables to be searched are John Cully, Ant Hodge and Alan Jones.

Cully drop his bags on the tables and looks at the bearded customs officer and in a seductive voice says, "Hello big boy, are them rubber gloves for my internal?" as he bends over and points to his bum in the air.

"Behave son or you'll be arrested," says the bearded customs officer.

"Hmmmm," replies Cully. "Handcuffs are my favourite sex toy, you're so dominant big boy."

The bearded customs officer gives Cully an icy stare. He puts his hand inside his bag and the gel and Vaseline go on his gloves as he pulls out the underpants.

"What's that?" snaps the beaded customs officer as he takes off the gloves and puts them in the waste bin.

"Oh, they're my Armani underpants, I wear black most nights, do you like them?" asks Cully winking.

"No, I'm asking what's that stuff in them?"

"Oh sorry," replies Cully. "That's from the other night, when we were watching porn about bearded men. I must have got too excited and filled my undies," says Cully as he winks at the bearded customs office.

"That's disgusting that son and watch your tongue that could get you in trouble," snaps the bearded customs officer.

"That's a bit harsh sir, it's not an arresting offence is it sir?" says Cully as he looks at Ant Hodge and sniggers.

Ant Hodge is standing getting his bag searched, the teacher-looking customs officer searches the bag and pulls out the jock strap where the hair gel, brown sauce and Vaseline are all mixed together. The teacher-looking officer picks it up, careful not to drop any of the contents inside the jock strap, "is that what I think it is son?" asks the teacher looking customs officer.

"Yeah, I'm afraid so," says Ant Hodge. "I was a bit loose that day."

"That is so wrong son. That is pure filth. Haven't you heard of going the toilet?" replies the teacher-looking customs officer.

"Of course," replies Ant Hodge. "It's hard finding a toilet in the middle of a football match, so you just shit where you stand."

The teacher-looking officer looks at Ant Hodge, "Is there any more of this in the bag shitty arse?"

Ant Hodge holding in his laugh shrugs his shoulders, "I'm not sure sir, you best check."

"No thanks," replies the teacher-looking customs officer. "You're free to go," as he drops the jock strap back into the bag. "Pure filth that son, pure filth," as he points him towards the custom officer with the passports.

Ant Hodge reaches out his hand "Thank you sir," the teacher-looking customs officer turns away declining the hand shake.

Alan Jones puts his bags down smiling at the fat customs officer, "Hello fatty, hurry up and check my bags, then you can trot over there and fetch my passport with your little piggy feet."

Not amused the fat customs officer starts checking his bags. He pulls out a bag of pies and puts them on the table smelling them. "What are these son?" asks the fat customs officer.

"They're pies fat boy, you know them things that you munch on, you've most probably eaten loads of them fatty," laughs Alan Jones.

"Pies are they son?" replies the fat customs officer.

"Yeah pies fat arse," replies Alan Jones. "This is England not Australia, we can eat pies little fat man, we are allowed to bring food back home with us."

"Yes, you're correct, this is England, food is allowed yes, cannabis pies no sir, we call that smuggling. It's a class B drug, you have fourteen of them. I'm arresting you on account of possession of a class B drug with intent to smuggle them into the United Kingdom," replies the fat customs officer.

"Fuck off, are you messing?" snaps Alan Jones as he looks at John Cully. "Is this a joke Cully? These are the pies Mills give me that you got me when we were in the Café Dell Duff."

"It's no joke mate, I told you not to go back for the pies, I told you Mills didn't have any left."

"You little shit Cully, you've stitched me up. I'm going to rip your head off."

"No, I didn't Alan, replies Cully. "I told you not to go for pies."

The fat customs officer calls over the customs officer by the exit to come and take Alan Jones away. As he's leads him away Cully shouts. "Don't worry Alan, we'll get you out."

Alan Jones looks back laughing, "Don't bother Cully, you've done enough, I know it's my own fault for my love of pies."

Next up is Chopper Moon, Todd Elliott and young Brian Cassidy. They fly past the customs officers without problems.

Pat Arrow stands at the table while his bag is getting searched holding a four pack of Carling. As he swigs the can the bearded customs officer looks at him and shakes his head saying, "It's a bit early to be drinking that isn't it? It's 9 in the morning."

"No not really," replies Pat. "To be honest, it's late for me because I work nights. Your morning is my night."

Shaking his head, the bearded customs officer replies, "Were you working last night then?"

"No, don't be silly mate it was my night off."

On the next table John Paul Anderson is drinking a can of Carling, he burps into the fat custom officer's face as he searches his bags.

"Hey, do me a favour lad, put your can down," says the fat customs officer.

"No, I won't, fuck off fatty, I'm not breaking the law," replies John Paul with a cocky attitude.

Ian Craig is getting his bag searched by the teacher-looking customs officer, he's cleared and free to go. He passes John Paul singing, "Fatty's going to get yer."

Pat is cleared to go and nudges John Paul saying, "I'll get us some more cans, hurry up."

The fat customs officer finds a chunk of cannabis in John Pauls shorts whilst searching his bag, "What's this son?" says the fat customs officer, as he puts the cannabis on the table.

"Oh, that's nothing," replies John Paul. "That's just my smoke fatty."

"Oh, is that right," says the fat customs officer. "Where I come from its called smuggling a class B drug into the United Kingdom, which is a crime that you get arrested for."

"No, no, no," replies John Paul wavering his hands in the air. "I haven't smuggled it in because I brought it with me from Liverpool when we left last week."

"Oh, I see, so you're a double smuggling criminal then," replies the fat customs officer as he waves to the waiting customs officers to take John Paul away to be detained. "Leave your can of Carling sir, it's a criminal offence to drink alcohol while you're under arrest, it's not allowed," the fat customs officer says in a cocky voice as John Paul is lead away to the cells.

Fred Kettle is searched by the bearded customs officer and cleared to go. Alex Sharp is searched by the teacher-looking customs officer and is freed to go. The last three to be searched are Kevin Chivers, Kevin Parry and Mark Barrow.

Kevin Chivers puts his bags on the table as the teacher looking customs officer searches Mark Barrow's bags and waves him past. The bearded customs officer goes into Kevin Chivers bags pulling bags and bags of ten pence pieces out of it placing them on the table.

"What's with all the coins son?" asks the bearded customs officer.

"It's ten pence's in the bags," replies Kevin Chivers.

"I can see that son, where did they all come from?" replies the bearded customs office.

"It's my savings," replies Kevin Chivers.

"Yeah so why did you bring it son?" replies the bearded customs officer not convinced about his explanation.

"I brought my coins so I could exchange them into Euros," explains Kevin.

"They don't change coins son, I have just weighed it, there is over six hundred pounds in coins in your bags," replies the bearded customs officer.

"I know that now," replies Chivers. "I nearly starved, I had no money to spend because of that coin rule. I'm wasting away."

The customs officer looks at the stocky build of Kevin Chivers but has no choice but to wave him through even though he's not fully convinced of his story.

Kevin Parry is last to be searched. "Hello boys, I see you're saving the best till last," laughs Kevin Parry as he tries to get them onside.

The fat customs officer starts to empty Kevin Parry's bags. He stacks 30 boxes of Golden Virginia tobacco onto the table.

"What's this?" enquires the fat customs officer.

"What do you think it is?" rants Kevin Parry. "I'm allowed to bring back as many as I want."

"Are these for you sir?" asks the fat customs officer.

"Of course," yells Kevin Parry. "Who do you think they're for?"

"So, you're a heavy smoker sir?" replies the fat customs officer.

"Yeah, why fat boy, what's with all the silly questions?" snaps Kevin Parry.

"They're not silly questions," replies the fat customs officer. "It's just not adding up, a heavy smoker with thirty boxes of Golden Virginia tobacco, with a total of three hundred pouches and yet not a cigarette paper in sight or a lighter, what do you do chew the tobacco?"

"No fatty, I don't," snaps Parry.

"Have you got your receipts for the purchase of these boxes of Golden Virginia?" asks the bearded customs officer.

"No, I haven't, why would I?" replies Kevin Parry. "I had them but they blew out my hand into the sea, it was windy on the way home."

The teacher-looking customs officer walks to the table saying, "Sir, we have just watched the ferry duty-free shop closed-circuit camera and we have identified you walking out of the duty free with boxes of Golden Virginia tobacco without paying."

"I don't think so mate."

"The camera never lies son, you're nicked."

Kevin Parry is led away to the cells in the customs section of Hull harbour. In the cell, Kevin Parry is greeted by John Paul Anderson and Alan Jones. As they're sitting in the cell, Alan Jones turns to Kevin and John Paul.

"What happens now lads?"

"We will be taken to the police station then charged," replies Kevin Parry.

Alan Jones looks John Pauls and Kevin in the face laughing, "Them customs officers are fucking daft, they didn't do a body search on me, I still have six of them pies in my pocket."

"No way," laughs John Paul. "Quick, share them out two each, let's eat the evidence."

"Fuck off," replies Alan. "They're too good to share."

"Don't be stupid Alan, its better if we're all stoned in here, let's all be on the same wavelength, plus you're anti-drug anyway," says John Paul with his hand held out.

"Yeah, your right, I'm anti-drug but I'm not anti-pie."

"Power to the people Alan, hurry up and share them out."

"Two for you John Paul, two for you Kev and two for me."

John Paul gobbles down his two pies in seconds as he turns to Alan saying, "At least we'll all be stoned and in a good place in this shit hole of a cell."

Parry munches on his pies, "These are the best I have ever tasted, nice one Alan."

"I know they taste lovely, it's a pity fat arse took them all off me, he's probably in his little office now eating them all, the little fat cunt."

Outside and free to leave, the players gather at the front of the doors, waiting for the coach to pick them up. As they see the coach approaching, the dark clouds in the sky burst open sending down torrential rain accompanied by eighty-mile an hour winds.

Chapter 14

The Hidden gems

As the rain belts down, the players wait in the foyer. Mick the coach driver manoeuvres his golden double decker coach towards the team.

Cass is met by Reid at the foyer doors. He looks into Cassidy's eyes straight faced saying, "We need to talk Cass, not now a bit later on the coach when it's quiet, just you and me in private."

Cass nods his head, "Okay Reid, I'm sorry if I've let you down."

Reid looks at Cass shaking his head replying, "You haven't let me down but you do seem to be letting yourself down if the truth is known but like I said we will talk later."

Chopper Moon walks out of the foyer and a seagull shits on the head. "Fucking bastard seagulls," shouts Chopper.

"That one is the cock of the harbour," laughs Birdy. The seagull sits on the top of the lamp post making noises at Chopper.

"Look at that fucking bird, listen to it, the cheeky twat, it's snarling at me," shouts Chopper as he takes a fifty pence piece out of his pocket and throws it at the seagull. He misses by miles.

Laughing, Kevin Bird shouts, "The seagull didn't move, it must have known that Chopper throws like he shoots a gun, it must know he couldn't hit a barn door, it's taking the piss out of him."

Chopper turns to Kevin Bird giving him an icy stare and shouts, "Shut it Birdy, or you be one bird I won't miss, you'll be getting a right hook to the head."

Birdy not amused replies, "All right Rocky take it easy, I was only joking."

The players make their way to the coach. Young Cass is met by a serious faced Chelsea whose hair is wind swept by the high winds and torrential rain.

He looks at Chelsea, "Why did you do that Chelsea? That was really stupid, you're studying to be a bannister."

"I'm not as stupid as you are big licks." Chelsea hands Cass his duty-free bags with the Golden Virginia tobacco and Rolex watch in it.

"Thank you Chelsea. Why did you do it?"

"I did it because I can see you're a good person, you have a heart of gold, there is a nice person somewhere in that scatty brain of yours. You're still young and a bit stupid at times but deep down I think you understand right from wrong, but you're getting sucked into trouble."

"I don't know what to say."

"You have talent Cass, use it wisely, don't be just another loser in life who has a story to tell in a drunken rage in twenty years' time, telling people you could have made it only for that thing you did wrong."

"I will try."

"No, do more than try, don't be that person that fucks up his life, be the person who gives it his best shot with no regrets, don't let other people guide you down the wrong path. Grow up Cass, use your talent to give yourself a better life, a clean healthy living life."

"I still can't believe what you did for me."

"I did it this once Cass. I'll never ever do it again. You're right I'm training as a law student, I want to be on the good side of the law and if you want me to be in your life as your girl or even as just a friend you need to grow up. Be a man not a stupid schoolboy who had it all and wasted it away, there are lots of people in that club, be that person who people talk about in a good way. Or do you want to be just another number in the prison system?"

"I understand what you're saying and hopefully I can make you proud of me Chelsea."

"Don't do it for me, do it for yourself, do it for Brian Cassidy, girls come and go, you have been blessed with a talent so don't waste it. People dream about having the talent you have been given."

"I know, I don't want to end up in prison."

Chelsea gives Cass a peck on the cheek as she leaves to make her way back to her coach. The wind is swaying her left to right with the rain pelting her in the face disguising her tears.

Cass yells, "Don't forget to ring me Chelsea, don't forget our index finger pact. I once had that pact with someone I fell in love with, but she forgot that pact and forgot me at the same time... It broke my heart."

Chelsea steps onto the coach her eyes welling up. She turns around coach stairs and replies, "When I know you have grown up, I'll consider ringing you. I won't break your heart, it's up to you to grow up be a man. I will ring you only then." Chelsea waves goodbye to Cass as she walks out of sight returning to her seat on the coach.

Max sees Peter Springsteen in the foyer and throws the kitbags into his direction. Max turns to Peter, "Here you are Peter, I think these smelly kits belong to you, we're finished with them. They fucking stink."

Ronnie interrupts Max as he kicks the kit bags. "What he means Peter, is that we're going in John Arrow's car now so we have finished carrying them for you, they go in the coach now."

Peter nods replying, "Okay, thanks Ronnie. I'll take them to the coach from here."

"Thanks Peter," replies Ronnie.

"What a pair of wankers them two are," whispers Peter to Birdy.

"I know Peter. That Max made me carry the new Russian kit in that room, they were telling porky pies to the custom officers, the horrible deceitful bastards."

"I can't wait to see the back of them Birdy to be honest."

Max is walking next to Ronnie like a man on a mission.

"Ronnie we're home and dry now. Do we have to travel with these horrible fuckers?" Ronnie gives Max an icy stare as they both head towards John Arrow's x5 BMW with the cups in tow.

"Shut up Max, just play the game." Max and Ronnie are joined by Bob and John Arrow at the car. John Arrow opens the car doors.

Max rips off his Golden Dock tracksuit top turning to Ronnie saying, "Thank fuck for that, I can take this fucking horrible top off now."

Ronnie shaking his head whispers to Max, "Get the fucking top back on till we are home and dry."

"We are home and dry."

"No, we're not, now get the top on."

Bob looks at Max shaking his head and turns to John Arrow and whispers, "Cheeky cunt, he should be proud to wear our colours."

Alex Sharp does a head count as the players get on the golden coach. He turns to Peter Springsteen saying, "That's fourteen Peter including you and me."

The players are greeted by Mick the coach driver in his brand-new double decker coach.

"Hello Mick, new coach hey? A double decker with an upstairs, hmmm very posh," says Chivers.

"What lad? All double decker's have upstairs. I hope you had a good trip, did any of you lot get me tobacco?"

"Fuck off Mick, you insensitive twat," shouts Kevin Bird. "Our mate, Kevin Parry has just been nicked trying to bring back tobacco for you. He's been detained and you're asking for tobacco? Have a word with yourself mate."

"I didn't tell him to rob it. I'm not fucking Fagin?"

Cass walks to the front of the coach carrying his duty-free bags. "How much did you say a box Mick?"

"Are you even old enough to smoke son?"

"What does that matter? I'm selling, are you buying?"

"Yes, I'm buying, I'll pay one hundred pounds a box."

"Well get your dough out then, show me your money Mick."

"How many have you got kid?"

"Six boxes of Golden Virginia," replies Cass as he hands them over. Mick counts out six hundred pounds and hands it to Cass.

"Fuck me Mick, you are fucking Fagin, you're dealing with the Artful Dodger there, Cass is no more than twelve years of age."

"Shut up Birdy, give your arse a chance lad," replies Mick.

"Yeah shut up Birdy, business is business," laughs Cass.

"Cass the tobacco king has entered the building," yells Birdy. Cass walks back to his seat. Kevin Bird is shaking his head.

"Fuck me Cass, if you fell into a pile of shit you would get up smelling of roses."

Cass smiles at Kevin Bird singing, "You've got to pick a pocket or two Kev, you've got to pick a pocket or two."

"Nice tune Cass," laughs Birdy.

Reid Johnson, not amused looks at Birdy saying, "He might be laughing and singing, smelling of roses now with that six hundred pounds in his arse pocket but going down that path that smells of roses soon fades and it turns into a shitty smell. He has to ask himself does he want to be a footballer or just another Jack the lad in prison?"

The coach goes quiet. No one dares to make a joke out of Reid's response.

Mick puts the boxes of Golden Virginia tobacco into a hidden compartment in the floor of the coach. As he locks it he smiles to himself.

"Mick, does that go into the suitcase compartment of the coach?" asks Pat Arrow.

"No," replies Mick. "It's a hidden secret compartment that can hold up to two holdalls."

"So, is this the smuggling coach then Mick?" laughs Birdy.

Mick looks at Pat. "Does he ever shut up Pat?"

"No, I'm afraid not Mick."

"He's hard work Pat."

"We could always tie him up and put him in your secret compartment."

"Nah, it's okay Pat, no shits going in there."

"I heard that Mick, yer cheeky git, this whole coach is a pile of shit." Snaps Birdy.

John Arrow puts on his black Ray-Ban sunglasses and beeps his horn as the x5 pulls out of the Hull harbour car park with Bob as co-driver, and with Max and Ronnie in the back of the car with the cups on their laps.

Chopper Moon and Fred Kettle run upstairs on the Golden Dock coach to catch up on sleep they have missed. Downstairs, Pat Arrow is sitting next to Kevin Bird. Opposite them, separated by the table is Mark Barrow and Ant Hodge. The next table is occupied by Reid Johnson, Kevin Chivers Alex Sharp and Peter Springsteen. The other table is occupied by John Cully, Cass, Ian Craig and Todd Elliott. Mick pulls off as the players sit at their tables chatting.

Mick has 'We are the champions' playing on the CD player.

"So, Pat did we conquer Europe like you said we would?" asks Ant Hodge.

"Yes, we did Ant, we did conquer Europe but it was at a cost, we have returned home four players lighter, one was injured in battle and three have been captured. They will be prisoners of war, we didn't expect any casualties but it happens in battle, but we did make peace with the Russians. So, if you were to sum up the journey, overall we did conquer Europe. When you look back you would say the mission was successful, so I'll drink to that."

Pat cracks open two cans of carling and swigs a can and places one next to him.

"Why have you opened two cans Pat?" enquires Kevin Bird.

"One for me and one's for my drink buddy John Paul Anderson who has recently left us."

"Pat recently left us? He has only been nicked, how's he going to drink that can from his cell?" Laughs Cully.

"It doesn't matter that he's in a cell, I'll open a can in memory of him."

"He's not dead Pat, he has just been nicked, that's all," replies Cully.

"I know that," replies Pat. "I'm doing this for him cos his cans always tasted better than mine."

"Oh, I see," replies Cully none the wiser.

"Pat how come in the match you saved everything but you couldn't save John Paul Anderson who's your best buddy?" asks Kevin Chivers.

"John Paul Anderson can't be saved Kev, the only person who can save John Paul is John Paul himself."

"I agree with you on that one Pat," pipes up Alex Sharp.

"It's true Alex, maybe a bit of jug will do him good, it might detox him, clean him of the drink and drugs. It might detox his body, be like a rehab for him, cleanse his body of the toxins, he could come out a world beater again."

"Maybe Pat. Maybe."

"I will drink to that Alex," replies Pat as he drinks off his can picking up the other can raising it into the air yelling, "long live John Paul Anderson."

"Go 'ed Pat my Son, you were fantastic today in goal," yells Ian Craig.

"Nice one Ian lad, like my mate Ted said today all good things come in small packages."

"So, are you and little Ted best mates now Pat?" asks Cully.

"Yeah me and Ted are like two peas in a pod."

"Peas in a pod hey, so you've both been sending each other little text messages you and little Ted then?" smirks Cully, winding Pat up.

"Less of the little jokes Cully or I will be texting Ted and giving him your number, telling him you're taking the piss out of small people."

"Oh, behave Pat it was only a little joke," laughs Cully.

Peter Springsteen looks over to Todd Elliott and says, "Hey Todd, that was a class goal today you showed awareness and your pace was frightening."

Todd Elliott looking surprised replies, "It was a tap in Peter."

"I know that," replies Peter Springsteen. "You showed great awareness and used your speed to get to it and score, with Cass leaving next season you could make that place your own."

"Oh, get to fuck Peter."

"I'm serious Todd."

"I could play in any position next season, you have your star player leaving, there is three players in the jug, another with a long season injury, you'll be lucky to have a fucking five a side team next season, never mind an eleven a side team." snaps Todd Elliott.

"Oh, we will have a team Todd," snaps Pat Arrow.

"A mid-table team maybe."

"No Todd, a league winning team. We will recruit the best players in the league, players will walk barefoot over glass and fire to sign for us, we're the Golden Dock and we shall never be defeated."

"Okay Pat, I'm on board, you have sold the dream to me."

The coach flows down the motorways towards home. Most of the players have fallen asleep except for Reid Johnson and Brian Cassidy. Reid looks at Cass saying, "I think it's time for that talk now Cass."

Cass nods his head and replies, "I'm all ears Reid."

"What I've got to say is short and sweet Cass." replies Reid.

"I know you only want to help me."

"I've tried to help you Cass and guide you to take the right path but at times you amaze me with your stupidity, you need to grow up really quickly and follow the path of your dreams and use your god given talent to be the best that your ability allows you to be. Cut out all the badness in your life otherwise, you will end up another sad statistic of a talent that has been wasted and ended up in shit valley or even worse in prison."

"I hear you Reid, I know where you're coming from."

"Have a think of what I'm saying to you Cass because I'm only saying it because you're like my brother and I want to see you rule the world, not fail and end up miserable for the rest of your life thinking how it could have been."

"I want to go down the right path, I know I need to grow up, thank you for the advice Reid I do listen to you. I've more respect for you than you know... I want to play professional football for a top team, but at times I think no one wants to sign me and that I'm not good enough, it scares me Reid that I'll end up a loser in life with not even a pot to piss in."

"You have got the talent, just use it wisely and stop doing the stupid things that you do, the cream always rises to the top and you're the crème de la crème Cass, so have a think about what I'm telling you."

"I listen to you Reid I really do, I saw Chelsea cry today cos of my stupidity and had you worried as well."

"What's that telling you?"

"It's telling me it's not the road I want to go down, that road will take me to a life of crime signing on the dole getting my money once a month, smoking pot staying in bed all day or even worse going to prison."

"Get your shit together then Cass and grow up, listen to me."

"I do," replies Cass, "Thank you for the advice."

The coach bounces down the motorway. Mick has Smooth FM playing on the radio. Cass and Reid have fallen asleep, the whole coach is snoring. Amsterdam has finally caught up with all of them.

In the x5 BMW, John Arrow is cruising home. Bob asks John to pull into the service station for a cup of tea and to stretch his legs

"We're nearly home now Bob." moans Max. "Can't you wait?"

"No, all that drinking and football is giving me cramp."

"Just stretch your legs in the car Bob," says Ronnie.

"I need to walk and stretch my legs and have a cup of tea."

"Tea and cake for two then Bobby boy," replies John Arrow with a smirk on his face.

Max looks at Ronnie shaking his head, "Tea and cake, fucking knobhead."

John Arrow pulls into the service station. It's still pissing down outside with gale force winds. Bob and John head straight for the café. Max and Ronnie walk behind them, cups in tow with Max muttering, "Pair of wankers."

Bob orders two teas, a scone and Fudge cake.

John Arrow tells Bob he needs the toilet for a number two and runs to the toilets undoing his belt on the way. As he gets to the toilet he goes in the end cubicle, locking the door behind him. Whilst he's in the toilet Max and Ronnie walk in still carrying the cups.

As Max and Ronnie stand at the urinals having a piss, John Arrow, staying silent, keeping out of sight, listens to their conversation.

"For fuck sake Ronnie could we not have left these cups in the car they weigh a ton?" moans Max.

"No don't be fucking stupid Max, they're platinum gold cups in a fake sliver coating with three million pounds worth of diamonds hidden in the marble bases, so do you really think it's wise to leave them in the car? We're home and dry in less than twenty minutes, then we can get away from this stupid fucking football team," replies Ronnie.

"Thank fuck for that Ronnie I can't stand this team, with that Bob and his gob cos we have the cups."

"We have still got the problem of them wanting the cups back Max."

"I know Ronnie, they'll want them when we get to the pub car park."

"They have got no fucking chance Max, they're getting melted down after we have taken the diamonds out of the bases."

"What will we do Ronnie?"

"We'll give them a grand each out of the twenty-grand which Ted Hike gave us to give them."

"But that's off him, he said give it to them because he enjoyed watching them in the match, *pure gold entertainment* was Teds words."

"Yeah, they were the words he used, we'll just tell them the money is off you and me. They will be non-the wiser, it will soften the blow of us keeping the cups with no questions asked."

"Yeah that's a good idea Ronnie," replies Max as they both wash their hands.

"*Pure Gold entertainment* that's a laugh, I thought they were shit."

"Me too Ronnie, and all that fuss about that Cass. He was shit too."

"Oh, fuck off Max, now you're showing you know fuck all about football, that Cass was fucking brilliant."

"Okay let's go Ronnie, I'm sick of talking about that team."

John Arrow gives them a minute, then stands on the toilet seat looking over the top of the cubicle making sure Max and Ronnie have vacated the toilets, he unlocks the cubicle, washes his hands then rushes to Bob to tell him what he has just heard.

"Really John? I can't believe it."

"Scouts honour Bob."

"The dirty bastards, the fucking dirty scum bastards have used us, the cheeky twats."

"Okay Bob, calm down these are hard-core gangsters, we're just normal working class people, say nothing, let's just see what happens."

Bob agrees but is fuming as they make their way back to the BMW x5. Max and Ronnie are waiting in the torrential rain.

"Hurry up Bob," shouts Max. "We're getting wet."

Bob replies under his breath, "I know you are, it might wash you clean you dirty horrible bastards."

"What are you saying Bob?" asks Ronnie.

"I said we can't walk any faster."

John Arrow opens the car with his fob key. The remaining part of the journey is in silence.

On the coach everyone is fast asleep. Chopper Moon is woken up by police sirens, he looks out of the back window to see four police cars behind the coach with their blue lights flashing and sirens blaring. He bolts downstairs waking everyone up.

"Wake up everyone the Percy Filth are chasing us!" yells Chopper.

Mick the driver looks in his mirrors, "Fuck me, they really are following us. I'll have to slow down and pull over."

John Cully jumps up shouting, "Right all throw your duty-free drinks and perfumes and any other shit that's dodgy into this bag." All the team and management empty their bags and put the dodgy stuff into the bag provided by John Cully.

Ant Hodge shouts to Mick, "Give us the key Mick for your secret compartment." Mick throws Ant the key who opens the secret compartment whilst Cully puts the bag in.

"Have you done it lads?" asks Mick.

"Yeah, it's sweet Mick," replies Ant as he gives him back his key. The police are alongside the coach beeping their horns, pointing at him to stop. Mick pulls over into the entrance of the service station. The police point and direct him into the car park.

The policemen get onto the coach with the first fat police officer shouting at Mick, "Hey, driver why didn't you stop half a mile back when we first put our stop signs on?"

"Sorry officer, I didn't see you with this torrential rain."

"I think you need to go to Spec savers then when you get home, did you not hear our sirens?" replies the fat police officer.

"No, sorry sir," replies Mick. "I can't hear anything because of the high winds." The fat police officer looks at Mick shaking his head. The thin sergeant walks down the coach aisle looking at all the players.

"Right, all off the coach, you're all nicked."

"What's the charges mate?" asks Cass.

"I don't need any son, get off the coach."

"We're champions of Europe, we can't be treated like this!" shouts a drunken Pat Arrow.

"Champions of Europe at what? Tiddly winks?" laughs the sergeant.

"No, at football, smart arse," replies Pat.

"Football you lot? There's only about nine of yers on the coach and three of them are old men."

"There's fourteen of us here, we have cups. There is -" John Cully kicks Pat under the table.

"Shut up Pat, tell them Fuck all," whispers Cully.

"Where are the Cups then?" asks the sergeant.

"We didn't get cups, he meant medals," replies Ant Hodge.

"I don't believe you son"

"And I don't believe your fucking counterparts nicked our three mates at customs when they were innocent," rages a drunken Pat Arrow.

"Innocent. Is that right Sir?" replies the sergeant.

"Yes innocent," snaps Pat. "But we won't let it lie, they were framed, we're going to start a campaign *free the Hull three*. They won't be locked up for long."

"That's good," replies the sergeant. "While you're setting up the Hull three, set one up for the Risley fourteen cos that's where you lot are going now."

"Risley prison?" asks Birdy.

"Yes son. Risley prison."

"No, we're not, we're going nowhere," replies Cass. "Where is your evidence to put us in jail? This is England, here you're innocent till proven guilty."

"Well the Hull three were found stoned in their cell with space cake wrappers and pie crumbs on the floor."

"So, what does that prove?" snaps Reid.

"It proves that your bags were searched but you lot didn't get a *body search*."

"I got strip searched dickhead, do your homework. I'm going fucking nowhere," snaps Reid.

"Well son, our counterparts at Hull customs have blown through and told us different," replies the sergeant.

"Yeah, that's where our innocent mates are being held."

"Innocent? They were seen on C.C.T.V. eating the space cake in the cell."

"It wasn't space cake it was Dutch pies," protests Cass.

"Dutch pies, space cake, it's all the same son. They're all laced with cannabis."

"Oh yeah, they're guilty," snaps Cass. "I'm guessing the C.C.T.V. has smell- a-vision?"

"No, why would it Son?" asks the sergeant.

"Well in a court of law you would need smell-a-vision to establish whether or not it was marijuana in them pies. Only smell-a-vision could provide that information as them pies could be as they were, just pies. As there is no evidence, no jury in the courts of Great Britain would find them guilty," replies Cass.

"Fuck me Cass, when did you eat the law book?" laughs Birdy.

"It's that Chelsea the law student, she's become a role model to him," smirks Ant.

"Hey lad's we've got Judge Law on the coach," says the sergeant to the rest of the police officers.

"Sergeant shall we get them all to get their bags and take them to Risley prison?"

Ant Hodge stands up from his seat and yells, "Fuck off you muppet, what are the charges?"

The big bearded officer standing at six feet four pipes up, "It's for the theft of items from the duty-free shop on the Rotterdam to Hull ferry."

"Are you having a laugh?" replies Kevin Bird. "Are you a comedian of some sort?"

"Do I look like I'm laughing son?" replies the Officer.

Kevin Bird looks over to Todd Elliott. "Hey Todd, sign him up for your talent agency, he's having a laugh, he's a comedian or he could even be an impressionist, doing an impersonation of a gobshite police officer."

"This is no joke," replies the sergeant.

"Where is your search warrant?" asks Cass.

"I don't need one dickhead, you lot weren't body searched at Hull customs."

"Well, where is your evidence to arrest us?" replies Kevin Chivers. "Is it not better that you search the coach and search all of us and our bags first and find your evidence before you arrest us? That way we won't be able to sue you for wrongful arrest because in this country you're innocent until proven guilty."

"Yeah, why waste tax payer's money?" snaps Peter Springsteen.

The sergeant steps off the coach and talks into his walkie-talkie. He returns telling everyone to get off with all their belongings, so that the coach can be searched. The sergeant points at Mick the driver, "You too sir, off the coach like everyone else."

The players stand on the tarmac in the pouring rain while six police officers search the coach. They check the baggage area, emptying all the kit bags onto the tarmac, whilst standing all over the kits.

Kevin Bird sees what the police are doing and turns to John Cully saying, "Have you seen them wankers standing all over are kits in their size nine bovver boots, thinking they're dead hard, bet their mums are so proud of them. During the war we had true hero pilots in the air battles *the dam busters*, now we have the wanker boys in blue ground force the *kit busters*."

The coach has been searched and the three kits are piled on top of the kit bags in the baggage area of the coach. The players get back on the coach carrying their bags. The sergeant stands on the hidden floor compartment as he checks each player's bag on the table. In the downstairs section of the coach, each player is searched then takes a seat. Last to be searched is Ant Hodge. As the sergeant is searching his bag he comes across the jock strap with the brown sauce in it.

"Is that shit you dirty bastard?" says the sergeant looking horrified.

"No, it's not Sherlock, its brown sauce." says Ant Hodge. "No wonder you've never made it as a detective, you're fucked now at your age with them observations."

Not amused, the sergeant empties his bag onto the coach floor. He looks at him and says, "Oh look at that, it looks like a pile of shit now. Pick it all up shithead."

Ant Hodge gathers all his stuff into his bag saying, "what a wanker you are, no wonder your wife is shagging the milkman."

"Shut it laddie," replies the sergeant. "Otherwise I'll nick you."

"Yeah, that's what the milkman does with your wife," whispers Ant under his breath.

The sergeant walks up and down the coach fuming because he has nothing to arrest them for. He walks to the back saying,

"You're all free to go." The sergeant makes his way off the coach with the rest of the police officers.

Mick starts up his engine as all the players wave to the police officers as they stand on the car park tarmac. The players start whistling out the theme tune of the classic movie 'The Great Escape' as the coach pulls off.

The x5 BMW pulls into the Golden Dock car park. Bob turns to Ronnie and Max.   "So, do we take control of the cups now Ronnie?" Max and Ronnie look at each other.

"So, is that a yes Ronnie?"

"No not yet Bob, we just need to get a tracker fitted in case they get stolen from the pub, just to be on the safe side."

"Are you fucking kidding me Ronnie?"

Max and Ronnie get out of the x5 BMW and get into their Mercedes sport-car saying, "We'll be back with the cups in twenty minutes Bob."

They drive off with Bob whispering, "Yeah, fuck off, you pair of horrible scheming bastards."

Back on the coach the spirits are high... They think they have pulled off the biggest heist since the Italian job; ten bottles of perfume, six boxes of tobacco, four sleeves of cigarettes, two bottles of Jack Daniels and a Rolex watch. They're banging on the tables singing the song from the Italian job at the top of their voices;

"This is the self-preservation society, this is the self-preservation society."

Peter Springsteen is dancing up and down the aisle of the coach playing air guitar.

Back in the pub car park, Ronnie and Max return minus the cups. They have been replaced by two cups a quarter the size of the originals.

"What the fuck are they Ronnie?" asks Bob fuming.

"These are your new cups Bob."

"Are you kidding? They're quarter the size of the original cups."

"I know, they're solid sliver Bob."

"This is a load of shit Ronnie, I need to ring Ted. I'm not happy about this."

"I've just phoned Ted and I told him about you not being happy about having to give the cups back after ten months, so he asked me to replace them with these two cups for you to keep forever. Me and Max are giving you twenty grand, a grand each for every single person on the trip."

"I would rather have the original cups," replies Bob.

"Don't be stupid Bob, they were never for keeps, these two cups are yours forever and you all get a grand."

"Whatever," replies Bob. Ronnie hands Bob the two cups and gives him the twenty grand.

"Smile Bob for fucks sake," says Ronnie.

"You're one for smiling Ronnie. I heard your nickname is the Joker," snaps Bob. Ronnie gives Bob a long icy stare.

"Come on Ronnie, let's fuck off there is no pleasing this team," snaps Max as he throws the two Golden Docks tracksuits on the car park tarmac. "Here you are Bob, you can have this shit back, they're no good to us now."

Bob picks up the tracksuits muttering under his breath, "The only shit here is you two."

John Arrow asks Max and Ronnie if they want to buy a lucky team ticket at two pounds a go to help the team funds. Max and Ronnie decline as they get in their car. Ronnie wishes Bob good luck, Bob just nods at him as they drive away.

The Golden Dock coach pulls into the pub car park. It's swaying as there is a party atmosphere on board.

Chapter 15

Homeward Bound

The golden coach pulls into the pub car park, it's 2pm and the rain has stopped. The players are in high spirits as they get off the coach into the path of a steaming Bob.

"Hello skipper, smile," laughs Birdy.

"Champions." shouts Chivers. Bob half-heartily smiles at Chivers.

"What's up with you Bob?" asks Chivers sensing something is not right.

"I'll explain in a minute Kev, when everyone is off the coach." The players gather together as Mick drives away beeping his horn. Bob explains to the players what Max and Ronnie have done.

"I knew they were horrible dodgy bastards." says Todd Elliott.

"Me too, I knew there was something shifty about them," says Kevin Chivers.

"That Ronnie and his mate Max are pricks, they've taken us for mugs," Bob says fuming.

"No, they haven't Bob, they're a pair of pricks, I agree with that," says Ant Hodge.

"They wouldn't even buy a two-pound lucky team ticket to support the team, the tight bastards," yells John Arrow.

"I can understand that," laughs Kevin Bird. "Everyone knows you fiddle them tickets, we all know one of the committee always win, even I wouldn't buy one of them tickets."

"Fuck off Birdy, you're just as tight as them," replies John Arrow.

"Forget about the tickets, I'm more concerned that them bastards have made mugs of us," says Bob.

"They haven't made mugs of us Bob," says Ant Hodge.

"Yes, they have, I hate them pair of wankers."

"We all hate them Bob," says Todd.

"They have taken the piss," replies Bob.

"No, they haven't Bob, we've been to Holland with free transport, coach's rides back and forth, ferries with cabins and meals, minibuses taking us everywhere. We have stayed in a top five star hotel and had lovely meals and the best times of our lives. We could write a book about this adventure and most of all we've conquered Europe and we all have a grand in our pockets. The cups that we have got we keep, even if they are quarter of the size of the original cups, these cups we keep for good. So cheer up. Forget about them two wankers, take the positives out of the trip."

"I guess you're right, thinking of it that way Ant, but them two twats will never get a warm welcome off me, if I ever see them again."

"Bob, none of us had ever seen them before this trip, we most probably won't ever see them again, we don't mix in their circle," replies Ant Hodge.

"I know Ant, let's not talk about them fucking pair of dogs."

Kevin Bird starts chanting, "*Who let the dogs out?*"

Bob starts smiling "Shut up soft arse."

"I will do Bobby boy, give me my grand," replies Birdy.

"Here you go Birdy, enjoy don't waste it. Treat the wife."

"Are you kidding Bob, that tight arse," laughs John Arrow.

"No John, he will treat the wife."

"I already have Bob, I bought her flavoured condoms and a tea towel in Amsterdam."

"He's not even married," laughs Todd.

Bob gives each player a grand out of the twenty grand he got from Ronnie and Max.

John Cully is met at the pub car park by his cousin Bert Cully.

"Hello Bert, You Okay? When can you play again?" asks Peter Springsteen.

"Not for another six months Peter, I'll start light jogging in three months," replies Bert.

"Okay Bert, when you're fit there's a shirt here for you."

"Thanks Peter."

"Bert will you see Colin Johnson?

"Yeah Peter, why?"

"I want him to sign for us, he'll add steel to the side. I tried to get in touch with him before the trip to take him to Amsterdam, his wife Jane said he was away doing double work for Robert De Niro."

"What? He's about seventy that De Niro, why do you want to sign a player that old?" laughs Chivers.

"Shut up soft arse you know he's not seventy, he scored a hat-trick against you last season," replies Peter.

"I know, I'm taking the piss, he's thirty-two and two of them goals were penalties."

"Anyway, stop taking the piss and shut up, I'm talking to Bert."

"Okay calm down, I'm joking Peter."

"Bert make sure you get him to Ring me."

"Okay Peter, I'll see him and tell him. I was gutted I missed the trip."

"Don't worry Bert, I'll fill you in about the trip on the way home," says Cully as he makes his way to Bert's car.

"Peter, this season has only just finished, why new players this early?" asks Birdy.

"If you want to be the best you rebuild early. Colin Johnson was the best player in the league by miles last year, it makes sense that he should sign for the best team."

"No Peter, you're wrong there. Cass was the best player in the league last season and the season before that," remarks Bob.

"I was discarding Cass in that statement Bob, he's on a completely different level altogether from any other player in the league."

The players say their goodbyes and make their way home. The last two to see Bob for their grand are Cass and Reid.

Bob gives Cass his grand with a sad face, "Don't forget us now Cass, will you?" he says with sadness in his voice.

"Don't be stupid skipper, I haven't even got a club yet," replies Cass.

"That won't be a problem Cass, you'll have every top team in professional football trying to sign you now." replies Bob.

Cass laughs saying, "Don't take the piss Bob."

"I'm not," replies Bob. "I think this trip has shown you that you can't mess about with the talent that you've got, you have to go down the right path to fulfil your true potential."

"I know that Bob, this trip has opened my eyes, it's made me realise I need to grow up sooner rather than later before it's too late."

"Cass, you will end up playing for the top team in the Premier league."

"I hope so Bob."

"You will Cass, you best not forget me. Will you come and watch us from time to time?"

"Of course, I will Bob," replies Cass. "I'll always come to watch, our Reid still plays,"

"I'm glad to hear that Cass."

"I'll always remember what I've learnt from you Bob."

Smiling Bob says, "Do you mean you'll always remember me being a role model with quick feet and having great skills on the ball?"

"No, don't be fucking stupid Bob, I'll remember how you lift up the cups, you glory hunting bastard," laughs Cass.

"I know Cass, it's a good feeling lifting up trophies."

Reid and Cass make their way home Bob shouts, "Good luck Cass, it's been a pleasure being your team mate."

Cass smiles, "thanks Bob, you will always be my skipper."

Bob grins saying to himself, "That complement is better than any cup I've ever won."

Charlie Reece walks out the pub and shouts to Bob, "Are them cups going in the trophy cabinet?"

"Yeah Charlie," replies Bob. "Make sure you give them a good polish."

"I run a pub Bob, I'm not a silver polishing company, that's four new trophies you've won this season."

Bob smiles as he walks away muttering to himself, "Yeah four trophies. It really is a grand old team to play for."

John Arrow asks Charlie does he want to have a go of the lucky team ticket.

"Yeah," replies Charlie. "I'll have two teams," and hands John Arrow four quid.

"What teams are you having Charlie?" asks John Arrow.

"It doesn't fucking matter," replies Charlie. "You fucking fix them tickets anyway, so I'm not expecting to win."

"That's shit, I haven't won in the last six months."

"Yeah, says you, in your expensive X5 BMW," replies Charlie.

John and Bob drive away beeping Charlie as he takes the cups into the Golden Dock pub.

Bob shouts, "Champions of Europe." at the top of his voice. Cass and Reid are walking over the Mab Lane field homeward bound. In the corner of the field a man is walking his dogs, a Jack Russell and a Staffordshire Bull pup when a big American Pit Bull runs over to the Staffordshire Bull pup smelling the pup. The Jack Russell puts its head up against the American pit Bull's head barking, warning the American Pit Bull to back off. Cass watches the dogs, pointing them out to Reid;

"That's you that Reid, you're the Jack Russell protecting me. I'm the Staffordshire Bull pup, that's what you're like, you'll take any one on, no matter what size they are."

Reid laughs and growls at Cass.

As they're walking on the tarmac path, Cass puts the Rolex watch in a bag with the Dsquared jeans and Givenchy t-shirt. He puts the six hundred pounds with the thousand pounds he got off Bob into the bag. Keeping the football boots and Hugo boss tracksuit he got off Ted Hike and the gold chain with the boxing glove pendant; he hands the rest to Reid.

"I want you to have all these, you're right, it's time I grow up, I want to follow the right path, chase my dream and stop playing Russian roulette with my life. I know one silly crime could ruin my life as a footballer and that is my dream."

"Behave soft-lad, I don't want your stuff," replies Reid. "You keep it, there's a few quid there."

"No!" says Cass. "I really want you to have them and all the money. I look up to you Reid. I did them things to impress you, but now I know you're not impressed by it."

"You're right, I'm not impressed Cass," replies Reid. "I'm impressed when you're on the football pitch shining like a diamond, when you're on the pitch you're THE KID THAT SPARKLES, you're the kid people watch and leave the ground amazed at what they have just seen."

"That's what I want to be Reid. I want to be that player, so please have these."

Reid takes the bag replying, "If it makes you feel better I'll take it off you. I regard you as my brother Cass. I only want to see you do good."

"I know that Reid," says Cass. "I look up to you. You're my role model in life, but I wish you wouldn't moan as much as you do. I don't want to inherit that of you."

Reid laughs and gives Cass a friendly kick up the arse. "Yer cheeky get."

"It's true though Reid, you do like to moan."

"Shut up soft-lad, are you coming for tea on Saturday?"

"Yeah, what's on the menu?"

"H, has got bacon ribs, potatoes and cabbage on the menu."

"Is that the meal your dad says the British army have before they go into every battle?"

"Yes, that's the one, he says he made it, his dad made it, his grandad made it and all the ancestors made it, whilst they were all army chefs."

"That must have been some meal the British army had going into battle. At one point or another the English have owned three quarters of the world."

"Tell me about it Cass, the English have fought everyone throughout history in their day."

"I know Reid, the English are fuckers, that's why we should be proud of Tommy, he always goes into battle brave as fuck with a full stomach."

"Who's Tommy?"

"He's the brave British soldier that's fights for Queen and country."

"Oh, you mean one of H lads that he and his ancestors have fed throughout history?"

"Yeah, that's Tommy," laughs Cass. They both jump over the wall at the end of Mab Lane.

"Right champ I'm off, see you Saturday. Real Madrid will have signed you by then."

"Reid, I don't think any clubs are interested in me."

"It's half two in the afternoon now, they'll be knocking your door down soon, now that your home having conquered Europe."

"I hope so Reid, I really do, I'm worried I might have blown my chance."

"Don't be stupid Cass, you're world class. Mark my words they'll be fighting each other to sign you now you've left school, now get home and stop worrying."

"Thank you, Reid, see you Saturday."

"Yeah Champ, you take care, see you Saturday." They separate and go in opposite directions. Cass reaches the top of his street, he sees the two telephone workmen.

"Are the phones back on now mate?" shouts Cass.

"Of course, they are kid, us two are the best phone fixers in the North West, they're all back on now," replies the workman.

"Nice one mate, did you get in touch with your boss to get the other fella to work his magic for you?"

"Who is the other fella son?"

"You know, the main man Johnny Crowe, did he work his magic?"

"Nah, did he fuck kid, it was me and my mate Billy, we have worked around the clock the last five days to get your phones back on," moans the workmen.

"Nice one mate, I'll have all me birds ringing me now," laughs Cass as he walks up his front path to his front door.

"Lucky *you*. The only bird that rings me is the wife asking for money or moaning," mutters the workman to himself.

It's 2.45pm on a Tuesday afternoon, Cass opens the door and is greeted by his mum.

"Hello lad, did you have a good trip? We've missed you. If you have any dirty washing put it in the kitchen on the floor by the washing machine. I'll do it now love," says Mrs Cassidy.

Cass goes into the front room where his dad is watching the golf, Mr Cassidy looks up. "Hello son, how did the trip go?"

"It was okay, we won the cup. I met this girl on the ferry, she's beautiful, her name is Chelsea dad, I think she's the one," replies Cass.

"Hmmm the special one, hey son?" Mr Cassidy says laughing.

"Don't take the piss dad, you're not funny," snaps Cass.

"Well Brian what do you expect me to say? You're too young to be falling in love, you have your whole life in front of you. Look at me. I married your mother young, it ruined my chances of being prime minister." On hearing this Mrs Cassidy stands in the doorway carrying more washing.

"Hello love, you okay, I didn't see you there," says Mr Cassidy.

"Prime minister hey? The only thing that let you down from being prime minister is that you're a prime dickhead, you might have become prime minister for the monkeys in the zoo, because you're thick, all your good for is watching golf." snaps Mrs Cassidy.

"That doesn't make sense mum."

"Neither does your dad son."

"Don't be like that love, it's my week off, you know I love you babe. Make me a cup of tea," says Mr Cassidy as he winks at Cass.

"Piss off, go and get one of your cabinet members to make you a cup of tea," snaps Mrs Cassidy as she heads back into the kitchen to do the washing.

"Have any clubs been in touch dad?" enquires young Cass.

"Yes Brian, the Brazil national manager knocked to see if you have any Brazilian in your roots. I told him you had none in your roots but you had Brazil nuts under your bed. I told him they had fallen out the packet and rolled under your bed, and that you're a lazy bastard that's left them there for your mum to clean. He said that doesn't qualify you for Brazil. He said if you had Brazilian nuts in your jeans you would qualify, so I told him I would get you to tidy your room and get you to put the Brazil nuts in your jeans, he spoke funny, so I was surmising he meant jeans, but he might have meant gene's," laughs Mr Cassidy.

"Stop taking the piss dad," snaps Cass. "I'm worried no one is interested in signing me, no one has rung, there's no queue at the door knocking to sign me. There's been no interest in me at all."

"Brian stop worrying." replies Mr Cassidy. "When you went to Holland on Friday, me and your mum packed our bags and went to Wales for the weekend. We only got back late last night and this morning we were out early getting the shopping in for when you got home. Let's just see what happens in the next few weeks son."

"Okay." replies young Cass as he goes out to the kitchen to empty out his dirty washing from his bag. As Cass walks out to the kitchen he hears a knock on the door. He makes his way to the door and as he opens it, he looks on in disbelief.

"Hello wee man," says the man at the door. "Is your father home?"

"Yeah," replies Cass in shock.

"Can I speak to him then wee man?"

"Dad, *dad*," shouts Cass. "Kenny's at the door, with two men in suits."

"Kenny, Kenny! Who's fucking Kenny?" shouts Mr Cassidy.

"King Kenny dad, Liverpool's Kenny."

"Yeah okay Cass, do you think I'm going to fall for that one? King Kenny at my door on a Tuesday afternoon? Kenny the arse shield, because that's how he used to shield the ball with his big fat arse," shouts Mr Cassidy from the front room.

"Shut up dad, it really is the legendary King Kenny, now get to the door, he wants yer."

Kenny smiles at young Cass, "I'm guessing your fathers a blue?" he says with a canny smile.

"At this moment, I'm more leaning towards him being an arsehole," replies Cass.

Mr Cassidy comes to the door and sees Kenny with two official looking men in suits.

"Hello Kenny," says Mr Cassidy. "I thought Brian was saying it's Penny from next door, our elderly neighbour... Come on through to the front room, make yourself comfortable, how can I help you Kenny? I'm a blue, but you were always my favourite Liverpool player," says Mr Cassidy.

"Aye is that right?" replies Kenny. "I thought Jim Royal might have been your favourite player, my arse," laughs Kenny.

"Yeah, you're Kenny the arse shield and my dad is an arsehole," laughs Cass.

Both Kenny and Mr Cassidy give Cass an icy stare. "Maybe not then," mutters Cass under his breath.

"Mr Cassidy, I'm here because Liverpool football club want to sign your son. I'm here to help him agree terms. We want Brian to sign now with your consent. My two friends in the suits are here with the paperwork, they're the main men at the club who oversee every signing at Liverpool football club."

"So where do you fit into the equation Kenny?"

"I'm here to get Brian the best deal from the club. We have been chasing after his signature for the past ten years without any success, so today we're here to get him signed," replies Kenny.

Cass looks at his dad not believing what he's hearing.

"Have you got any representation or an agent Brian?" asks Kenny.

"I haven't, but me mum has," replies Cass. "She's with *Artist Management*, Chris Smith is her agent."

"Does he have footballers on his books Brian?" asks Kenny.

"No, she only does extra work on the telly Kenny, but I know he has good actors on his books. Gary Bird and Rochey are on his books they're boss actors, the pair of them are always on the television."

"Brian, do you mind if I represent you during negotiations so I can get you the best deal? It's up to you if you would like to sign for Liverpool football club," asks Kenny.

Cass looks at his dad, "Can I sign dad?"

"It's up to you, do you want to sign? You're an Evertonian son," replies Mr Cassidy.

"I know dad and I will always be an Evertonian. I really want to sign for Liverpool. I think it would be a good move for me." replies Cass.

"Aye wee lad, not so quick, let's get you the best deal we can get for you first," says Kenny. Cass and his dad sit down with Kenny and go through the contract with the two suited gentlemen, who arrange for Cass to go for a medical the following morning.

Kenny gets Cass the best deal throughout the negotiations. Mr Cassidy and Brian are happy with the contract and sign on the dotted line.

Cass has signed a four-year deal as a Liverpool player via a medical. With all the paperwork finished, the two suited gentleman get up to leave with Kenny... As he's leaving the room he notices all of Brian's medals and trophies in the cabinet.

"There's a lot of medals and trophies there wee man," utters Kenny as he picks up the Sean Quinn challenge cup winners medal. Kenny looks at the medal, he stares into open space going into a daydream.

"Now that kid was a player with world class potential, he was the wild thing who was blessed with amazing talent, forever young Quinny lad, forever young." Mutters Kenny as he looks at the name SEAN QUINN. Kenny comes out of his daydream and puts the Sean Quinn challenge cup winner's medal back into its rightful place. As he walks to the door, young Cass turns to Kenny.

"Hey Kenny, I think you should be Sir Kenny, it's ridiculous that you're not a Sir."

"Aye wee lad, I've never wanted to be a school teacher," replies Kenny with a wry smile.

"No not that type of sir, a knighthood for all you have done in football and for all the hard work you've done outside of football, Sir King Kenny suits you," replies young Cass.

Kenny looks at Cass with his trademark beaming smile saying, "What's meant to be will be," as he reaches the door and says his goodbyes.

Cass and Mr Cassidy return to the front room and start dancing and jumping up and down, Mr Cassidy starts shouting, "We have hit the jackpot, it's like winning the lottery."

"Liverpool, Liverpool, Liverpool," shouts Cass.

"Now hey Brian, we will have less of that, this is and always will be a blue household."

Mrs Cassidy comes to the front room and gives Cass a big hug.

"That's my boy, you little beauty, you wear that red shirt with pride, take no notice of that arl blue nosed git."

"I never do mum." Mrs Cassidy gives Cass a big kiss on the head.

"Hey, less of the old," sniggers Mr Cassidy to his wife.

"Brian didn't you watch the news last week?"

"No mum. Why are you asking me that?"

"The reason, I'm asking you Brian is because last week Kenny was on the Queens Honours list and he's getting a knighthood and you're telling him he should be Sir Kenny."

"How was I supposed to know that? I have been out the country since Friday."

"Don't you read the newspapers?"

"Yes, I do mum."

"It's a waste of time him with newspapers love he only reads the sport and doesn't get past page five," laughs Mr Cassidy.

"Must be like father like son then," hisses Mrs Cassidy.

"Alright love leave it out, I'm agreeing with you."

Cass and Mr Cassidy sit down and discuss Brian's future when there is another knock at the front door.

"There's the door, go and answer it Brian," says Mr Cassidy.

"Piss off dad, you get it," replies Cass laughing. "I play for Liverpool now, I don't answer the door." Mr Cassidy gets up to answer the door. As he opens the door, he's greeted by Brian's best mate Neil Parks who is standing alongside *Big Duncan*.

"Hello, Mr Cassidy," says Neil Parks. "Big Duncan has been pestering me all weekend to bring him here to see you and Brian. I kept telling him Brian was away in a football tournament but he didn't believe me, he was having none of it, so it's now Tuesday afternoon and he's dragged me here."

"Hello, Mr Cassidy, I hope you don't mind me knocking at this time?" Duncan says in a quietly spoken Scottish accent.

Mr Cassidy looks at Big Duncan and is awe of the man, "Hello Duncan, they said down in the pub in real life that you're as big as King Kong. I think they're wrong you look even bigger than King Kong in real life, our toffee lady Gladys Street will always be safe whilst you're at the club, no-one will try to run away with her, not even King Kong."

Duncan smiles saying, "Thank you Mr Cassidy, King Kong was massive but he was shit in the air, he wasn't a very good header of the ball."

"I've seen you score time after time in the air. You would have even beaten the Red Baron in the air, the German's would have been shit scared of you."

"Aye, Mr Cassidy, I know the Germans were shit scared of Andy Gray in the Bayern Munich game many years ago."

"Gray was good Duncan but you're a legend."

"Mr Cassidy, I want Brian to sign for Everton, that's why I'm here, the gaffer told me to get him down to Finch Farm to sign professional forms."

"You best come into the front room Duncan. That's where Brian is sitting."

Mr Cassidy brings big Duncan and Neil into the front room. Cass is lying on the couch with his feet up, he sees Neil walk into the front room and looks up.

"What are you doing here shithead? Can't I have five minutes peace away from you?"

Big Duncan walks in behind Neil.

"Is that your new best mate Neil? I've only been away five days," says Cass.

"Shut up Cass, you know you're my bestie," replies Neil.

"Sit up Brian, we have a legend in the house."

Neil Parks takes a bow saying, "Thank you Mr Cassidy."

"Not you soft arse," snarls Mr Cassidy. "We have Big Duncan in our presence, he's a true-blue living legend."

"What does he want Dad? Have we won season tickets for next season?"

"He wants you Brian, Big Duncan has been asked to take you to Finch Farm, for you to sign forms for Everton."

"Well we have a big problem then dad, don't we? Because thirty minutes ago I signed for Liverpool." replies Cass.

"What was that?" asks Duncan.

Changing the subject young Cass says to Big Duncan, "Hey Duncan, my dad was in the pub last week and his mate asked him what he would do if he caught Big Duncan in bed with his wife, my dad said he would do nothing because she's not his wife."

Duncan looks at Cass puzzled. "Me dads mate scratched his head, he then repeated the question, saying if it was my dad's wife what would he do? My dad replied, he would ask you if you were warm enough and offer you another blanket if you were cold."

Big Duncan in shock says, "I'm happily married son, I'm not sleeping with your mum."

At this point Mrs Cassidy walks into the room saying, "Don't flatter yourself Big Duncan, in gobshites world you're a living legend." She points in Mr Cassidy direction. "In the real world you're just like the rest of the male species, you're only good for sitting on your arse watching sports on the television, while us women rule the world. Now I've got washing and ironing to do, so if you don't mind I'll leave Mr Cassidy to continue to admire you while I get some work done."

Mrs Cassidy leaves the room Neil Parks, laughing says to Big Duncan. "Get told big man." Duncan gives Neil an icy stare.

"Do you like the subs bench, Parks?"

Neil puts his head down and mutters something under his breath out of Duncan's earshot.

"Duncan is it true or just a myth that when Wazza cut his knee in training at Finch Farm that he bled blue blood, that blue blood ran down his leg from his knee?" asks Mr Cassidy.

Big Duncan turns to Mr Cassidy and says, "Mr Cassidy I'm not obliged to answer that but what I can tell you is that in years to come it will be written in Everton folklore that when the prodigal son returned he had royal blue blood running through his veins."

Mr Cassidy has his mouth open wide has as he listens to Big Duncan.

"It's a shame he went to play in America, working with him opened my eyes... In training he was seconds ahead of everyone with his thinking on the ball, he had pure natural talent; he was world class."

"I know, I was gutted, he really is a true-blue. I know he went to the man shite but in hindsight he had to leave to fulfil his career, he's a born winner and as much as it's sad to say, he wouldn't have won what he did if he had stayed at Everton," replies Mr Cassidy.

"The day he returned, his face lit up Goodison Park, he was that happy to come back. All he kept saying was who's our first match against? I'm home where I belong."

"That is a joy to hear Duncan, is it true he didn't want to leave the second time? I heard he was welling up at the thought of leaving yet again."

"I could understand that Mr Cassidy once Everton has touched your heart it never leaves you."

"I understand he had to leave the first time, just like the Beatles had to leave Liverpool for London in the sixties. You have to go certain places to become the best in the world, us Scousers can understand that as long as they don't forget where they came from, we are fighters in this city, we've had to be since Thatcher and her predecessors tried to make this a forgotten city. It will never work because Scousers are too strong-willed to lay down and be trodden on. Scousers are like yeast they always rise to the top, they are born winners."

"Okay dad, calm down, jib the lecture."

"I thought I was back in my history class there Mr Cassidy," Neil says laughing.

"Let's get back to business Cass do you want to sign for us?"

"I would have loved to have signed but I can't because thirty minutes ago I signed for Liverpool."

"I'm sorry Duncan. I would love Brian to play for Everton."

"It's okay Mr Cassidy, we would have loved him at Finch Farm, I'm gutted he won't be signing for us." Mr Cassidy apologies to Big Duncan about Cass signing for Liverpool.

"Don't worry Mr Cassidy, I can see you're a true blue, it's just unfortunate that Kenny got here first. I wish Cass all the best for the future." Duncan bids the Cassidy's farewell as he leaves the Cassidy household with Neil Parks in tow.

Mr Cassidy waves them off as the phone rings. Cass jumps up.

"I'll answer the phone, it'll be Chelsea."

"Liverpool, Everton now Chelsea, when will it stop?" laughs Mr Cassidy.

Cass picks up the phone, "Hello is that Chelsea?"

"No, no, it's Jose from United," comes the reply in a foreign accent.

"Oh, hi Jose, its Brian Cassidy here."

"Well it's you I want to speak to Brian." comes the reply.

"How can I help you Jose?"

"I want you to sign for the biggest club in the world son," replies Jose.

"Josie's Giants?" replies Cass.

"Yes, that's us son."

"I'd be no good for your team Jose as I'm only five feet ten inches and if your club is the biggest in the world, they must all be giants. I'd be too small, I wouldn't fit in," says Cass laughing.

"I like your quick-thinking Brian, are all scousers comedians?" laughs Jose.

"No, only the funny ones…"

"I've been ringing you all weekend Brian, I could not get a connection. I even drove to your house, so you would sign for United but there was no one at home."

"Oh, sorry about that Jose the phone line has been down, it was only fixed today."

"It's a tough estate where you live Brian, no one was in when I knocked."

"I've been in Holland in a football tournament and my mum and dad have been to Wales for a long weekend Jose," replies Cass.

"I drove my car onto your estate," says Jose. "As I got out my car a young kid no older than ten years of age asked me did I want him to watch my car for a fiver? I said no to him and told him it was okay as I had guard dogs in the back of the car, the little fucker asked me could my dogs put out fires? I was in shock. They grow up fast on your estate."

"I know they learn fast here Jose. That Tommy Scott and Jamie Murphy from the band *Space* lived on this estate. Tommy wrote that song 'Neighbourhood' about this place.

"Out of curiosity I asked the kid why I would need him to watch my car? Quick as a flash this ten year old replied otherwise when you get back to your car all your car windows will be smashed as he stood there flicking a stone up and down, so I said to the kid that I would pay him a fiver the agreed fee he asked for. So I then went to your house got no answer, so I returned to my car where the ten year old boy was standing with his mate. I give him his fiver and the cheeky sod looked me up and down saying, 'it's a ten spot mister not a fiver'. I looked at the boy and replied you said a fiver kid, he stood there bold as brass him and his ten-year-old mate, both standing by my car flicking stones up into the air and catching them with hatred in their eyes and said it's a fiver each mister, so I paid the other fiver and drove off as fast as I could. I was thinking of hiring them as car park attendants at the training ground," laughs Jose.

"They make them tough up here Jose, it's the battle of the fittest that survives around these parts, it's not like your posh Chelsea pad."

"I could see that, so Brian are you interested in signing for United?"

"I would have loved too Jose, but one hour ago I signed for Liverpool." replies Cass.

"Oh, no way, I'm too late?"

"Yeah, sorry Jose I would have loved to sign for your club."

"I'm gutted Brian, you were top of my list, I wish you good luck in your career Brian," replies Jose.

"Thank you, Jose," replies Cass as he puts the phone down.

Cass looks at his dad, "King Kenny, big Duncan, and Jose, who's next? Do you think Pep will knock or ring?" says Cass with a grin the size of a giant banana.

"At this point son I wouldn't be surprised if the England manager knocked."

Cass looks at his dad saying, "Dad I feel like a miner in a pit of gold with all these clubs trying to sign me." Mrs Cassidy walks into the room and hands Cass his mobile phone.

"Here's your phone son, I picked it up today, it's all fixed. I felt ashamed in that phone shop today."

"Why mum what, happened?"

"Betty Saidie served me and she said your mate James who owns the shop, said I didn't have to pay because you're going to be the next best thing since sliced bread and that Jen Lambert and Lisa Cantwell were giving me dirty looks because I didn't have to pay."

"They weren't giving you dirty looks mum, they were just looking at you in shock because you're the mum of the best-looking kid on the estate."

"Shut up Brian, next time you can go get it yourself, Liverpool player or no Liverpool player." Cass thanks his mum and switches on his phone, it takes a few minutes to update. Cass opens up his phone scrolling through his text messages and his missed calls.

"Look at that dad?" says Cass. "I've got five hundred missed calls and seven hundred text messages that I missed whilst my phone was in the shop getting fixed."

"Look dad, I've got a missed call from Chelsea!"

"No way Brian, Chelsea football club?" yells Mr Cassidy.

"No, better than Chelsea football club, it's Chelsea the girl I met on the ferry, the law student," says Cass with a big cheesy grin on his face.

"Oh, that girl," replies Mr Cassidy.

"She didn't forget me, index lives on."

"Index whose index? And as for forgetting you, she was with you this morning. I don't think she's going to forget you in half a day Brian."

"Oh, shut up dad and look at how many football clubs that have tried to contact me."

Mr Cassidy scrolls through Brian's phone laughing. "Brian, by the look of these messages, you have had a missed call and text from nearly every football team in Britain, so going by this you're definitely on the right path."

"I want to follow the right path and make everyone proud of me."

"Brian, you can hold your head up high, you can follow your destiny, be remembered for the good things you do, on and off the football pitch. Make sure people talk about and remember the football genius Brian Cassidy."

Professional footballer, Brian Cassidy, walks slowly to the back garden, onto the green grass. He looks up at the clear blue sky and ponders what the future has in store...

THE END

Follow on https://twitter.com/KidSparkles

31386763R00145

Printed in Poland
by Amazon Fulfillment
Poland Sp. z o.o., Wrocław